Knight of the Wicked Heart

The Eglinton Knight series
Book 3

Margaux Thorne

ARE YOU SIGNED UP FOR DRAGONBLADE'S BLOG?

You'll get the latest news and information on exclusive giveaways, exclusive excerpts, coming releases, sales, free books, cover reveals and more.

Check out our complete list of authors, too!

No spam, no junk. That's a promise!

Sign Up Here

www.dragonbladepublishing.com

Dearest Reader;

Thank you for your support of a small press. At Dragonblade Publishing, we strive to bring you the highest quality Historical Romance from some of the best authors in the business. Without your support, there is no 'us', so we sincerely hope you adore these stories and find some new favorite authors along the way.

Happy Reading!

CEO, Dragonblade Publishing

PROLOGUE

Eglinton Castle, Scotland August 28, 1839
The Eglinton Tournament

THEY WERE CHANTING her name.

To be fair … it wasn't *exactly* her name. Actually, it wasn't her name at all. But they didn't need to know that impertinent fact. They were directing their chants at her. *For her.*

And it was glorious.

In all her nineteen years, Lady Louise had never experienced anything like it. To have people scream and smile and clap and holler *for her.* It was magnificent. Awe-inspiring. Life-affirming. Ego-building. Another person—a better person—might have kept it all in perspective. The crowd was cheering for the tournament. After an interminable day of waiting, the spectators were thrilled for the joust to finally begin. Their unbounded exuberance had nothing to do with her or who she was pretending to be.

And yet Louise continued to stand there.

In the middle of the field, in front of the lists, on top of her horse, with the rain pummeling down, Louise allowed the glorious adulation to invade her soul and soak into the marrow of her bones.

Was this what it was like to be a man? Louise wondered from behind the mask of her helmet. Was it so easy to be loved and accepted? Because she certainly hadn't earned it yet. None of them had. The moment they had entered the lists, the storm had forced the knights and their entourages to instantly hide under the cover of pavilions, protecting their lances, shields, and other cumbersome equipment before the jousts began in earnest. All pomp and ceremony had been dead on arrival.

Except this.

Lord Eglinton, the tournament organizer and ancestral owner of the grounds, had ordered the knights to come out of hiding, to present themselves to their beleaguered audience.

Louise hadn't needed to be told twice.

Lined up alongside the thirteen other participants, she accepted her due—or a knight's due.

After their obligatory show, most of the other combatants retreated to the safety of their tents. Louise's horse flicked its head, annoyed by the raindrops battering its face. With stiff steel gauntlets dwarfing her hands, she clutched the reins tightly.

Louise held her ground in the muddy field while the applause played the sweetest music in her ears.

The armor she wore wasn't made for her body. The armet helmet sat awkwardly over the top of her head, rubbing harshly against her scalp. The chain mail and breastplate were so heavy she was certain the vertebrae of her spine were smushing together. Louise was grateful she was still riding. She feared the second she had to walk she would instantly trip in the sabatons that were exuberantly fashioned into long points at the end of her toes, mimicking a court jester's shoes.

Despite all that, Louise had never been happier in her life. The pain was fleeting; that celebratory music would last forever in her mind.

In the end, riveted by the moment, Louise unsheathed the sword she wore at her side and thrust it in the air. The crowd rewarded her grandstanding with a monumental roar of approval.

Whoever said that the pen was mightier than the sword had been wrong, Louise decided.

Clearly, they'd never held a four-pound English longsword in their hands.

Louise was imbued with might and possibility. If she wasn't cloaked in so much armor, she would have pinched herself. But she wasn't about to take her costume off anytime soon. She wasn't about to let the crowd in on her little secret.

Women—especially marquis's daughters—weren't knights. But Louise didn't want to stay a knight forever—one day would suffice.

And then she would disappear. Across the ocean.

How in the world had she gotten here?

Had Louise known one little word could change her life so much?

Yes.

CHAPTER ONE

Two weeks earlier
London, England, the Offices of J.M. Harvey

J. M. HARVEY, editor of the *London Town Crier,* gnawed at the inside of his cheeks, his flamboyant walrus mustache twitching like the second hand of a clock.

Lady Louise forced herself not to move, not to wiggle, not to twist her fingers in her lap. She reminded herself that she *belonged* sitting in this dark office, sitting across this wide mahogany desk, positioned in this plush leather chair. And she could not behave any differently. However, the positive thinking did little to relax the tight knot in her belly that made her want to retch all over the fine Persian rug.

After an interminable pause, Harvey lifted his lips and tapped his yellow-stained teeth together, granting Louise an apologetic smile. "And you say we've met before?"

Louise held back a monstrous exhale of exasperation, instead revealing a tight smile of her own. She'd worn her "serious" dress today: dark blue with very few ruffles and lace, but it still cinched her chest like a giant's fist. "Six months ago. I came in to see you about a travel-writing position. I brought you stories that I'd written. Our meeting was brief, but you told me I ... lacked experience."

That wasn't entirely true. Louise was being diplomatic. The editor had grandly informed her that she was a woman, using the word as a catchall for everything that was wrong and unacceptable for the position—and the world, for that matter.

Harvey's bloodshot eyes peered at her quizzically. His spindly gray eyebrow hairs twisted toward her like the claws of a decrepit monster. "Yes … yes … I think I remember." His smile formed into a grimace. "You seem … ah … different."

Different was as polite a word as she was going to get for it.

"Yes, since I've seen you last, I've taken up exercising."

"Exercising?"

Louise's smile would not crack. "And eating more to compensate."

"Yes," Harvey replied slowly. "I can definitely see that."

Louise. Would. Not. Crack.

Harvey's nose scrunched. "I think I recall now. You wrote me a story about Bath."

"Yes, Bath!"

"Bath." He repeated the word as if it was a spinster cousin asking to live in his house indefinitely. "Not very exotic."

Pulling back her shoulders, Louise scooted to the edge of her seat. "You mentioned that—"

The editor threw up a hand like a wall blocking her next words. "Now I remember!" He lounged back in his seat with great self-importance, crossing one ankle over his opposite knee. "I told you that women travel writers made no sense; they don't have what it takes."

Louise's temper began to percolate, her cheeks blushing—and *not* in an endearing way. "Yes, I know—"

"You see, women are too meek for travel. They don't have the endurance, the curiosity. The gentler sex requires comfort and pampering, a fine home to feel safe from the scary outside world." Harvey gazed off into space, as if starry-eyed for this ideal woman. "Real men grab life by the tail. They say 'yes' to whatever experience life throws at them. Women, on the other hand, ask for permission."

Louise's jaw almost snapped under the pressure. "Yes, I know," she replied through gritted teeth. "But after all that, you told me that the only way I could make it as a writer is if I said 'yes' as well. So ..." She stifled the excitement tickling her belly. "I did."

Kicked out of his reverie, Harvey blinked. "What's that?"

"I took your advice."

"I didn't give you any advice."

Louise nodded. "You told me to say 'yes.' You told me to stop being afraid of the uncomfortable. You told me to be daring."

"No, I didn't!"

Louise nodded again, her voice harder. "You did. And I took it. I came here to tell you that next week, after the Eglinton Tournament is over, I will be aboard the *Clementine* bound for the Sandwich Islands."

Harvey slammed himself toward his desk, throwing his elbows on the expensive wood. "You cannot be serious. Had I been drinking? What time did you visit me?"

Louise blanked. What did that have to do with anything? "I'm not sure. Late morning, perhaps? You didn't appear to be drinking."

Harvey's head collapsed into his hirsute hands. Every part of this man had an abundance of hair. "Late morning? I most definitely was!" His shoulders shook, and Louise worried he might be crying. It surely wasn't the response she'd been expecting. A muffled "The marquis is going to kill me" filtered out from between his fingers.

And they said women were emotional. Louise needed to get the editor under control. "Don't be concerned about my brother. I'm not telling him—or my mother—before I leave. I've written them a note that they will find after I'm gone. It will explain everything and tell them not to worry about my safety. I have a plan, and everything is under control."

Oddly, Louise's words did little to quell Harvey's anxiety. If anything, he retreated into himself even more as he wailed, "Christ! A single woman—nay, a single *lady*—running off alone to dance with the natives …"

"Sir, I assure you I won't be alone … or single. As I said, I have a plan."

Harvey's red face popped out from his clutches like a raging volcano. "What do you mean you won't be single?"

For the first time in this conversation, Louise felt like she'd finally found solid ground. The muscles of her feet spread and flexed inside the tight confines of her sensible leather boots. "As you said at our last meeting, I may be young and perhaps a little naïve"—Louise disregarded Harvey's demonstrative *humph*—"but even I know a lady shouldn't travel across the entire world without a companion, no matter how determined and ambitious she may be. Do not fret, sir. I will have a solid ring on my finger before I march on the *Clementine*'s gangplank."

"Oh …" Harvey considered Louise, his apoplexy receding along with his beetlike color. "Well then, I suppose that's not the worst thing. But I think you should call it like it is—a honeymoon." He passed a hand over his face before standing and expelling a great exhale. "I need a drink."

Harvey walked to the bookshelf that lined the wall of his office. Bypassing the knickknacks and novels, he went straight for the crystal decanter filled with a brown liquid. He loaded a balloon glass, tossing back the contents in one fluid gulp. That didn't surprise Louise overly much, though the fact that he refilled the glass right away did.

This time, Harvey raised the glass toward her. "To your marriage," he said before downing the liquid. He poured another glass, but showed some restraint, holding it in his hand while he leaned against the shelves with a pensive expression. "Why sneak off? You're getting married. Your family must be delighted. You aren't so long in the tooth … yet. Why the hurry?" He brought the glass to his mustache before he stopped, and his lips curled away from his teeth as a thought came to him. "You're marrying beneath you, aren't you? Yes, now I understand."

Louise hated to admit it, but his guess stung her pride. As did the "long in the tooth" comment. "I most certainly am not. My husband-to-be is perfectly respectable."

The glass perched on Harvey's lip. "Then why the hurry? Why the clandestine departure?"

He made her sound like a common thief, not an intrepid adventurer. Louise's knuckles whitened as she clutched at the reticule in her lap. "If you must know, my brother isn't particularly fond of my fiancé, regardless of his superb social standing."

Harvey's mustache curved to his cheekbones as he sneered. "Better to ask for forgiveness than permission? Is that right?"

"Something like that."

Louise eyed the ormolu clock on Harvey's desk and, thankfully, realized she'd overstayed her welcome. Her mother was expecting her home so they could dress for the Earl of Sinclair's ball together. Usually, Louise could feign sickness or talk herself out of another exhausting *ton* event, but this ball was especially important to her mother, and Louise was loath to rock the boat, since soon she would be countless nautical miles away on one. Sinclair's was the last ball before the Eglinton Tournament, and was being held in its honor. Everyone who was participating in the event would be there, showing off their gaudy and priceless medieval apparel to all those who weren't fortunate enough to find a ticket.

Louise was one of the *extra*-fortunate ones. Her mother had pulled strings and secured her a position as one of the ladies-in-waiting to the tournament's Queen of Beauty, Lady Seymour. So not only was Louise attending the event, she was also one of the "lucky" few with the honor of parading into the lists along with the knights and their retinue. It was a dream title that any unmarried lady of the *ton* would have killed for.

Not Louise.

She'd been indescribably furious when her mother informed her about the situation six months ago. The last thing Louise had wanted to do was spend her time following the other ladies-in-waiting while they watched the knights prep and practice in London. All that simpering and gossiping ... It only pointed out just how mismatched Louise was to her peers. Loneliness—especially when one was surrounded by others—was the most debilitating feeling.

But then she'd had her meeting with Harvey. And everything changed.

Louise had decided to say "yes" to what *she* wanted to do. If Bath wasn't glamorous enough for J. M. Harvey and the readers of the *London Town Crier*, then she would go someplace that was. She'd booked a ticket to the Sandwich Islands the very next week and spent the ensuing five months preparing for the journey. Everything else was history. She'd been able to compartmentalize the silly, archaic tournament in the back of her mind, smiling and listening to others gape about it as she dreamed about the exotic islands. While everyone else had been dragging on about the past, Louise had been looking straight into the vast ocean of the future.

Now—*finally now*—after an enduring summer, it was time to begin her journey.

Louise gathered her reticule and stood up from the chair. "Again, thank you for seeing me today, Mr. Harvey. It will be a while before I am in your office again. I just wanted to say how much I appreciated your advice. My life has been completely turned upside down by my decision to grab it by its tail, as you said. I only ask that you remember me when I come back and consider publishing some of my stories. I promise they won't be anything like Bath. Now, if you'll excuse me. I am to attend the Sinclair Ball, and then I will be off to Scotland. Have a good day—"

"Wait!" Harvey slammed his glass so hard on the shelf that Louise was surprised it didn't shatter in his hand. He rushed in front of her, grabbing her shoulders so they were square with his, not caring one iota about the impropriety of it all. Louise couldn't fault him. In all honesty, she was delighted by the whole impudent exchange.

"The Duchess of Londondarry is the tournament's Queen of Beauty and you're one of her ladies-in-waiting, aren't you?"

Louise nodded, holding her breath at the noxious smell wafting from his mouth.

Harvey gripped her shoulders even harder. His words came fast and violent. "And you'll be staying in Eglinton's castle, a part of the procession, sitting in the grandstand along with all the blessed few?"

Louise tried to pull away; she didn't know where this was going, but by the manic look in Harvey's eyes, it didn't feel safe. *Safe* … She recalled his words from earlier. "*… a fine home to feel safe from the scary outside world.*"

Louise held her ground, nodding again.

"Do you have any idea how fortuitous this is? We need to celebrate." Harvey didn't wait for an answer. He retreated to the bookshelf and poured two glasses this time. "Here," he said, shoving one glass into her hand.

Louise was certain her eyes bulged out of her face. She shook her head adamantly. "Sir, please, I cannot—"

Harvey took a sip and released a long "aaaahh." "So, all that talk before was a load of nothing, then? Whatever happened to saying 'yes'?"

Louise wasn't a simpleton; a person didn't become editor of one of the most popular dailies in London by playing fair, but she was still shocked by how Harvey knew just where to stab his words and how hard to thrust.

He narrowed his eyes and grinned playfully. "A man would drink it."

Louise cocked her head. "This early in the afternoon?"

"Most definitely."

Louise stared at the brown liquid. There was nothing remotely appealing about it. The smell alone was already making her stomach roll. She should have thrown it in the editor's face and escaped the room with her head and dignity intact. But that was what a lady would do. That was what the old Louise would have done. And Louise was not that person anymore. Louise was an adventurer and a writer and would soon be leaving London and the word "no" behind.

"Fine," she answered begrudgingly, tipping the crystal glass against her mouth. She emptied the contents as quickly as she could. The retribution was swift and painful.

It was like swallowing fire, swallowing hell and Satan and every knife and sword ever made. The caustic liquor flamed down her neck, causing Louise to cough right in Harvey's perplexed face.

Then came the pounding. "Christ, girl," he said, slapping his heavy hand heartily on her upper back. "This whiskey is expensive. It's meant to be savored."

"I was …" Louise hacked some more. "I was following your lead. *You* didn't savor it."

"The hell I didn't," he said, relenting on his whacks. Taking Louise's glass, he walked back to the decanter, filling it once more. "Try again," he ordered her. "Slowly, just like a fine wine."

Louise refrained from informing him that she didn't like wine either. But she did as he said, taking one very tiny sip. This time her lungs didn't burn like the apocalypse … much.

"Now we're celebrating." Harvey laughed.

"What exactly are we celebrating?" Louise asked, marveling at how light her head felt all of a sudden. She was warm all over; it wasn't altogether unpleasant.

"My idea!" Harvey said, his eyes twinkling. "You see, dear girl, my readers only have the tournament on their minds; they eat up everything we print. Only, Lord Eglinton isn't dealing us a fair shot. He's being stingy. For some ridiculous reason, the earl won't allow our reporters to stay in his castle. It's got dozens of rooms, but we have to keep our reporter in the town that's two miles away!"

Louise's brow creased. She'd never considered herself slow on the uptake, but she had no idea what this had to do with her. "I'm sorry to hear that," she said, only because she thought it was time to make a noise.

Harvey huffed, running a hand through his puffy gray hair. "It's hardly conducive to getting the story—the real story."

"And that is?"

"The real Eglinton Tournament!" he exclaimed. "You see … Eglinton just wants us to write about the jousts and battles, which is all well and good, but I'm looking for more."

"More?" Louise gulped.

Harvey's smile widened from ear to ear. "*More. And you're just the writer who's going to give it to me. Consider it a travel piece—to Scotland—to medieval times.*"

It felt like someone had grabbed the strings of Louise's corset and pulled with the strength of ten men. "Me?" she hiccupped. "But I'm just a lady-in-waiting. What will I see?"

Irritation flashed across the editor's face. "Everything! You'll be in the thick of it. Think of it as practice, a way to study the natives before you actually get to the Sandwich Islands."

Louise laughed. Was this funny? She honestly didn't know. Suddenly, everything seemed humorous. She took another sip of her drink. "Mr. Harvey, I don't think you understand. I don't want to be a part of the Eglinton Tournament. I'm just participating to make my mother happy. To be honest, I hate everything about the event. It's pure nonsense. Frivolous."

"Of course it is!" Harvey bellowed, the cords of his neck straining under his collar. "But what does that matter? You're a writer. You go to the story, and Scotland is where the story is." He rubbed the bottom of his chin. The rasping noise put Louise into a daze. "You do this for me, and I promise that I will publish every single article you bring back from the islands—front page."

Louise startled. *Front page?* She couldn't even comprehend the magnitude of change that would happen to her life after something like that. Then again, it was getting harder comprehending anything right now.

She took another sip, mulling it over. Harvey was right—drinking the alcohol slowly definitely helped it go down smoother.

"And, if the interest is there," he continued, "I'll see what I can do about turning it into a book."

A book!

How was she still standing?

When Louise had first learned of it, the Eglinton Tournament seemed like a giant waste of time. Three days of jousting, mock battles, balls, and dinners in southern Scotland ... Who would ever want to take part in something like that?

Everyone, that was who.

England had a new, young queen and, thanks to authors like Sir Walter Scott, had become obsessed with all things medieval. Capitalizing on this romanticism, the Earl of Eglinton and his friends had devised the tournament as a way to step back in time and embrace a bygone era, where knights roamed the country-side making a living and a name while defending the Holy Land and fighting in mock battles. Hysteria for the event had spread like wildfire—but it had stopped at Louise. She could never see past the masquerade. All she saw were men with nothing better to do playing dress-up.

"And if I say no?" she asked.

Harvey raised a prickly eyebrow; Louise already knew what he was going to say. "I thought we weren't saying 'no' anymore?" He tapped his fingernail against his crystal, his expression growing solemn. "Well, for argument's sake, if you say 'no' then I might just have to pay your brother a visit tonight. After all, no one would blame me for tipping him off that his very own sweet sister was thinking of eloping against his will and sailing to an island filled with cannibalistic barbarians."

"They're not cannibals!" She hiccupped. At least, she didn't think they were.

Harvey snorted. "That's the least of your worries."

He had her; they both knew it. As Louise sighed in defeat, Harvey clinked his glass against hers. She looked down to see if anything spilled and found that her balloon was almost empty.

Where had it all gone?

Does it matter? Louise drank the remainder and handed it to Harvey to refill, which he did grinning. What was the harm in one more glass? She still had plenty of time to get back to her mother. Louise was *celebrating* with the editor of the *London Town Crier*. It was almost too good to be true. This was what happened when you said "yes" to life and acted as a man would. This was what happened when you stopped asking for permission and started doing what you wanted. Doors opened. All Louise needed to do was walk through them.

So, she had to write about the lousy tournament before she left. She could push aside her disdain and disinterest for a single day and pay attention. Like Harvey said … she could use it as practice. The knights and ladies taking part were as foreign to her as the people she was sure to meet at the islands—probably even more. What a wonderful outcome! How did she not recognize it before?

This time when Harvey and Louise clinked glasses, she was the one with the silly grin on her face.

"To new beginnings," he toasted.

She beamed. "To new beginnings."

"More people will be at that tournament than were at the queen's coronation," he exclaimed. "You will be a part of history. Just remember, the mark of a brilliant travel writer is one who can make his reader believe he was there. So, make me believe that I'm sitting front row during the jousts. Make me see the splendor. Show me the real Eglinton."

Louise lowered her lips to the dark liquid, her smile faltering. Her confidence waned while she considered what she'd signed up for. Because there was nothing real about the Eglinton Tournament. She'd known that from the very beginning.

CHAPTER TWO

LORD CHARLES COULDN'T wait much longer. He was receiving too many gawking side glances as it was. Being a quasi-celebrity came in handy when trying to catch a woman's attention in the middle of a crowded ballroom—however, it wasn't the most desirable trait when trying to go incognito in Trafalgar Square. It had to be the hair. Not many men of his station kept it as long as he did, down to his shoulders. The newspapers always made a special mention of it—as did his mother. Charles would never give her the satisfaction of telling her, but maybe she was right. He should have cut it a long time ago.

Another gasp sounded as a pair of middle-aged women strolled past him down the National Gallery steps. Charles quickly ducked his head and turned away, wiping his sweaty palms surreptitiously against the sides of his coat. August in London was a miserable time; he couldn't wait to escape the city. The rancid smell of the Thames was enough to make someone desert the capital and never come back.

Usually, Charles would have decamped to the country by now, but he'd stayed in order to make an appearance at the Sinclair Ball. As one of the Eglinton knights—some might argue, the most famous one outside Lord Eglinton—it was his duty to be at the ball to represent the tournament, something he had taken very seriously since the event's inception. But if Charles was being honest with himself, there was another reason he'd stayed in town. And that reason was finally walking down the National Gallery's steps.

Charles sprang into action, sauntering toward the entrance with the casual, devil-may-care grace that the newspapers applauded him for. His wheat-colored hair worked in his favor this time. Even with his top hat, it attracted notice at just the right moment.

"Lord Charles, what a wonderful surprise bumping into you!" Sir Martin Archer Shee, president of the Royal Academy, said, smiling warmly. The older gentleman climbed back up two steps so he could be at the same eye level as Charles. "I feel like I haven't seen you in ages, though I have read plenty enough."

Charles held back a grimace. "The newspapers love to have a story," he agreed. "But you've been busy yourself."

Shee's beady eyes widened as he took a dramatic breath. "Indeed, the Summer Exhibition is a great undertaking. I hope you don't misunderstand me when I say I'm always relieved when it's over."

The men shared polite laughter.

"I hope you had a chance to see it," Shee went on. "Although I could understand that your schedule was full of practicing for the big day."

"No, no," Charles replied. "I came more times than I am willing to admit. It was spectacular as always. Turner's *The Fighting Temeraire* was extraordinary."

"You think so?" Shee asked, concern shading his brow. "You didn't think it too ... bland?"

Charles rocked back on his heels. "Bland? Turner? Never. The steamboat pulling the ship acting as a symbol for industry pulling the nation was brilliant."

"Yes ..." Shee glanced away, one cheek pinched, as he was still not clearly convinced.

Seconds dragged on, the two men standing on the steps as

Trafalgar bustled around them.

Charles was losing his nerve. It was now or never, but the words clung to the back of his throat crying mutiny. He shouldn't care what Shee thought; he didn't really need to know his opinion, did he? What did it matter, anyway?

It was not like Charles wanted to be an artist … not really. He was the Earl of Somerset, for Christ's sake. Earls were too busy for this sort of nomadic, philosophical, head-in-the-clouds pastime. Earls had hobbies. But, for some reason, art had never seemed like a hobby to Charles. Though being an earl did.

Shee turned back to him expectantly. "Well … I'm so glad to have run into you. I waited too long and couldn't get tickets to the big day, so I'll wish you good luck now. I just know you're going to do splendidly. A true credit to our nation."

Shee tipped his hat and had taken a step down when Charles finally regained control of his faculties.

"Why was my drawing declined?" he blurted. Charles closed his eyes; all he wanted to do was retreat into himself like a snail in its shell. However, he'd done it. He'd said what he'd come to say. Best to deal with the consequences like a man. He was a knight, after all … wasn't he? A lance barreling toward him didn't frighten him in the least. Why did criticism from an art master make him want to hide under the nearest rock?

Shee paused in his step. He winced, the wrinkles around his eyes dragging down as if he'd known this question might come and thought he'd almost escaped without having to encounter it.

The Royal Academy received thousands of admissions for the Summer Exhibition every year, and it only accepted a small percentage of those. One would think Shee would be more comfortable dealing with the men he and his fellow judges deemed not worthy to show. Though, Charles allowed, perhaps Shee had less experience encountering earls he'd deemed not worthy.

"I meant to call on you at the club," Shee began slowly. "I wanted to speak to you about that in person." He raised his hands helplessly. "But, as you said, it's been a busy summer."

"Of course, of course," Charles answered, trying to put the older man at ease. "I know I haven't trained at the Royal Academy like some of the others—"

"Naturally," Shee cut in. "You spent your youth training to become an earl!"

They were at a standstill, each trying to out-polite the other.

Charles bit his tongue. People outside aristocratic circles always thought it was such a monumental thing being a lord, when in actuality, there wasn't much to it. Perhaps that was why the *ton* put so much effort into keeping people away. If the average person got a glimpse beyond the curtain, they might realize all that scraping and bowing wasn't necessary.

"Thank you, yes," Charles said, "but I thought this year … well …" He could feel the sweat drip from his neck down his back. "I thought I had a chance."

The pitying expression Shee returned almost broke him. "Oh, my lord," Shee said breathlessly. "You did. Your work was very, very … good."

"Good?"

Shee nodded, gaining traction. "Very good, but …"

Charles hung on to that word like it was a thin branch saving him from falling to his death. "But?"

"Well …" Shee shrugged. "Different is all well and good. Art is the perfect place for different, though your drawing might have been a little *too* different. Too … real."

"Too real?" Charles felt like one of those trained parrots, echoing everything his master said.

Shee's teeth tapped together as if he were contemplating whether to keep going. Charles almost wished he wouldn't. "It wasn't a matter of talent. You have that, my lord. It's clear to anyone. But …"

"But …?"

"It's the subject matter. We found that it lacked a point of view. It was too ordinary and mundane. People want to *think*.

They want beauty and classical elements made new. You painted women looming in a weaving shed. Not very awe-inspiring."

Charles was like a hot air balloon losing all its fire. He tore off his hat, wiping his brow with the back of his hand. Not very gentlemanly of him, but he didn't feel like a gentleman right then. He didn't feel like much of anything. Regardless, he couldn't contain the heat from his response. "Ordinary life, however mundane to you, can still be beautiful, and certainly has a point of view."

"Quite right, quite right," Shee replied, his feathers slightly ruffled. "I was just surprised, that's all. I thought you'd give us something more in line with the tournament, something harkening to King Arthur and Lancelot, something noble. That's what the people expect from you—London's mythic hero!"

Charles laughed, though there was nothing friendly about it. "Have you walked the streets lately? There's nothing nobler than working day in and day out for your supper."

Shee cocked his head, his mouth screwing up as if he was seeing Charles for the first time and didn't know what to do with him. It occurred to Charles that thanks to his title and the countless newspaper articles, the world had a firm idea of who and what he was. And they loved it. Anything counter to that ruined their fun. He was the shining knight, the playboy earl who left a bevy of beauties in his wake, closing in on thirty years of age with no heir and no hint of settling down (despite what his mother thought). That idea of Charles was the people's escape. And here he was, trying to ruin that. Or, at least, that was what Shee thought. It was written between the lines of his face.

After a bumbling pause, Shee lifted his shoulders helplessly. "There's always next year, my lord." He gave Charles a solid pat on the arm. "Good luck in Scotland. Everyone knows you'll put on quite the show."

AN EMPTY TOWNHOUSE didn't appeal to him, but Charles didn't feel like being swarmed at White's either. He considered traipsing down to his best friend's home, but Lord Edward, Marquis of Marlborough, was a bit single-minded these days trying to nab an heiress. Charles had no doubt Edward would hook Miss Georgiana in the end. The man had a knack for making even the direst situations go his way.

Without thinking, Charles ventured out of the square toward Pall Mall. A park might do him good—any park; it didn't matter. Nature always had a rejuvenating effect on him. So why couldn't he draw it? Wouldn't that make his life easier? Landscapes were always fashionable and "awe-inspiring," never too … mundane.

Mundane. That word stabbed him like an ice pick to the chest. Charles had never been considered mundane in his life. Though to be fair, Shee wasn't calling *him* mundane—just his point of view.

Well, as Shee said, there was always next year. Or maybe it was time to put these childish dreams behind him. Charles had an estate to run, though thanks to his forward-thinking late father, it ran itself deftly and lucratively. He had a name to uphold, though thanks to his mother, the family's respectability was in capable hands. He had the tournament to attend, though in a few short weeks that would be long over. Charles's art—or, more importantly, his curiosity on what made something art—was his and his alone. Giving it up seemed inevitable and yet untenable.

A woman. Yes, that was what he needed. Just a few hours in a silky, pillowy bosom to take his mind off his troubles. Most times, it was the only thing to do the trick, and Charles was smart enough not to mess with a good thing.

He veered off the road into St. James Square, cutting across to Mayfair. London's preferred madam kept a house in the fashionable area, and she valued discreetness just as much as she valued the coins in her pocket. The arrangement worked for Charles, who never could settle on a mistress. The arrangement always seemed too vulgar for him, like keeping a wife but cheating her out of the respectability of the position.

He was almost past the center statue of William III when a giggle tickled his ears. Ethereal, like a dream that stuck just at the perimeter of his youth. Charles realized he'd heard that giddy sound before, but not in a very, very long while.

Skirting the old king, Charles quickly found what had attracted his attention. If a wind had been present, it would have knocked him clean on his arse. Lady Louise—his best friend's sister—was sitting on the bench alone next to the statue, lost in some type of hilarious conversation … with herself. Or maybe the statue.

A few others enjoying the fine weather paraded past, giving Louise the odd stare, but she didn't seem to notice. She was simply too enamored with joy.

Charles's next discovery truly surprised him. Joy looked fine on Lady Louise. Fine indeed. It wasn't often, but whenever he spied her at the rare *ton* event, her face was marred with the kind of disapproving scowl that would make a mother superior jealous. Not now, though. An ebullient smile painted itself across her creamy, full face, and her clear eyes were as blue and cheerful as the cloudless sky. Even with her bonnet covering most of her head, Charles could still make out the sparkle the sun cast on her auburn hair. She never cut hers either. He remembered that. It was loud and full, like a burning bush.

He *also* recalled that Lady Louise did not appreciate his company. Not one bit. Never had. His very existence seemed to annoy her, which naturally made teasing her so enticing when they were children.

Fortunately for him, Charles's memory was the only one on that point, because when Louise noticed him standing in front of her, her mouth kicked up even more. The ice pick that had been needling Charles's chest instantly melted, and he felt fine. Fine indeed.

She popped up from the bench, nearly upsetting her plain, very serious bonnet. Charles never understood why Louise dressed so drab in her muted colors. Not that it took away from her classic beauty. Hell, if anything, it might even enhance it. Especially now that she'd put on weight. It had caught his eye that summer, but standing so close to her, he could finally appreciate what the extra pounds did to her slender frame. Louise seemed softer to him now, and yet stronger. Succulent and lethal.

"Charles!" she damn near screamed, approaching him a little too closely by Society's standards. She wobbled on her feet, and Charles swiftly steadied her curvy hips before whipping his hand back. Anticipation shot through him as he waited for her rebuke, but nothing came. Nothing but honey came from those plump pink lips. "Of all the men to run into today, I run into my old nemesis. How are you?"

Charles wasn't sure how Louise did it, but she made "nemesis" sound like "old friend," which they were ... in a way. Thanks to a strong friendship between their mothers that had carried over to Charles and Edward, they'd spent many happy summer days together in their youth, though Louise, who was almost a decade younger than her brother and Charles, usually spent them by herself or spying from a distance.

Charles's heart grew light, the lightest it had been all day. Perhaps the curmudgeonly woman had turned over a new leaf, was ready to accept him as a true friend and let their old, adversarial relationship run on its merry way. He was surprised by how much he instantly wanted that.

But then Louise burped and covered her mouth with another of those adorable, long-lost giggles, and Charles surfaced from his delusions. Lady Louise wasn't happy to see him; she was drunk.

His body tensed with rage. And questions. So many questions. Why the hell was a marquis's daughter sitting in the square all alone? Why was she soused? And who in the bloody hell had gotten her that way? It was an unusual, reputation-murdering situation if Charles had ever seen one, and he'd accumulated his fair share.

Action was needed. Along with answers.

"Lady Louise," Charles began slowly. "How … what …" He couldn't seem to land on what he needed to know first.

"Since when are you lost for words?" she asked cheekily. "Usually, you're the first person to talk." She wrinkled up her pert nose prettily. "And the last one to talk, for that matter."

Charles laughed despite himself. Even with the alcohol clouding her mind, it hadn't taken long for her viperish tongue to strike. It amazed him how much he enjoyed their verbal sparring.

He reached for Louise's forearm, relieved that she let him steer her toward the path out of the square. She only tripped on her feet twice. As was the custom, most of fashionable London was in Hyde Park seeing and being seen, so Charles felt confident he could get the sotted girl home before she made a scene that they would both regret. Or maybe only she would regret it. Charles didn't think he would ever want to. It wasn't every day that he had the termagant on the back foot.

"I'll do my best not to offend you with my insipid conversation," he remarked dryly, "if only you'll be so kind as to tell me how you found yourself here. I'm mighty curious."

"I bet you are," Louise replied, giving him more of her weight. She raised her pointy chin, closing her eyes to the heavens. "I've been celebrating."

"Celebrating? With whom?"

Her long eyelashes flickered, and she narrowed her gaze at Charles. "I knew you were going to ask me that, and I'm not telling."

"Why the hell not?" he returned, the words shooting out sloppy and fast, like a novice unloading his first gun.

Louise sighed dreamily, and Charles's attention swayed on the wonderful way her bosom fought against the strain of her matronly attire. Why hadn't he noticed how well-endowed Lady Louise was before? Oh, right. Because she was his best friend's sister, and she acted like nothing less than a shrew in his presence.

Only, she wasn't acting like a shrew now. She was supple and soft and malleable and damn close to friendly. *And* she was drunk.

"All right, so you won't tell me," he said, directing them onto St. James Street. "Then at least explain why you were sitting in the square alone."

"I needed to think."

"But when I came upon you, you were speaking."

"Haven't you ever thought out loud before?"

That brought him up short. "So, you were thinking out loud, then?"

Louise chuckled. "No, dear boy, I was talking to William."

Charles had to shake his head to get past the "dear boy." It was a first to be called that. His breath caught at how much he enjoyed it coming from her lips. "William who? You mean the statue?"

"I was bouncing ideas off him."

This was getting out of control. Charles had to wonder if it wasn't something a little more insidious that she'd been imbibing. Was her mind completely addled? How the hell was he going to explain that to her brother?

He decided to go with it. "And how did that turn out?"

"Quite well, actually. King William was quite the adventurer himself, so he approved of all my plans."

"And did he give you good advice?"

Her voice was dry and slapped him like he was an incorrigible child. "No, Charles. He's a statue."

Well, then. At least she knew the difference. He was heartened by that fact.

"I must confess," she went on, "I also took a seat because I became a bit … turned around."

"Turned around?"

Under her bonnet, Louise's already pink cheeks colored even more. "I forgot how to get back to the house. Don't look at me that way. It's perfectly normal!"

"You've lived in that house all your life!"

She pinched his arm. Hard. "Not *that* house. We're staying with Lady Davenport. My mother wouldn't dream of impeding my brother's privacy. Unlike mine," she added bitterly. "Not to mention it's part of her grand scheme to get Lady Diana and me to be friends."

Charles slowed his steps. He was familiar with Lady Davenport's residence, and they were close. Also … Lady Louise hadn't spoken to him this much in years—maybe ever. He was hesitant to end the conversation now. Louise's speech was comforting to him, rolling and mellifluous as well as straight and to the point. In a world of flirting and innuendo where no one meant what they said, she was a breath of fresh air, even under the stench of whiskey.

"And you don't want to be friends?"

Louise snorted. "We couldn't be more different. It's a losing battle."

Charles stayed quiet. There was no reason to argue with that. When Lady Diana spoke, it was almost as if she purposely tried not to say words that had more than five letters in them. Louise's mother should have known better.

As if she'd read his mind, Louise said, "My mother is determined for me to get along with all the tournament's ladies-in-waiting. That's why she got me the position in the first place. She thinks it will help my social standing and, naturally, help with the husband-finding. Bleh. As if I care about that."

Charles was treading on thin ice. He chose his next words carefully. "Mothers tend to want what they think is best for us."

Now, he was the one who should have known better.

"Ha!" She dragged him to a stop and thrust her finger into his chest. "Then why haven't you married Lady Charlotte yet? Everyone knows she's waiting for it; your mother is telling the whole world it will happen any day now. The two golden gods of the *ton* blinding us all with their holy matrimony."

Charles had plenty of experience with drunk friends turning from pleasant to furious in a matter of seconds, but the fury unleashed by Louise made him take a step back. Her finger followed him, pressing into his coat. Was she jealous? No, not

Louise. Anyone but Louise.

He cleared his throat, ready to defuse the situation, but she wasn't having it. "What a coup for Lady Charlotte. You are the shining beacon of the Eglinton Tournament. Everyone's favorite knight. London's perfect hero."

Charles started to speak, but she cut him off, on a roll now.

"Oh, I've read all the papers. How could I not? But how stifling that must be, being put in such a box where everyone thinks they know you and has a say about who you are or what you do. I don't think I could live like that. Even with all the accolades, it seems … terrifying."

Charles's mouth slammed shut. As always, the woman hit the nail on the head. That was why she had such a difficult time navigating their circle. Louise didn't have it in her to pretend. She saw things the way they were, and not through the rose-colored glasses that members of the aristocracy preferred. Her bluntness could be harsh, but it wasn't cruel or mean-spirited. She had an opinion and, unlike many ladies of her station, refused to keep it to herself.

Louise was the antithesis of Shee, who danced around his criticism so as not to trample on Charles's ego. But that conversation had left Charles more confused than ever. With Louise, he always knew where he stood. And that was so fucking welcomed.

"… I mean, I'm not saying that I am above them all … your supporters … that is. You don't know this, but I was quite infatuated with you when I was younger. Horribly so. But I think it's normal for a young girl to have a crush. And you were always around, always showing off, always playing at being a conquering champion with Edward. I didn't have a chance, did I?"

Should he make her stop? Louise's loose tongue was divulging a veritable treasure chest. The more she spoke her truth, the more he craved it. Charles hadn't realized how starved he was for authenticity, and Louise could only ever be Louise.

Unsticking his own tongue, he replied, "Your brother and I knew you were watching us. We saw no harm in it."

Louise blinked. "How awkward." She laughed.

"Not at all. I'm only surprised that you loved what you saw. You ... uh ... never gave any indication of that before."

Louise tugged him to stop again, startling Charles with the challenge in her expression, the haughty indignation of her form, a luscious form that his body was quickly reacting to. "I said I watched. I didn't say I *loved* it. It was a silly girlhood crush, no more, no less. Also, you used to draw... It was fascinating to me. You even sketched me one time."

"You remember that?"

"Of course," she replied. "I was six, and I'd never felt so special in my life. I thought you were as talented as Hans Holbein."

Charles laughed. "Not quite."

"Nevertheless, you were still talented. Everyone thought so. Do you still draw, or are you too busy being the Earl of Somerset and the Knight of the Sun?"

"Do you still have the sketch?" he asked, avoiding the question. He could see it in his memory—the skinny little girl in profile with the upturned nose and overly sober expression. That little girl had sat as still as a statue for as long as he'd asked. She'd believed in him. Sixteen-year-old Charles had believed in himself too.

Louise's countenance sharpened. "No. Like I said, I was six. I'm not sure where it is."

"Ah ... probably for the best."

"Why?"

"No reason."

Charles inched her back into his side. Even with the whiskey, she still smelled like Louise, all tart and spicy, electric to his senses. The pull only seemed to grow stronger the longer they talked. Unfortunately, he could see the Davenport townhouse ahead; their interlude was at an end. He slowed his pace, but even that barely helped. "To your point, what my mother thinks and what is going to happen are two very different things."

From the corner of his eye, he saw the tension in Louise's

mouth dissipate, her lips falling open just enough for her teeth to peek out. "Oh …" Her grip tightened around his arm. "Well, the same goes for my mother."

"Is that why you were celebrating with …" He trailed off, hoping she was befuddled enough to fill in the blank.

Her smile was approving. "You think you are so clever, don't you? Why do you want to know so badly?"

So I can find that bastard and beat him to a bloody pulp. Unless … she had a beau? That couldn't be right. Edward would have told him. Nevertheless, Charles would beat that lovesick puppy to a bloody pulp as well. Courting a woman like Louise was special— it did not involve whiskey.

He shrugged. "You know why."

They reached the front steps of the Davenport residence. Realization lit Louise's features, but her lips puckered, almost like she was as disappointed as Charles that they had reached their end together.

"I'm here," she replied wistfully.

"You're here."

She released his arm. *Reluctantly?* "I suppose having a knight around isn't such a bad thing every once in a while."

Charles's words left him before he registered what he was saying. "I could give you anything you wanted, Louise, whenever you needed it." It struck him that he probably had never said anything so truthful in his life. Later he would tell himself it was because he'd always thought of Louise as a younger sister; he was just being helpful. But that explanation would hold little water and do nothing to curb the lingering effects of their enchanting and unusual walk together.

She smiled, her entire face alighting into a magnificent tableau. "Such pretty words for a knight."

"I mean them."

"Knights never mean what they say."

"That's gentlemen."

"Too bad for you, since you're both."

"What if I could be something different?" Charles wasn't sure what he was asking, but her answer seemed vitally important to him.

She regarded him curiously. "Do you want to be someone different?"

"Sometimes," he allowed. "Don't we all?"

"I don't know why, but I think I believe you."

"You should."

Louise squinted one eye, as if appraising an artifact, judging if it was authentic. Then she slapped a hand against his chest. "If you really are telling the truth, then let me give you some good advice. Grab life by the tail."

Charles snorted. "That's it?"

"That's it," Louise answered, mighty proud of herself.

Where in the world had she heard that nonsense? Charles nudged her toward the door, if only to touch her one more time. Perhaps it was the lovely weather, or perhaps not, but she was so warm and inviting under his skin. "You should take a nap, Louise."

She shrugged him off, catching her feet while she stumbled. "I'm not tired in the least; besides, I have to go to the Sinclair Ball tonight. Mother's orders."

"You will not be doing that. Tell her you're sick."

She frowned. "But I'm not sick, and it's one of the last times I'll see her for a while. I want my obedience this week to be a balm to her. It's a way for me to tie up loose ends."

One of the last times? Balm? Up to this point, Louise had made *some* sense; Charles didn't know what to make of the last comment. "What do you mean? Are you going someplace?"

She swayed back and forth with the hand she waved in front of him. "You don't need to worry about that."

"But I do worry—"

Louise jammed her finger up against his lips. "Shh," she said, leaning into him, her face just inches away. His lungs filled with her spicy scent—and anticipation. "You're spoiling the moment."

He opened his mouth against her finger, tasting her skin. "What moment?"

She stared at the action. "You know … I'm happy I saw you today."

"You needed me to help you home."

Her smile was slow and enchantingly evocative. "Not just that. It allowed me to tie more loose ends."

"With me?"

Louise nodded.

Charles was never scared. But he was terrified now. He swallowed. "Go inside, Louise."

She didn't budge. "Before I go, I need to do something I've always wanted to do."

His voice sounded weak and gravelly to his ears. "Who were you with today, Louise?"

She lowered her finger and edged closer. The blue of her eyes was ringed with a layer of gray, like a storm battling for supremacy with a perfect day. Two locks of hair had fallen from her bun, framing the sides of her face. Charles yearned to hold on to them, never allow her to leave.

But she had every intention of leaving him. Wasn't that what she was trying to tell him?

For the remainder of his life, Charles would remember the way her tender lips felt as they settled over his; the way she secured herself to him like it was the most natural thing in the world; the realness that overwhelmed him when she captured him with her forthright gaze. And he would remember what Louise would say right before she altered him forever: "I lied to you before," she whispered in his mouth. "I was always watching you and only you … and I loved everything I saw."

CHAPTER THREE

L ADY DELILAH BURST into the room.

"Louise! What are you still doing in bed? I came in thirty minutes ago to tell you to get up!"

She snatched at the covers tangled in between her daughter's legs and yanked them with a strength that belied her thin stature.

Louise peeked open one eye and then promptly shut it, realizing immediately that it wasn't a good decision. Just that tiny act alone made her stomach feel like she was standing at the bow of a ship in the middle of a roaring tempest.

Her tongue felt overly large and chalky as it slid over her teeth. Everything seemed dry, like moisture had been sucked from her skin while she'd been asleep.

Asleep. How long had she been out? And how had she gotten into her bed? Sifting through her fuzzy brain, Louise vaguely recalled meeting with Mr. Harvey. Had that been only this morning? And then she'd gone for a walk ... and gotten lost? But then a statue came to her rescue. Or was it a man? No ... not a man ... it was a knight.

A knight!

Louise popped up from the bed, grabbing her head and middle as each part battled for relief from its pounding misery.

"Oh, good, you're finally listening to me," Lady Delilah replied blithely. "Now, don't dawdle. We're running late as it is. I'll send Susan in to get you ready, and then we'll be off. We mustn't keep Lady Davenport and Diana waiting."

"Mother, please," Louise said, her sad, pathetic voice reminding her of a frog on its last legs. "Can't you see I'm ill? I can't possibly go to the ball."

Her mother chuckled, marching over to stand in front of her. Tucking her hand under Louise's chin, she raised her daughter's face, inspecting it with the solemnity of a monk. "You look fine to me," she announced, twisting Louise's head back and forth. "Maybe a little green, but a little powder will do the trick just fine."

Lady Delilah released her hold, and Louise collapsed back to the bed, her neck no longer offering any support. She curled into a ball, hugging her knees. "Mother, I beg you. Let me stay home tonight."

"It's your own fault," Lady Delilah replied over her shoulder. "I told you not to go for a walk. You've tired yourself out." She waded across the room to inspect Louise's gown hanging in the bureau. A masterpiece of craftsmanship, the Elizabethan-styled piece reflected all that was admired in the Virgin Queen's court. From its delicate golden embroidery to its deep yellow silk, it was created to complement Louise's rich, fiery hair. Even with the financial issues Louise's late father had forced the family to endure, Lady Delilah had spared no expense on her daughter's tournament wardrobe. To her, it was an investment.

"I'm not just tired, Mother," Louise groaned into her pillow. "I truly don't feel well."

"Ha!" Lady Delilah said. "Like you didn't feel well at the Jacobson Ball? Or like when your head hurt so bad you couldn't attend Gage's picnic? What about the Wellfleet musicale? You insisted that your throat burned so wickedly you were afraid you had consumption! I asked two doctors to sit with you that night."

"Didn't stop you from going to the musicale, though," Louise muttered.

"I heard that," her mother snapped. Lady Delilah patted the

sides of her light auburn coif even though not a hair was out of place. She sighed, moving back to her daughter. "Now, don't forget to tell Queen Jane how beautiful she looks tonight. A lady-in-waiting must be many things, but her most important role is to be a champion for her queen."

Louise curled back her top lip, feeling a sweat breaking out at the nape of her neck. "I think you're taking this tournament too seriously, Mother. The Duchess of Londondarry isn't a real queen, remember? She's just the Queen of Beauty. Besides, it would be redundant. No doubt, the fifteen other handmaidens will have already beaten me to it."

"A lady never tires of being told she is magnificent, and Lady Jane Seymour is no different."

"I would."

Lady Delilah chuckled. "Oh, my love. You have so much growing up to do."

Louise straightened her arms, attempting to pick herself up from the bed, but soon gave up the herculean effort.

Her mother pressed on: "And for pity's sake, join the groups, don't just stand on the outside looking in like you always do."

"I'm perfectly fine there," Louise said into the covers. "I like being on the outside. It's the right place for people like me."

"People like you?"

"Wr-writers," Louise finally said.

A coldness swept over the dowager's fine features so swiftly, the sweat on Louise's back vanished. "Writers?" her mother repeated in a tone dripping with malice. "I thought we were over that."

"No. *You* were over that."

"Is that so?"

"Yes, that's so."

"Huh," was all her mother replied. But it was enough to make Louise feel like a giant bucket of ice-cold water had just been thrown over her head and her dreams. "What about marriage and children?"

"What *about* marriage and children?"

Lady Delilah's tone was nonchalant, but Louise could tell her mother was boiling just underneath the surface. The marchioness was too well bred to start a row while a guest in someone else's home, but that didn't mean she wouldn't get her licks in where she could. "A writer's life is barely conducive to a family. And you are a marquis's daughter. You have responsibilities."

Louise buried her head in her sheets. She'd heard all this before. "I know my responsibilities, Mother." She craned her neck around. "And you have nothing to worry about. I want a family. Plenty of writers manage to have them."

Her mother huffed. "Like who? That Jane Austen you love so much surely didn't."

Louise lifted her chin. "Mary Shelley."

Lady Delilah gasped. "You mention that woman to me? Do you want me to keel over in the Davenports' home?"

Fine. Louise had to admit that probably wasn't the best name to throw out, since it was well known that Mary Shelley and her husband had an affair before they were married, resulting in a pregnancy. Louise found it all rather romantic, though her mother thought the couple was one step away from eternal damnation.

Lady Delilah wiped her hands on her skirts as if the conversation was leaving a grimy trail on her pale skin. "All I ask is you try, that's all. I can't be the only one moving the family name forward. Someone must show face, declare to the *ton* that our family is still here and not completely fallen off the earth."

It made Louise's skull feel like it was splitting in two, but she managed to roll her eyes. "No one thinks that way."

"Of course they do," her mother countered. "Your brother is no help. He doesn't even pretend to try anymore. Why ... he's too busy chasing after that button maker's daughter."

"Miss Georgiana Spence," Louise reminded Lady Delilah. "She's an heiress; you should approve of that. And I wish you would stop speaking badly of Edward. He's only doing what he has to do because ..." Her words dropped off. Speaking about her father's unsavory ways was never wise. For all that he'd done—gambling away their fortune and selling off anything he could get his hands on to pay off his mountainous debts—he still held a strange hold over his widow, who refused to ever remonstrate his actions. "I applaud Edward for his business. He's creating a new life for us. I wish you could see that."

Lady Delilah snorted. "All I can see is that he's digging into our ancestral land and pulling up ... pulling up ..."

"Ancient lizard dung?"

With a ferocious scowl, Lady Delilah palmed the side of her head as if Louise's headache had turned contagious. "Don't say those words to me! My own son ... in trade!"

"There are worse things," Louise said. *Like having a daughter run off to the Sandwich Islands without so much as a by-your-leave.*

At that thought, Louise's conscience begrudgingly made an appearance, and she swallowed the lump of phlegm coating her parched throat. She'd resolved to be the best daughter she could be before she boarded her ship. Needless to say, things weren't going as planned.

"Darling," Lady Delilah began gently. "I know you think I'm being hard on you. I know we are two different people, and you don't enjoy these types of events—"

Louise scoffed.

Her mother went on. "But please understand that I'm doing this because mothers know what is best for their daughters. I'm only thinking about you; I'm trying to secure you a future befitting a marquis's daughter. This is your destiny. You were raised to be a lady who would take a place in the *ton*. Your father would be beyond upset that you haven't married a suitable young man yet. You're almost twenty!"

Louise wondered if the alcohol was still controlling her mouth or if she'd just snapped, because what she said next was obnoxious, even for her. "Then perhaps he shouldn't have wasted the majority of his life losing our fortune and being a complete and utter wastrel!"

Louise didn't move—couldn't move. It was as if she'd reached up across the bed and slapped her mother. Lady Delilah stood still, her mouth pinched, her expression agonizingly blank as her daughter's words hung in the air between them, sucking up any chance of understanding or empathy. The mother/daughter relationship was never an easy one to navigate, and in one instant, Louise had burned the map and thrown it out to sea.

Lady Delilah broke up the silence, clearing her throat. She smoothed the skirts of her dress, and all Louise could do was watch those lovely long fingers that had once been the envy of so many when they held the arm of a dashing and young marquis. A man she'd thought would cherish her and place her above all else.

Louise burned in shame.

After an agonizing delay, her mother finally spoke. "Your father loved you—loved all of you."

He had an interesting way of showing it. Enough damage had been done. Louise kept that comment to herself.

Her mother continued. "Susan will be up shortly. Please don't make us late. People will talk."

At the sound of the door closing, Louise dug her head into the pillow, replaying her mother's last words in her head. *People will talk.* Oh, yes they would.

"Oh, Mother," Louise lamented in her pillow. "You forgave Father for all his troubles. Please find it in your heart to do the same for me!"

LOUISE FIDGETED AT the perimeter of the group, taking long, deep breaths. *It's almost over. You can go home soon,* she told herself every minute or so, calming her rolling stomach.

If Louise hadn't felt so completely foul, she would have been proud of herself. She'd managed to get dressed in her insanely heavy medieval ensemble (with the help of her maid Susan) and put one foot in front of the other to arrive at the Sinclair Ball on time. Her mother had wasted little time foisting her off on Lady Diana, and together the young women joined the other ladies-in-waiting who sycophantically laughed at whatever their Queen of Beauty said.

The sixteen handmaidens formed a tight circle around their queen, each taking a turn "oohing" and "aahing" over her extravagant ensemble. It was whispered that Lord Eglinton had anointed Lady Jane as queen because they had a *robust* friendship, but others dismissed that rumor, saying that it would have been unseemly to have an unmarried woman in the supreme role. The duchess wasn't the most beautiful woman in the *ton*, though she made up for it with perfectly fine features and formidable comportment.

Lady Jane had not taken to Louise. But even Louise could admit that her "oohing" and "aahing" were decidedly not up to snuff.

It had been that way all summer. Louise always joined the other women at the balls and events, lagging on the very edge of their circles, laughing when it was expected, answering the few questions that were lobbed at her, putting in the least amount of effort she possibly could while doing as her mother asked. None of it had amounted to anything, including the lifelong friendships Lady Delilah had hoped her daughter would make. Those other ladies—the cream of the *ton*'s young society—had no interest in Louise, nor she in them. Their cares and concerns were too disparate. The only thing they shared was the blue in their blood, and even that never stopped the others from verbally cutting Louise from time to time just to check the color.

True to form, no one was giving much consideration to Louise that night. And perhaps her green pallor had dulled their claws. Louise could barely lift her neck from her butter-colored slippers for more than a few seconds at a time without gagging. The ballroom, as elegant and resplendent as one would expect, was much too bright for her. Candles and golden chandeliers glistened across Lord Sinclair's packed space, causing the exorbitant jewelry to sparkle like fresh snow against a morning sun. Louise's senses were attacked at every angle, and her head responded by ringing as viciously as the bells at Westminster Abbey after a monarch's coronation.

However, there was another reason she kept her gaze down. And *he* was on the other side of the room. Though that convenient fact hadn't stopped Charles from catching her eye as soon as she and Lady Diana joined the group of ladies. He was grinning the annoying grin that told Louise that while her memory might be hazy on what had transpired that afternoon, his was not.

As the young people continued to chatter around her, Louise fought through the dusty attic of her brain, trying to recount what exactly she had divulged to her childhood enemy/crush. She hadn't told him about her destiny with the *Clementine*, of that, she was sure. Even *slightly* out of her mind, she wouldn't risk ruining her plans.

She was *almost* sure, anyway.

And she couldn't have told him about her deal and subsequent *celebration* with Mr. Harvey, either. If Charles had attacked the editor for sharing his alcohol, news of the event would have already spread like wildfire over the ballroom.

No. Louise was certain the only thing she had to be embarrassed about was that Charles had caught her after she'd had *a little* too much to drink. *And* she might have been having a full-fledged conversation with a statue. That was all. Not too horrifying. Just horrifying enough.

But the fact that Charles wouldn't stop staring at her gave Louise the sinking suspicion there had to be more. Or maybe he was just teasing her. He liked to do that; he'd spent most of his childhood doing it. He and Edward had delighted in pulling her hair, calling her a baby, and making her cry when they refused to let her join in their games. When they'd gotten older, they lorded their age and education over her, traipsing off to Eton, being men about Town, gossiping about girls they admired right in front of Louise as if she didn't matter. Girls who barely had two cogent thoughts to rub together. Girls who giggled and waited for the paltry scraps of attention that the handsome boys threw at them.

All Louise ever wanted was to belong, to be taken seriously. For them not to see her as a future lady, but as a person with ideas and thoughts—a person whose future actions mattered. But Edward and Charles had been too busy being boys and then men. Too busy hoarding all the important futures for themselves.

But whereas Edward had grown out of that egotistical stage and was currently making good on his industrial endeavors, working with the rapidly changing times, Charles appeared to stall. Only too happy to be loved for being an earl, loved for being handsome with his ridiculously long golden hair, loved for being clever with his sardonic, razor-sharp quips, he'd become a rake. Less a man of substance and more a man of hedonism.

A man like Louise's father.

From her usual place at the sidelines, Louise had watched her boyhood hero become everything she despised in the world. *And* be celebrated for it. *Congratulated* for it.

Like now. Towering on the other side of the crush with his hands clasped nonchalantly behind his back, not even noticing all the women—and men—walking by him hoping to catch his gimlet eye. Hoping to snatch a word, a comment, even a grunt of his time. The ridiculous man hadn't even dressed in costume, and no one dared rebuke him. All the other knights had shown up uncomfortably fitted with hose and doublets, starched collars and silk shirts. Some poor fellows even took it a step further, piercing an ear. Pearl bobs hung from their throbbing pink lobes.

But not Lord Charles. He'd dressed as smart and plain as any gentleman, wearing his black tails and crisp white shirt. Even his buttons were dressed down without any diamond embellishments. The Knight of the Sun, Charles was the less to their more, and the *ton* couldn't kiss his backside enough.

Just as Louise had kissed him. Not his backside. But his

front … lips!

She gasped. More like shrieked. Lady Jane cut off from another one of her roundabout stories, and the entire group gaped at Louise's outburst.

No. No. No. No.

It didn't happen. It couldn't have. There was no way she would have kissed Lord Charles. In the middle of the day outside Lady Davenport's townhouse. Harvey's brown drink could not possibly alter a person that much, could it?

Louise's heart seized. She placed her hand on her chest, feeling the bone corset underneath her gown cut into her lungs. How could she have done it? When she was almost free! Was it a form of self-sabotage? Secretly, was she afraid to leave and hoping for someone to stop her? She hated to break it to herself, but kissing Lord Charles wasn't the way to go about it. For all the articles written about his knightly attributes, Charles was a rake, pure and simple. Kissing him wouldn't bind him to her; if anything, it might drive him away quicker.

Case in point. Louise's heart found just enough of a steady rhythm for her to lift her eyes from the chalky floor. Charles's relaxed form was no longer leaning against the far wall, and a quick scan informed her that he had deserted the room. Her muscles released. He'd just been teasing her, wanting her to worry about what she'd done. Charles might laugh from a distance, but the idea of his confronting Louise about the kiss was ludicrous. It would mean he would have to return to reality, and the Knight of the Sun was one of the many men in that ballroom who wouldn't be doing that anytime soon.

"Louise, darling, are you all right? Your face is positively white, like you've seen a ghost."

Louise swiveled toward the familiar voice to see the Honorable Royce Merton. No, no longer that. Ever since his elder brother had died in the spring from a hunting accident, Royce had become the heir to his father, the Earl of Merton. Royce was now titled Viscount Merton. It would take some getting used to for

Louise, though it appeared that Royce was getting on well enough with the change.

Standing before her in a dashing Knights Templar ensemble, her friend tossed his head self-importantly as he stretched tall, losing his balance enough to stumble slightly. His curly blond hair flopped against his brow. Louise didn't have to wonder at the cause. Last year Royce had told her that his anxiety was so debilitating that he needed to drink to even set foot in a ballroom. However, lately, Louise had smelled liquor on his breath *whenever* she came upon him, alone or surrounded by giddy dancers.

Regaining his composure, Royce studied her, fluttering his almost-white eyelashes. "Louise? What's wrong?"

She shook her head, placing a reassuring hand over his forearm, steadying them both. "Nothing. It's nothing. My dress is a bit tighter than anticipated, that's all. Why do men always get to be more comfortable?"

Royce glanced ruefully at his flowing white tunic and cape, both emblazoned with a blood-red cross across the center. "You won't be saying that when you see me in Scotland," he groused, color creeping like a weed from his collar to his cheeks. "My armor is a menace. I can barely move in it, let alone joust. Why did I agree to be a knight in this wretched tournament?"

"Because you can't refuse your mother anything." Louise laughed before quickly squelching it when Royce shot her a look. He never could make fun of himself, though he rarely minded laughing at others when the occasion fell in his lap.

She tried not to judge her friend too harshly in that respect. Royce had an affinity for hiding in the drapes at these events just as much as Louise did. That was what had initially drawn them to each other. While their peers danced and enjoyed the heady freedom of burgeoning adulthood, Royce and Louise commiserated on their unfailing feeling of "otherness."

After the death of Royce's brother, Louise had worried that his "otherness" would fade in the eyes of the *ton*. A viscount was distinctly different from a second son, regardless of any lingering atypical behavior. Even Royce's odd delight in spending days cooped up in his country home, playing with his guinea pigs, could be disregarded on account of his ancient title. Aristocrats were known for their eccentricities, after all.

But that hadn't been the case. The young ladies of the *ton* avoided Royce just as stridently as they avoided Louise. And Royce did the same right back. He might have been an unusual friend, difficult to decipher at times, but he was proving to be just what Louise needed. In fact, he was doing her the greatest favor of her life, and she wouldn't soon forget it.

Which reminded her … She crowded toward Royce—as close as her cagelike Spanish Farthingale skirt would allow—and lowered her voice. "Are we all set, then?"

Royce dropped his attention from the whirling dancing pairs on the floor and echoed Louise's clandestine tone. "Of course. Of course," he said, his Adam's apple bobbing.

Louise almost wished she'd curbed her furtive demeanor. Subtlety wasn't Royce's strong suit. He looked like he was being questioned by the Spanish Inquisition.

"Are you still on board?" she asked, raising her voice and her chin. *Nothing to see here. Nothing at all.* "You haven't decided to back out, have you?"

"What? No! I would never do that to you!" Royce said, causing more attention to be cast their way. "I promised to take care of you, and I will."

It wasn't lost on Louise that he picked up his tenor just as he spouted the last bit of his speech. Despite always peering in from the outside, perhaps Royce wanted to be a knight more than she thought—or at least be seen as one.

Did the poor man really think he could offer her protection? Royce might be an inch taller than her, but Louise was certain she could beat him at any competition that relied on physical strength—especially since she'd started her exercise regimen. Not one for outdoor pursuits, Royce was a regular beanpole.

Louise returned a reassuring smile, dashing the negative

comments from her mind. For better or worse, he was her partner, and seeing him in anything other than a positive light would not benefit her now. "Good," she answered. "You can't fault me for checking. I know I'm asking a lot of you."

Royce patted her hand. "Don't you worry about that." Wrinkles formed over his brow. "Is that why you're so worked up? You really do look a fright, darling. How about I get you some champagne? It's one of life's greatest remedies."

Louise's stomach curdled. The idea of putting anything into it gave her the chills; however, Royce was standing there all self-important, enjoying the idea of being her savior so much she didn't have the heart to deny him. She had to remember that it wasn't just her reputation that would take the hit when she boarded the *Clementine*. His social standing—however small—was also at stake. Although Louise couldn't help but be annoyed that she would bear the brunt of disapproval and ostracization. Anyone who thought differently was just plain naïve.

She gave Royce a polite nod and watched him make his way through the crowd toward the refreshment room, her anxiety relenting more the further away he was. He wasn't only her first choice to accompany her to the Sandwich Islands—he was her only choice. And he would have to do. There was no other way.

Honestly, she'd been surprised that he'd taken to the idea so readily six months ago—especially when she had told him that he could only bring two of his guinea pigs with them. It was quite the concession on her behalf, since even thinking about the coarse animals made Louise's skin crawl. But it was just as she'd informed Mr. Harvey—Louise was not a simpleton. There was no way she could sail all that way without some form of protection. If Royce wanted to believe he was providing muscle, she would let him. She would never tell him that what she needed from him most was his name. A married woman who traveled with her husband was always above reproach.

Lady Delilah would be so proud. It seemed marriage was in the cards for Louise after all.

CHAPTER FOUR

CHARLES WAITED FOR Royce to leave. Starting tedious conversations with the new Viscount Merton was not something he made a habit of. What was the halfwit obsessed with? Mice? Some kind of rodent, Charles was certain.

What kind of man focused all his energy on rodents in lieu of hunting or sport? Charles couldn't trust a man who didn't like to sweat, who refused to push his muscles and insanity to the breaking point in search of greatness. There was nothing great about the Honorable Royce Merton—strike that, Viscount Merton.

Why did Louise refuse to acknowledge that blatant fact and let the simpleton skulk around her? She knew how Edward felt about the spineless viscount; her brother couldn't stand Royce, considered him an untrustworthy, odd duck. And yet she persisted with the friendship.

At least Louise had the good sense to send the fool on his way. Royce was heading toward the refreshments and was probably going to bring back champagne. Bloody idiot. Had the man never experienced a hangover before? Champagne was the last thing she needed.

Lady Louise needed *him*.

Charles didn't even flinch as that thought seared through his brain. Over the course of the day, he'd gotten used to it and decided to stop fighting it. It was Louise's fault. She shouldn't have kissed him. Now Charles knew what it felt like to have those luscious lips pressed against his, the sweet taste of her mouth, the lavender scent of her hair scaling the walls of his bachelor heart. The effortless way he could act like himself around her. To Louise, he would always be simply Charles. Not Lord Charles, or the Earl of Somerset, and certainly not the Knight of the Sun. Just Charles.

It didn't matter that Louise was the sister of his best friend. It barely registered that she was determined to find fault with him at every turn. Louise had thrown the dice. She'd set the table. She'd overindulged and told the one man she shouldn't have a deep, dark secret. That, once upon a time, she'd loved him.

Charles was just the bastard to never let her forget it.

Glass of punch in hand, he maneuvered around the dancers. He kept his eyes on his target, not wanting to miss one iota of emotion displayed on Louise's pitiful face.

Her scowl was expected. But there was uncertainty there too in the pastel bags under her eyes, in the ravaged skin of her bottom lip that she bit at when she was nervous. Charles's fingers strained against the glass. In front of everyone, all he wanted to do was wipe the pad of his thumb over that bottom lip and declare to all that he was the source of her trepidation—and her pleasure.

The chatter of voices surrounding Louise became noticeably lighter as he approached.

Nodding to the others in her group, Charles thrust the punch into Louise's hand. The stubborn woman refused to accept it.

"Take it," he muttered, amusement and annoyance battling within. "You look like you could use it."

Louise closed her eyes, sucking in a deep breath. Poor thing. Charles knew exactly how she felt, and he wouldn't wish it on his worst enemy. "I can't," she said dismally. When she opened her eyes again, they were glassy, like she was fighting back tears. "I'm afraid I'll be ill if I do."

Charles ducked his head, leveling her with a look. "Trust me to know about these things," he replied. "It will do you some good."

She threw him a wary stare, but eventually relented. Her hands shook as she brought the fruity punch to her lips and took a minuscule sip. "There. Happy?"

He shook his head. "Not yet, but I will be."

"What is that supposed to mean?"

"It means," Charles answered, crowding her space, "that I won't be happy until we talk about what happened today. After I get some answers, we can move on."

"Move on?"

Charles flashed a smile. "And we can start kissing again. As much as you like. Whenever you like. Which I think will be a lot. I am quite good at it."

Louise's mouth dropped open. For a second, Charles braced himself for her actually being sick. Fortunately, only words came out. "I ... What ... You are not!" she flailed.

Taking her arm, Charles used her irate confusion to guide her away from the eavesdropping group. "What? You think you're better? Always so competitive," he drawled in her ear.

Louise's hair was as straight as the hedges of an English garden, but a tiny patch of baby wisps curled and danced around her ears. That alone was the incentive to stay close, not that he needed it. Charles's body had been tense, at the ready, ever since he spotted Louise in the ballroom. He was drawn to her like she was a magnet, itching to put his hands on the dip of her waist as he had that afternoon.

He'd been too caught off guard to do much when Louise kissed him. Charles had gotten over the shock just quick enough to appreciate the power vibrating under her clothes, the simmering, pent-up desire she'd been shielding for so long. She was like a bomb just waiting to go off, and Charles was determined to be there when the time came. Hopefully, sooner rather than later, of course.

She jerked in his hold. "Stop touching me. I don't want you to touch me."

He chuckled, leading her to a corner near the veranda where she could breathe in a rich dose of cool air. "That's not what you told me earlier. You told me you loved when I touched you, said you loved everything about me, actually—and have for a long time."

He was taking creative license over their earlier conversation, and Louise didn't seem to know the difference. Shame was naked on her face as it crumpled in dejection. For the first time, Charles's conscience nagged at him. She looked like a sailor who'd just woken up in a whorehouse after his first night back on dry land. He didn't want her to be ashamed of what she'd done. Aghast … maybe. Confused … sure. But never ashamed.

Louise peered out into the night, releasing the kind of exhale that made her lips flutter. "I didn't say all that … did I?"

"Would it matter if you did?"

She took another sip of punch. "Yes," she replied into the liquid. "Because none of it is true. And poor marks on you for taking advantage of me. Some knight you are!"

Charles's temper flared. Not for her lying, but for Louise calling out his character. He might have done some stupid things in his life, but taking advantage of a woman had never been one of them.

"I'm not the one who poured the whiskey into your cup!"

"Shh! Keep your voice down," Louise whispered, raising her glove, stopping just short of his mouth. It was exactly what she'd done to him earlier. It didn't take long for that glint of knowing to pass over her, and she dropped her hand.

"Only if you tell me what you were doing this afternoon before I came upon you."

"I already told you," she said cagily. "That's none of your business."

"You have made it my business."

Louise's mouth formed a straight line. "I most certainly have not." She dismissed him, turning back to the dancing. "Thank you for the punch, my lord. I feel better already, but please don't think you have to look after me anymore. I can take care of myself."

Charles snorted, narrowing in on the sharp upturn of her nose as she stood in profile. He wished Louise still had his sketch of her; he had a feeling not much had changed. Still stubborn, still so sure of herself.

Marquis's daughters were such pains in the arse—which was precisely why he'd never dealt with one before. "Like how you took care of yourself this afternoon? You couldn't even find your way back home."

He wasn't sure how Louise managed it, but her spine straightened so taut it looked like it could snap. "Your knightly good deed is done; I won't require any more."

"Oh, but what if I want to give more?" he said silkily, cocking his head so it angled just perfectly at the slope of her neck. Like most other ladies at the ball, Louise was wearing one of those ghastly hoods that looked like she was balancing a house on her head, but Charles still had access to her long neck, could still admire the tendons as they pulsed and pulled in reaction to his every word. He affected her. Despite what she wanted to believe.

"I … I do not require it."

"Just tell me who you were with," he purred, his words causing goosebumps to rise just behind her ear. "You owe me for helping you."

"I … I … owe you nothing."

"You used me in front of everyone," Charles went on, secretly pleased as her eyes bulged out at the word *everyone*. "In the middle of the day, for all to see, you kissed me and ruined my reputation."

"You'll live," she replied dryly.

He grinned. "Will I? I can't be so sure."

"Oh, there you are!" a voice sounded, breaking the spell of their moment. Charles jerked his head back to find Royce in front of them, a perturbed scowl on his round, baby face. "I've been looking for you everywhere. Why did you run off when you knew I was getting you champagne?"

Louise snatched the drink from Royce and downed it in one swallow. Before Charles could react, she shoved the empty flute, along with the punch glass, into his startled hands and lunged into Royce's arms. "Do forgive me. I'm so glad you're here now, though. Just in time. Is that a waltz starting up? Yes. Good. Let's go."

Charles reached for her, forbidding any movement. "I don't think that's a good decision," he said, arching one brow. "You're still greener than a tree frog."

"That's hardly sporting," Royce remarked. "Besides, we're celebrating. A dance is in order."

Even in the most violent moments of his life, Charles had never understood the concept of "seeing red." But that was no more. He saw it now, in its crimson, bloody glory.

"*Celebrating?*" he asked.

Louise ignored him. "I told you already, Lord Charles. I am none of your concern; I can take care of myself."

With that, she towed her puppy to the middle of the dance floor and settled in for the dance. She looked mighty proud of herself … and mighty bilious. Any other day, her yellow gown would have highlighted her bold amber hair, her pale coloring, but today it only made her appear washed out and sickly.

Charles should have left the ball, wiping his hands of the whole affair. The silly chit thought she could handle any situation. She thought she could drink like a man, make decisions like a man, and disregard him like a man. Well, then she could deal with the repercussions of her hubris.

But Charles didn't leave.

He stayed and waited. He was getting awfully good at waiting.

Because he'd been correct when he told Louise that she should listen to him in situations like this. Lord Charles, Earl of

Somerset, Knight of the Sun, had been drunk enough times to know copious amounts of alcohol and twirling around in circles rarely mixed.

So, when Louise's cheeks ballooned up like chipmunk's and she got that crazy look in her eyes, Charles appeared at the ready. Yanking the couple apart in mid-stride, he threw Louise back into the corner, where she generously tossed up all of her bad decisions.

With his form blocking her body, and the band blocking her gagging sounds, Charles had indeed saved the day. Well, not for Royce. Charles made sure that the poor bastard was lodged in the corner, directly in the line of fire.

CHAPTER FIVE

L ORD EDWARD, MARQUIS of Marlborough, perched against the side of his desk, arms firmly crossed. Louise had never considered her brother to be one for drama, but the incredulous expression he leveled on her made her rethink the decision to stop by his home that morning.

"I just don't understand," he said, scratching his head. "You were sick in the corner of the ballroom? Why didn't you run outside?"

From her seat, Louise gave her brother an unmistakable, exasperated glare. "What an idea, brother! Too bad you weren't there to direct the whole awful scene!" She flung up her hands before flopping them down on the padded arms of her chair. "I wish I could have made it outside, Edward, but time simply didn't allow for it."

Her brother answered with his typical frown, clearly not accepting her answer. He wasn't one for letting matters sit. If he believed something was remotely possible, then he was going to do it, with little to no regard for what others thought.

It was one of the reasons why they got along so much better now that they were older. Louise might still be annoyed that Edward refused to cut the wastrel, Charles, out of his life, but she could respect most everything else he was completing in his adulthood. Most impoverished lords would have given up, sold off their homes, or, worse yet, taken out loans to cover their profligate spending habits. Not Edward. After he took over the marquis title and realized their father had left the family with next to nothing, he'd worked tirelessly to recoup their fortune. Currently, he was in the process of funding a mine on their estate that would dig up fossilized reptile bones and use them for manure.

He was forward-thinking, that brother of hers, and Louise adored him for it.

"But why did Mother make you go? You told her you weren't feeling well, right?"

"Of course!" she replied. Honestly, she felt like she was on trial here. Did Edward actually believe she'd wanted to be sick all over Royce and Lord Sinclair's velvet drapes? "But you know Mother. She's determined to make something of me. And, apparently, I'd cried wolf too many times for her to take me seriously."

Edward raised an eyebrow, one side of his mouth twitching in amusement. "Huh. Serves you right, then."

"You're a fiend."

"A fiend who only wants the best for you." With a drawn-out sigh, he straightened away from his desk, and his tall figure loomed over in brotherly concern. "I'm sorry I wasn't there, Lou. But you know how I hate those things. It's not fair that you have to deal with all those people on your own."

Her brother's honesty startled Louise. They were as close as any two siblings could be, but the Englishness in their blood acted like a wall blocking them from taking their regard too seriously. They preferred to show their love through little jabs and cutting comments. Louise wasn't sure why; it just always seemed safer that way.

"I'm fine," she said, shifting in her seat. "I know what all of those people think of us, how they gossip behind our backs about how far we've fallen. Truthfully, I couldn't care less. I have plans for my life that don't involve their opinion of me."

If her brother could understand anything, he had to understand that.

Edward held her stare for long, measured heartbeats, analyzing her, deciding whether he believed her or not. Without blinking, Louise held that stare.

After another stiff moment, he broke, replying, "I know that. You can handle anything, but you shouldn't have to. Once I get this business rolling, things will change for the better, you'll see. I'll be more available. Until then, let's just thank our lucky stars that Charles was there to save you with his quick thinking. My God, what would have happened if he hadn't spotted you in the crowd when he did?"

Louise pressed her mouth shut. She wasn't about to tell her brother that Charles had been watching her the entire time. She'd felt his disapproving attention while she was on the dance floor with Royce. And she surely wasn't about to tell Edward about the contentious conversation they'd shared before she made the silly decision to waltz. The only lucky stars Louise was going to thank were the ones that kept Charles mum on the subject as well. She assumed the two men told each other everything. It seemed there was a limit to their friendly chats.

"When do you leave for Scotland?" Edward asked, altering her trail of thought. "Should be soon, yes? Lord Eglinton will probably host those taking part in the tournament a few days before it begins."

"Mother and I are traveling with the Davenports tomorrow. I just came to ask if I'd see you there. If not"—a lump abruptly formed in Louise's throat—"I thought I would say goodbye now."

He grimaced. "Goodbye? I'll see you soon enough. I'm escorting Miss Spence and her mother to Marlborough House after the tournament. I want Georgiana to get to know you and meet the girls."

A bold move for her brother, who, in the past, was as no-nonsense about marriage as he was about his business endeavors.

Louise had estimated that this was a marriage of convenience, but by the look of her brother—the way his voice grew deeper and more resolute when he mentioned his potential fiancée—she realized she might have been mistaken.

Louise stood up from her chair. She hated lying to her brother; evading the truth was turning out to be just as distasteful. "I am not sure about my schedule after the tournament. We might miss each other." She bit at her bottom lip, desperately holding back any emotion that threatened to spill. Louise loved her mother, she loved her three younger sisters, but leaving Edward was proving to be more than she could handle. He was the one person who tried to unearth the real her and accepted everything that he uncovered, prickly bits and all.

She twisted toward the door. The few short steps over the carpet were too far for her, and her feet stuck in place. "Good luck with Miss Spence," she said softly, ignoring her brother's bewildered expression. "And good luck with the mine. I have no doubt you'll be successful."

"Is everything all right? Are you sure you aren't still ill?" Concern clouding his face, Edward reached for Louise slowly, handling her with the care one usually reserved for consumptives … or lunatics. "You're awfully pale. Maybe you should reconsider the tournament? I'll have a doctor sent to the Davenports'."

"No, no," she returned, shrugging him off. "I'm fine. Just tired. I'll rest before the journey. I *have* to go to the tournament. I owe it to Mother. I wouldn't miss it for the world."

Worry abating, Edward chuckled at her about-face. A day had rarely gone by when Louise hadn't complained about the insufferable event. "Et tu, Brute? The excitement has finally gotten to you, hasn't it?" He chuckled. "I thought we were two of the last holdouts. Now I'm utterly alone thinking the whole thing is rubbish."

Louise laughed with him, the levity gradually ebbing all the would-be tears away. *Oh, Edward! If you only knew why I needed to get to Scotland!*

Not for the first time, she wondered if Edward would despise her for leaving. Was she pushing their sibling affection too far? After surviving the despicable actions of their father, she knew that Edward couldn't abide liars. Would he ever forgive her, or would he eventually understand that leaving England was a step that she needed to take?

Louise consoled herself by believing that it wouldn't take Edward long to come around to her adventuring and travel writing. Now, whether he ever came around to her choice of husband was something different entirely ... Royce wasn't exactly Edward's cup of tea. Her brother approved of obsessions (mostly of the financial or business variety), but Royce's infatuation with guinea pigs was a river too wide to cross.

Before Louise could lament on that fact, the door to the office swung open and Charles's wide shoulders filled the doorway "Oh, good. You're here. I wanted to catch you before I left—"

His body locked into place. The insufferable man recovered quickly, tearing off his top hat to reveal his golden hair and even more golden smile pointed squarely in her direction. Panic set in as he bowed.

Then Louise felt the rumbling in her stomach, and her throat tickled. *Not again!* she thought, clamping her hand over her mouth.

CHARLES FLEW INTO action, snatching a vase off Edward's mantel and dumping its dead flowers and old water on the floor. Holding it under Louise's chin, he couldn't tell who was more surprised by his quick thinking—her or him.

From the corner of his eye, he watched Edward slink away behind his desk. From experience, Charles surmised that was a sound decision. Edward was the kind of person who would be sick if anyone around him was, whether he'd had too much to drink or not.

Holding his breath *and* the vase at the ready, Charles felt Louise reach out and cover his hand with her own. It was a light touch, tentative in nature, but that didn't last long.

"Please move the vase," she choked out, deflating her cheeks as she nudged the vessel away from her nose. "If I have to keep smelling that disgusting, stale water, I really will be sick. And you won't have Royce to shield you this time."

"Royce?" Edward asked from his safe space. "What does Royce have to do with anything?"

Charles straightened, placing the unused vase and its putrid smell in the middle of Edward's cluttered yet organized desk. "Oh, nothing," he said, his focus glued to Louise. Her color was returning, and she appeared on the mend. "Poor old Royce was just in the wrong place at the wrong time."

"You could say that," Louise said, pulling back her shoulders. A tiny swath of sweat peppered the top of her brow, just under the brim of her straw bonnet. "You could also say he was placed in the wrong place at the wrong time."

"Agree to disagree," Charles replied easily with a wave of his hand. "It's not important. What *is* important is that you need to get home." Before she could open her mouth in protest, he had already directed her to the door.

Over his shoulder, he heard Edward say, "Wait. You're leaving already? You just arrived."

"Sorry, old friend—duty calls. There's a damsel in distress, and I just remembered I have a meeting with my solicitor before I go to Scotland. I'll drop your sister off at the Davenports' first, since it's on the way."

Poor Edward was at a loss for words, though Charles was confident that he wouldn't argue. The man had enough on his plate with work and his potential fiancé. Charles had no doubt Edward would have helped his sister home if the situation called for it, but the relief on his face was evident.

"Write to me, Lou," he called out just as Charles and Louise entered the foyer. "I want to make sure everything is fine."

"Don't worry about your sister. She can handle herself," Charles said arrogantly, repeating the insane comment she'd delivered to him at the ball. He lowered his voice for only Louise to hear. "And she's in good hands."

At least she was polite enough to wait until the front door slammed shut before she struggled out of his protective embrace. "Don't hold me like that," she grumbled. "It isn't right."

Charles *humphed*, using his long stride to match her hurried, disgruntled pace.

"I hope you haven't been drinking—or *celebrating*—again. It doesn't seem to agree with you."

"No, I wasn't drinking!" she replied, aghast. "I haven't eaten much today, that's all. My stomach gets upset when it's empty. What in the world are you doing here? Are you following me now?"

"Don't flatter yourself, darling. I was merely stopping in on your brother to ask about his travel arrangements to Scotland."

Louise kept her eyes straight and her face placid. "Then why aren't you still there?"

"Plans changed. I thought accompanying you would be more enjoyable."

"You thought wrong."

"I am never wrong."

Like she hit a brick wall, Louise stopped instantly. "See? There. Right there," she said, narrowing those blue eyes with an intensity that might have made a lesser man falter. "When you say things like that, I quite literally want to pull my hair out. Such conceit!"

Charles *tsked*. "Don't do that. Your hair is one of the most beautiful things about you. I can't wait for the night when you let me take it down and run my fingers through it."

She blinked. "What? Who?" She closed her eyes, praying for patience. "Why are you doing this to me? Why now?"

Charles couldn't stop himself. He reached up and tucked a

thin piece of red hair back behind her ear while Louise froze as motionless as a stone. "I told you. I'm not doing anything. You started all this, and now I am determined to finish it."

Her head fell back as she peered up at the sky. It was another beautiful day in London, no rain to be found; however, Charles doubted she was admiring the various shades of carefree azure. He gave Louise her time, and when she came back to center, he was rewarded with an expression that was less murderous than the one before.

"Charles, please," she began, her tone calm and frightfully diplomatic. "I can't pretend to understand what this is all about, but I'm not the little girl you once knew, and I don't have time for these games. I have too much to focus on over the next couple of weeks. I beg of you to have mercy and leave me alone."

When he opened his mouth to speak, Louise hurried to continue. "Thank you for helping me in the park; thank you for coming to my aid at the ball. I know you get some sort of sick pleasure out of teasing me, but I'm not a child anymore, and I can't keep playing with you. Despite what you think … all this dressing up you've been doing, running around with a sword … you are not a knight. Everything's fake, and this is no fairy tale. Do you understand that? I'm not a damsel in distress waiting for you to save me. Now, I apologize, but I have to go."

Her eyes were big and bright, and, for a second, Charles recognized the little girl he'd spent so much of his youth avoiding. The little girl that never stopped talking, never stopped asking questions. The little girl who thought she could wield a battle-ax with the strength of ten men. The little girl who never asked for help, only someone to play with. The little girl that he'd dismissed and said no to time and time again.

Unfortunately for her, old habits died hard. Charles would have to say no one more time. "I'm sorry, Louise, but I can't do that. I am not teasing you, nor am I playing games. I want you. You will be mine, just as you said you wanted to be. Mine. Now and forever."

The finality of his words shifted something in Charles. He'd heard of men recounting tales of seeing their lives flash before their eyes during a deathly, fearful encounter, their whole worlds wrapped up in one or two measly seconds of introspection.

With his declaration, Charles felt the same clarity, only fear wasn't the impetus. He visualized the next fifty years of his life with this red-headed woman. He pictured arguments and laughter, children and adventure, warm fires and warmer nights, long kisses and lingering looks. Real conversations, original debates and vicious companionship.

Peace overwhelmed him. Pure, unadulterated peace.

And then Louise slapped him. In the middle of the sidewalk, not caring one fig if anyone bore witness. She slapped Charles so hard that he heard a ringing in his ear. Still, it didn't compare to the church bells that would ring after they were married. What a bloody romantic he'd become!

Since Louise didn't seem to worry about a crowd, then Charles wouldn't either.

He shot his arms out and circled her waist, plastering her against his body. He blocked all outrage with his mouth as he plundered Louise quickly and mercilessly, kissing the woman with every ounce of passion he could muster. It wasn't hard. Though he was.

His body reacted to the woman in his arms and strained for satisfaction. But he would be grateful for this kiss and only this. There would be time enough for the other things. Fifty years, if he had his way.

Louise fought him at first, resisting his overture, turning her mouth this way and that, making it as difficult as possible for him to meet her lips fully. When he'd had enough, Charles bit her lower lip, holding her in place while his tongue surged inside her mouth, sweeping the holy land with a frantic grace. He'd planned to woo her, not scare the shit out of her. But it was Charles's equilibrium that was rocked. His ardor raged too hot, his anticipation too great. He couldn't stop at one kiss, and brought his hand up to cup the side of her face, skimming over her downy cheeks with the rough tips of his fingers. Why the hell hadn't he done this sooner? What had he been waiting for?

Louise. He'd been waiting for her to take the initiative again. Well … she could start the next kiss.

As her resistance gave way and her lips succumbed to his, a fluid dance overcame them. Louise still didn't use her tongue. Her shoulders caved in toward him, and he raised his hand to rest in the middle of her back, the sacred dip between her shoulder blades. Charles exerted no more pressure; he merely left his hand there, that light touch enough to feel the vibrations of her body, to touch the fervor that had taken hold.

Louise was the first to break the embrace, canting just far enough away to look at him. Her lips were pink and wet, and she licked at them as if lost in bewilderment.

"Was that fake?" Charles demanded. "I dare you to answer truthfully. And then go ahead and tell me what you feel for me, what you have always felt for me, is fake."

"Why now?" Louise asked. "After all this time … why now?"

He smiled ruefully, lowering his head. "You said this wasn't a fairy tale, but maybe it is. Maybe I was asleep, and your kiss held the power to wake me."

Her lids lowered, and her face fell as if heavy with exhaustion. "I don't have that kind of power."

Charles's hands tightened over her hips. "I think you do."

"I'm leaving," Louise said blankly.

"I know."

"You can't follow."

"Just answer the question," he growled. His patience was at its end. He needed to hear her say it; he needed her truth. "Was that fake?"

"No," Louise answered, the words dragged from her by an invisible thread. "It wasn't fake."

Pure, hot, unmitigated victory charged through Charles's veins. He closed in on Louise again to claim the prize, but she jerked away too fast, edging out of his hold.

"But it wasn't real, either," she said, leaving him alone in his fairy tale.

CHAPTER SIX

CHARLES WAS IN a foul mood.

It had been escalating ever since his encounter with Louise the week before, and it continued to spread like a poisonous spider spinning a web around his pride. He'd thought the trip to Scotland would ease his suffering. The naked splendor of the land had never failed to lift his spirits in the past, and yet, as Charles sat uncomfortably in the deflated plush of the old armchair in the corner of Lord Eglinton's drawing room, he found he could barely muster a hint of the excitement bouncing off the walls from the other men.

With only one more sleep before their debut, all of the tournament's knights had finally descended on Eglinton's castle for the long-awaited event. The fourteen men had been training for the past six months and were at the precipice of showing off their skills and brawn for the fawning crowd. There were whispers going around that close to one hundred thousand people would be present to watch the knights perform. That staggering bit of information had brought some of the men up short, which was probably why some of them were drinking—nay, celebrating—so heavily. These lords and gentlemen of the realm had never been a part of a real battle and had no idea how to assuage their jitters. Drinking seemed as good an idea as any to curb the stage fright.

Charles, on the other hand, paced himself. The last thing he wanted was to wake up with a groggy head that could slow his instincts. The idea of one of these simpletons getting the best of him on the big day was beyond ken; however, he reminded himself that anything could happen when horses and weapons were involved. The lances might have been blunted, but that didn't mean Charles still couldn't be knocked off his seat. And thanks to all the attention he'd received in the newspapers, he had a blazing bull's-eye on his chest. There was no paucity of knights who yearned to provide the blow to send him on his arse and receive their shining moment in the sun.

Lord Eglinton clinked his fingernail against his glass and ambled to the center of the room. Like a seasoned actor on the stage, he spun in a slow circle, catching the light to his advantage, clearing his throat to snuff out the conversations. "Gentlemen, please, if I may," he started, his tone deep and commanding. Charismatic and rather eccentric, Lord Eglinton had never met an audience he didn't like. At only twenty-seven, he was tall and fit, with a youthful, round face he tried to conceal with a pair of bushy sideburns. Though not great friends, he and Charles ran in similar circles, and Charles considered him a good sort and a damn fine horseman. In addition—and perhaps the most important mark of character—the earl had follow-through. When Eglinton first mentioned the tournament, not many believed something so vast and detailed could ever come to fruition. And just look at them now!

Though it had to be said, hundreds of knights had initially signed up for the day of jousting and the numbers had dwindled greatly soon after. The ones last standing were not *le crème de la crème.* Not many understood at the time just how costly their involvement would be in the tournament. Thanks in large part to Charles's lucrative estate (and the fact that none of the previous earls of Somerset had ever had to sell off their possessions), he already possessed a suit of armor to wear for the day, as well as a proper mount. Many others were not as lucky. Attics and antique shops had been pillaged across Europe to find the items needed, and even when found, few could afford the hundreds of pounds to purchase them. The thirteen other men standing with Charles in that well-appointed room weren't necessarily the most fit, most energetic, or most youthful. They'd had the most money, pure and simple.

And they were all champing at the bit to show it off.

"Thank you, my fellow knights," Eglinton went on when the room stilled to an eerie reverence. He placed a guileless hand over his heart. "I can't tell you how overjoyed I am to experience these next few days with you. It's been a journey, but we're here!"

Whooping and clapping showered across the smoke-filled room.

As he let the accolades wash over him, Eglinton's expression turned serious. "It is a good day when a man can look around and see so many like-minded spirits. We all know why we're here. And I applaud your resolve. It wasn't easy. Then again, it never is easy to be on the right side of history."

The atmosphere quaked as the men lumbered up tipsily from their seats. As they were unwilling to relinquish their glasses, the knights' applause was awkward and a little messy, but no one in that room noticed. If the men wanted to boast and pat themselves on the back, then they would.

Charles was the only one left sitting. He blamed one person for his distinct lack of enthusiasm. *Damn Louise.* Her words cracked over him like a runny egg. *All this dressing up you've been doing, running around with a sword ... you are not a knight. Everything's fake, and this is no fairy tale. Do you understand that?*

Of course he understood that! But why couldn't she try to understand his point of view? Earls and viscounts, dukes and foreign princes—what did they have if not their pasts? They sure as hell didn't have too much money left these days. Many of them were predominantly landowners, and their coffers were dwindling along with their tenant rents. Industry was quickly becoming king, and unless this generation of aristocrats got on board investing in the future, they would be left behind. Just like the knights they were desperately attempting to emulate.

These ideas weren't new to Charles. He'd considered them before, but there was something about the current mood, the grandiosity of the present company, that made him give greater credence to Louise's remarks. It was the way Lord Craven was on his fourth glass of brandy and wobbling on his thick legs so much he had to be nudged away from the hearth. It was the fact that Lord Glenlyon had shown up at the castle with no fewer than seventy-three official bodyguards—all ridiculously kitted out in a specially made uniform of a blue jacket, short tails, green plaid, white and red diced stockings, and a blue Glengarry bonnet. Oh, and bagpipes! Charles mustn't forget the bagpipes. It was damn near impossible anyway, since Glenlyon made sure they were playing constantly outside the castle.

Britain was known for its love of ceremony, but Charles was beginning to wonder if the Eglinton Tournament had just a bit too much pomp. Not enough substance.

Of course, it was quite clear he was in the minority with that opinion. Just as Shee had informed him outside the National Gallery, the people weren't looking for the real or mundane. They wanted to be awed, inspired. For better or worse, the men in that room were deemed awe-inspiring thanks to their lineage, even Lord Royce, who stood by himself, tucked away in another unfortunate corner. The dolt kept peeking inside his shirt and laughing. Charles was certain he had some kind of rodent stuffed in there. Lord knew what it was doing to elicit the giggles.

"It's we who should be thanking you, Eglinton," Craven slurred, brandishing his drink in the air, spilling most of its amber contents. "You called out the queen's grievous offense and are making good on your promise. Whyever did she think she could take the crown and change everything along with it?" he asked his fellow knights. "She may be our monarch now, but we must remember she is still a young woman who needs to be shown what is right and what is wrong. And her coronation was wrong!"

"Quite right," Glenlyon said, slapping Craven on the back and then holding him up so he didn't fall over. "We were denied our due! The prime minister spat in our faces by canceling the monarch's state dinner with the peers, as well as the ceremony of the royal champion after the coronation. He relegated us to the side … us! Peers! If you could have heard all the people who came up to me saying how they missed the royal champion's ceremony. Tears in their eyes they had. Such a missed opportunity."

Charles doubted that. The previous monarch was crowned seventeen years before. Other than the Dymoke family, who had performed the ceremony for the last six hundred years, who could remember something as silly and inconsequential as the royal champion's ceremony?

Meant to take place after the first course of the state dinner with the peers, the ceremony would commence when the royal champion appeared in full armor on top of his caparisoned horse, preceded by a flurry of retainers and trumpets. Three times the Lancaster herald would call on anyone willing to fight the champion if they disputed the monarch's acquisition of the throne. The champion would throw down his gauntlet in dramatic fashion, knowing full well that no one would pick it up. Then there would be plenty of toasting and drinking and vowing until the champion back-pedaled his horse away from the monarch's table.

As far as ceremonies went, Charles had to allow it wasn't the worst. But to cry and whine so much over its loss?

But cry the peers did, bemoaning the demise of feudal traditions and whimsies that made England what it was. That made *them* what they *were.* The idea of the tournament was born soon after. "A return to a romantic era" was how the event had been advertised. A return to gallantry and chivalry that was so desperately missing in present society.

Charles grimaced as Lord Jerningham hurried to the corner, audibly relieving himself in the pisspot, completely disregarding the screen that was there for that purpose. Better yet, Jerningham—the Knight of the Swan—could have retreated to an empty room …

Jerningham's trumpetlike flatulence did nothing to halt the conversation.

"My only hope is that the queen will take heed and learn from her mistakes," Eglinton went on. "But I hate to say it … she hasn't shown any signs yet. Just look at her meddling with poor Peele."

"Are you talking about the bedchamber debacle?" Craven asked, his eyelids almost completely shut now. How in the world was the man still standing? Charles marveled.

Eglinton nodded, raising his brow with a self-important air. "The very one. Not even two years on the throne and the girl thinks she knows everything already." He *tsked*. "Won't even switch out her Whig ladies-in-waiting even though it's the right thing to do. Obviously, gentlemen, we know where the queen's loyalty lies, and it's not with the Tories."

"We're being hemmed in on all sides, I'm afraid," Jerningham announced, coming back from the corner, wiping his hands on the back of his trousers. "The queen, her ministers, the bloody industrialists … don't they understand that we, the peers, are the heart and soul of this country?"

Charles had had enough. He unstuck his tongue. "And yet we sit around and harp about the queen and her ladies when there are more important things to discuss."

Every neck in the room swiveled his way. "Such as?" Jerningham huffed.

Ready for the question, Charles ticked his answers off his fingers swiftly and concisely. "Oh, I don't know. How about our invasion of China, or maybe the steamship that just crossed the Atlantic from Bristol, or the damned corn laws, for Christ's sake!"

The air fled the room. Charles saw all the pairs of eyes blinking at him and realized he'd stood up during his diatribe. What had gotten into him? This wasn't the time or the place. These men were just talking as they were wont to do; why had he felt the need to bring reality into the stuffy environment? It was already too full as it was with cigar smoke, bittersweet alcoholic notes, and dreams of better days ahead.

Charles expected a commotion, but the laughter surprised him. All at once, great, inelegant belly laughs of confusion and astonishment.

"Christ, Somerset." Eglinton cackled. "You almost had us for a second. But that was wonderful. Yes, why don't we all sit around and discuss Hong Kong? Yes, let's get on that. It's not like we don't have a joust to prepare for tomorrow!"

Craven stumbled over to Charles. "I had no idea you were so funny," he said after a sloppy gulp from his ever-present glass. "I thought you were just a ladies' man. I think I want to knock you on your arse even more now."

"Don't mind him," a snide voice said from across the room, cutting through the merriment. "Somerset has had a lot on his mind lately."

The knights spread like the Red Sea to display the one who had been quiet up until then. At first glance, it was easy to understand why. Lord Jacobson sported a hideous bruise on the right side of his face. The blues and purples traveled all the way from his jaw to his hairline. Empathy was lost on Charles; in fact, his fingers itched to put a matching bruise on the other side. Jacobson had deserved it. He'd been caught making nasty comments about Louise, citing reasons why he wouldn't lower himself to court her. Once Edward had found out, he'd responded firmly and decisively with one heavy punch. The altercation had happened weeks ago, but the effects were still colorfully apparent. Edward always did have an explosive right hook.

"What's that, Jacobson?" Eglinton asked, pulling himself together. "Why is Somerset so put out?"

Jacobson's gaze latched on to Charles. The corners of his lips lifted in a tiny smile, but the effort cost him, and pain sparked in the whites of his eyes. "I heard that Charles was rejected from the Summer Exhibition—again," he replied snidely. "It seems our very own Knight of the Sun wants to be an artist, but he isn't as great at everything as people like to believe."

Too overwhelmed in his anger, Charles let the others respond for him. "Who told you that?" someone asked.

Jacobson shrugged. "A friend."

Eglinton guffawed. "Jacobson, you don't have friends."

"An acquaintance, then," Jacobson allowed, glaring at his host.

Charles held his ground, waiting for all the teasing and questions to follow. Just because he wasn't used to being the butt of jokes from his peers, that didn't mean he couldn't stand and take them like a man. Let them have their say. Let them sneer at all the hours he put into learning; let them ridicule his need for purpose; let them baffle at the idea of an earl not being content to be an earl. Charles could take it. It might even do him good to get it off his chest. Maybe there were others who'd encountered similar disoriented episodes and could provide advice.

But in the end, only Craven—the valiant Knight of the Griffin—had the courage to ask the one question that, apparently, they all had been thinking. Right before he passed out on the chaise in front of him.

"Do you get to draw naked women?" he asked, tripping over his feet, face-first into the crimson cushion. His voice garbled against the velvet. "I'd do it too if I got to draw naked women. You really are a lucky bastard."

"No," Charles answered tersely.

Craven's laughter bubbled through his drool. "Then what the fuck's the point?"

CHAPTER SEVEN

WHAT WAS IT about a man who couldn't mount his horse that was so funny?

Was it the fact that he was weighed down by three-hundred-year-old German armor that was biting into his pudgy skin? Or was it that those around him insisted on calling him *Sir Knight* while they encouraged him during his failed tries?

Even with all her good breeding, Louise couldn't look away, which, she reminded herself, was her job for this triumphant day—tournament day. Mr. Harvey had ordered her to write about the real tournament. Well, it didn't get much more real than a knight not being able to mount his horse. Like Louise was passing a gruesome carriage crash, her eyes refused to budge from the Earl of Craven's ignominious scene. She bit the inside of her cheek, forcing herself not to laugh.

She needn't have bothered. No one was looking at her anyway. All attention was on the earl as he attempted to haul himself on his noble—and patient—steed for the fifth time. He was red-faced and drenched with sweat, and his neck muscles bulged as he strained to throw his stubby, short legs over the horse's rump, only to be knocked to the taunting ground once more.

A barking laugh slipped out of Louise, but she immediately squashed it with a contrite look of concern. It was all so incredibly funny and very, very pathetic.

But hardly the most pathetic thing Louise had witnessed so far that morning.

That dubious award went to the procession that Louise was currently waiting in. The procession that was currently over three hours late for its own event. The procession that showed no signs of departing the castle anytime soon.

It was an inauspicious start for the Eglinton Tournament. An inauspicious start indeed. Louise couldn't wait to get back to her room to work. It was almost too easy. This article was practically writing itself.

"Darling, why are you here all alone?" Louise's mother asked while gracefully elbowing a couple of medieval squires out of her way so she could stand in front of her daughter. Though a big proponent of the event, Lady Delilah had eschewed the request to dress in historic garb. She appeared comfortable and refined in her dark blue silk day dress with an open neckline and loose sleeves.

She plucked at Louise's voluminous skirts, patting them down and fluffing them out at various intervals.

A steady pool of sweat had been dripping between Louise's shoulder blades for the better part of an hour. The sun had been bright and plentiful as she'd waited outside for the others to gather, and her costume—equipped with layers upon layers of heavy damask fabric—was not conducive to summer temperatures. The accessories were even worse. The high neck ruff strangled her throat, the huge pearl earrings made her ears burn, and the rigid head gable was starting to give her a crushing headache.

But none of that mattered. With her soft red hair arranged back in a high, plaited bun, Louise looked like Queen Elizabeth come back to life. More importantly, she looked like she belonged. That, and that alone, was what her mother cared about.

Louise swatted the older woman's hands away. "Stop fussing, Mother. It's too hot for that."

Lady Delilah scoffed, though she did halt her exertions. "Don't be so dramatic. There's a lovely breeze."

That was true. A welcomed gust had developed over the last half-hour as forbidding clouds formed in the sky, blotting out the sun.

"You should be over by the other ladies," her mother chided, hands poised to begin nudging again.

Louise took a step back, but not in the direction her mother wanted. She had no intention of joining Lady Jane and her ladies-in-waiting until the last possible moment.

"This is not how you make friends," her mother said. "You can't always be on the outside looking in."

Louise scowled. Not this again. "Look around, Mother," she said, gesturing to the crowd forming around them. The procession *had* to begin soon. Louise couldn't move without slashing pantaloon-clad legs with her skirts. "I couldn't be more in the middle. In fact, I would argue I am so in the center of things I am in the beast's belly."

"Really, Louise." Lady Delilah *humphed*, her face agog. "Where do you come up with this nonsense?"

Mercifully, they were saved from further conversation by the Knight of the Griffin. It seemed that Craven had finally admitted defeat. "Hey, you there!" he cried to a passing squire, snapping his fingers irritably. "Get me a chair."

Louise might have imagined it, but she thought she heard the earl's horse release a snort of relief. The poor animal had been granted a reprieve from the incessant yanking.

"I'm not a fan of horses, but I do hate to see an animal in distress," Royce said, joining Louise and her mother.

"Lord Royce," Lady Delilah replied with rigid poise. "Look how fearsome you are in your armor. The Knight of the Falcon. I'd hate to face you today in the lists."

Royce tossed his head ruefully, and his curly blond hair flopped against the wind. His lips twisted together as if each of Lady Delilah's words pricked him through his steel breastplate.

He opened his mouth to respond, but Louise's mother silenced him with a long finger swiping between them. "It was so wonderful to see you, Royce, but I think I see Lady Natick calling me over. I haven't spoken to her in ages. I better say hello before you all retreat to the field. But do keep my daughter company, will you?" She gave Louise a knowing look. "She's being entirely too bashful today. Perhaps you are just the thing to coax her from her shell."

With one last arched brow in warning, no doubt reminding Louise to smile and be as congenial as humanly possible, the marchioness left her daughter in the unmarried hands of the Knight of the Falcon. Louise didn't even stop to wonder if Lady Natick really was in the crowd.

"I can see your mother is in her element," Royce joked. "But how are you holding up?"

Louise found one of her first smiles of the day.

"I'm fine enough, though not as well as you," she answered, appreciating the gleam of Royce's suit. Underneath all that armor, he'd transformed into a person to be reckoned with. "You look like you're ready to smite a dozen surly dragons, at least."

"You're being kind," he said with a polite dose of humility. The crowd knocked him closer to Louise, and her nose twitched. Royce smelled like wood chips and fur—even more than usual. "However, I have no intention of being formidable today. Between you and me, I hope someone knocks me out early so I can get back to the castle. I even think I might fall off my horse and pretend to get hurt. The babies don't like to be alone for long. I think Sir Pigceval is sick. He didn't look at all well when I left him."

Perhaps it was Louise's imagination, but the wood chip smell intensified. "How many did you bring with you?" she asked, terrified of the answer. "And surely you left them safe in a cage."

Royce's incredulous expression was answer enough. "Never! I couldn't keep them enclosed all day. I'm not a monster."

Despite the heat, Louise's skin went cold. It was one thing to bring one's guinea pigs to another's castle. It was quite another to let them roam free in a room all day. But Lord Royce wasn't your average lord. He wasn't even your average person. For as long as Louise had known him, he had had an exuberance for the small rodents, giving each one its own name and backstory. She'd never seen it, but he'd told her all about the miniature village he'd built in his country house in the Lake District that housed all his little pets in cavy splendor. She'd always tried to be polite enough when he entertained her with their adventures, and yet all Louise could ever think about was the awful odor that must pervade his halls.

She attempted to keep her voice level, though her skin began to itch. It always did when they spoke of his guinea pigs. "Does Lord Eglinton know you brought the pigs?"

Royce evaded her gaze, swiping some dirt off his silver ensemble. "I didn't think it was important enough to tell him. All will be well. They listen to me."

They?

"Royce," she said slowly. "How many did you bring?"

"Just a few ... All right, ten."

"Ten!"

Stiffly, he tossed up his armor-clad arms. "Well, they all wanted to come. What would you have me do? I couldn't break their hearts! They're social creatures, Louise. They don't like to be left behind."

"But what about the plans? In a matter of days, we're leaving here to sneak off to Gretna Green before meeting the ship. I told you that you could only bring two. Please don't tell me you're bringing them all?"

"On that savage voyage? Of course not," he said, taken aback. "Don't worry your pretty mind about that. I've got it all figured out."

For some reason, his confidence didn't bolster hers.

Suddenly, the ruff around Louise's neck was strangling her even more. She had no real love for Lord Eglinton. But she couldn't help but feel terrible for the noble knight who might come back to his castle after vanquishing his foes and find it eaten through by a bunch of neglected guinea pigs.

The image of all that coarse fur, those little scampering feet, the sharp, devilish teeth, made her entire body revolt. Louise longed to tear at her clothes to scratch at her skin. It felt like thousands of ants were crawling up her legs.

She was sharing a room with her mother at the castle. What if one of the pigs got out? What if it found its way to her bed and snuggled up under her sheets just waiting for her? God forbid, what if it ate her toes while she slept?

Louise's chest pumped. She couldn't breathe. Her clothing was so damn heavy and restrictive, but no match for a smart rodent. Sweat began to pour down her temples as her vision clouded.

Royce was still talking. In her haze, she couldn't hear him, but his lips were moving. She thought she heard "whiskers" and "claws," and that just added fuel to the fire of her paranoia. She had no love for furry little animals. But she especially hated when they were loose in the same place as she.

Louise stumbled back, bumping into a few musicians who were practicing their flutes. Angry glares were tossed back at her, but she paid them no notice. She needed to get away. She could practically feel wet noses, their brambly feet. She could feel them chewing on her slippers and running up her legs.

No. Not her legs. Her ears!

Soft fur nuzzled against her lobes, and Louise couldn't take it anymore.

She did what she'd wanted to do ever since her mother told her she'd be a part of the Queen of Beauty's court at the Eglinton Tournament six long months ago.

Louise screamed bloody murder.

CHAPTER EIGHT

T HE FUR WAS replaced by a growl in Louise's ear. "What the hell is the matter with you?"

A pair of large, strong hands gripped her shoulders.

Louise opened her eyes to find the only thing worse than ten starving guinea pigs lunching on her toes. Charles.

"Stop shaking me," she said, wiggling out of his clutches. He rearranged the helmet he carried in the crook of his arm. A long, thick red plume sprouted from the top, and Louise blinked, suddenly realizing what had happened. "Did you stick your *plume* in my ear?"

Charles answered with a soft, crooked smile. "Who would do something like that? Never me. Why did you scream?"

"I thought I saw a guinea pig." She grinned maliciously. "But no, it's a different pig altogether."

Charles's emerald eyes held hers shrewdly before he let out a low whistle. "Very clever," he said.

"Only when compared to you," Louise returned with a smile.

Charles cocked his head. "Really? Are you still pretending to hate me? After everything we've been through."

"I have no idea what you're talking about," she said breezily. That was a lie, of course. But she'd rather strip naked and let guinea pigs feast on her for days than acknowledge his comment.

Charles shifted his stance—and his gaze. "When your brother

told me you were a lady-in-waiting, I couldn't believe it." He started low, working his way up her body. Louise didn't know how he did it. Even with all her layers and ruffles and lace and pearls, she still felt horribly bare beneath his frank perusal. The man was a cad and a rake and every other vulgar word she couldn't think of at the time. But he was also charming—and handsome. Horribly so.

His eyes returned to hers, with a hint of appreciation on his freshly shaved face. "I thought you would have called in sick today, but this surprises me. You look …"

Her corset constricted her breath. What? How did she look? Did it matter? *God. Yes.*

Charles rubbed his square chin a few times before dropping his hand. "You look … perfectly capable of ordering someone to be beheaded."

Louise tried so hard to keep her spirits from sinking. She held on, clutching them with all her might, but they still fell like they'd been filled with lead. Served her right. Why was she begging for compliments, anyway? *She* was the one who'd run away from *him* the last time they'd been together on the street outside Edward's townhouse. She shouldn't crave—nor did she deserve—a kind word.

She lifted her pointy nose. "So very clever."

He graced her with a little bow. "Well, I try."

"Not too hard, I hope. You might hurt yourself," she quipped, rolling her eyes when he merely laughed. He was always laughing at her. "And you look …"

Charles took a step back, giving her more room to make her appraisal. As if she needed it.

She'd seen him in his armor often enough. Her mother had made sure Louise was present for every one of the knights' practices during the summer. However, that didn't diminish the magnificent scene he presented in front of her.

For starters, Charles was one of the only men wearing armor that was his own—or at least from his family. Perhaps that was why it fit so well. He didn't need to squeeze into it like Craven, nor did he look the least put out by its unyielding steel. Simply, it looked made for him, exemplifying that he came from a long line of men fashioned for battle and glory. The steel was thin and molded with curves so delicate and refined that Louise had no trouble imagining he could dance in it, just like medieval warriors did in the past to limber up before a coming battle.

However, that was the last thing she would tell him. Charles was well aware of his appearance. "You look … stiff."

Stiff? That was rather weak.

A mischievous grin widened across Charles's delighted face. "Stiff? Yes, I suppose I rather am."

Why did she feel so uncomfortable all of a sudden? "Well, I am sorry for it."

"Don't be," he replied. "I rather like it … from time to time."

This conversation was ridiculous and only getting more so. Why wouldn't he just leave?

"Don't you have someplace you need to be?"

The question cajoled him out of his teasing. Charles blinked a few times before regarding the crowd while it continued to swell around them. If the procession didn't move soon, Louise was afraid they'd all burst together like an overinflated balloon.

The procession was close to half a mile long. It was as bloated as a corpse and just as stagnant.

The entire party still had to snake its way down to the lists and grandstand that Lord Eglinton had built especially for this day. The earl had spent the better part of the last year planning the entire weekend, and had spared no expense. When one's goal was to resurrect a medieval tournament, one didn't skimp on the details or worry over the bottom line.

However, with all his meticulousness—the historically accurate banners and heralds, lances and swords he'd commissioned, the tickets he'd sold, the nationwide hysteria he'd created, the hours of exercises he'd organized with the other knights—it seemed no one had practiced how to form a line.

Charles didn't seem to mind as much as Louise. Of course, he never seemed to mind anything. Why would he? Worries and problems never dared ruin his days. He was rich and titled, handsome and witty, and his whole life was a series of events dedicated to bacchanalian pleasure. And to Louise's ever-living disappointment, he didn't see the problem with that. He'd told Louise that her kiss had awakened him, but she was confident he was merely sleepwalking through the motions.

"I think we've got a little bit of waiting left," he said easily. "Lord Glenlyon still has to get his bodyguards in check."

Louise snorted. Bodyguards? She looked past Charles's shoulder to watch the Scotsmen gather—all seventy-three of them. The colorfully dressed men filed around their lord as if they were ready to die for him in battle … bagpipes poised at the ready. Though Louise had to admit, there was something about men in kilts … those bare knees … It was all quite thrilling.

"See something you like?" Charles asked, forcing her focus to snap back to him and his crooked smile.

She huffed. "Oh, please. I am just taking all this in." After all, it *was* technically her job. She threw an arm out. "This performative gallantry is so unnecessary. Do you know how many women and children are starving in London right now? Families are being thrown off their farms for not being able to make rent. People are working from sunup to sundown in factories and can still barely make enough money to feed their families. Children are lost on the streets with no homes to go to at night, and yet we are here. Playing. Acting like none of that matters. Instead of using his money to actually do some good in the world, Lord Eglinton is putting on a medieval tournament to entertain his silly friends. It's all so … disappointing. No wonder people say the aristocracy is out of touch. How much more out of touch can we be? How can you take part in this? How can you just prance around on your horse pretending the world is some fairy—"

"I'm sorry, what?"

Louise swallowed. She hadn't meant to say all that, but there was a fire inside her, and once she opened her mouth, it had all spilled out.

And Charles hadn't heard any of it. He shook his head. "I'm terribly sorry. Can you repeat that? I missed some of it. You should have seen yourself. Your face got so serious!"

Louise's spirits sank—again. She didn't even try to hold them up this time. She should have known her speech would land on deaf ears. Especially his … the darling of the tournament. "Never mind," she replied lifelessly. "Don't listen to me."

"My favorite words out of a woman's mouth."

Louise's lips tightened, and she was rallying to give Charles a good set-down when he stopped her with a raised hand.

"Oh, I'm just teasing you. You used to know that. Even laugh a little once in a while. I understand what you are saying. I might even have said something similar last night. It is all a bit much."

Was that true? Or was he just trying to get on her good side?

"Sorry if I don't feel like laughing anymore." Louise shrugged, looking away, not able to hold his gaze, feeling even more foolish than before. Even though there were only fourteen knights taking part in the joust and melee, there were over two hundred people involved in the procession: musicians, heralds, squires, pages, and archers … all desperate to be a part of the grand spectacle. "It all just seems so … remote."

"Oh, I suppose it is," Charles drawled, surprising her. For a moment, he allowed himself to be serious. She liked the way it looked on him.

They stood in companionable silence. Louise waited for him to say more, but nothing came. It seemed that one sentence was to be the only concession he gave her.

She crossed her arms. "So, are you going to tell me why you stuck your plume in my ear?"

"I told you. I didn't. I was merely walking past as you were speaking to that odd fellow."

Odd fellow? Royce! When had he left? More importantly, why hadn't she noticed?

Charles continued. "My plume must have had a mind of its own."

The wind kicked up, and as if it knew it was being discussed, the plume fluttered against Louise's chest. She knocked it back with an indignant flick of her hand. "Why does your plumage have to be so thick and long?"

His smile widened. "It doesn't *have* to be. It just is."

Whatever that meant.

"What could you possibly have been talking to him about, anyway?" he went on. "Every time I turn my back, you're whispering to him."

Louise frowned. "Who?"

Charles nodded behind her. She twisted to catch Royce fighting through the crowd. Her scream must have frightened him—or maybe it was the guinea pig that he, most likely, was hiding under his breastplate.

"He's not odd. Well, not *that* odd."

Charles cocked his head, and a lock of dark blond hair fell over one eye. Louise desperately wanted to brush it out of his face ... or pull it until he screamed.

"Since when are you so nice? You know as well as anyone he's an oddball of the first order."

"I am nice!" she railed. "Just because I don't fall for your lazy charm like every other female of your acquaintance doesn't mean I'm not nice!"

"No ..." he replied slowly. "The fact that you never have anything pleasant to say to me and you like to throw mud cakes in my face makes you not nice."

"I was four years old, and you and my brother had just finished locking me in the chicken coop! You deserved every dung-filled cake."

Charles only laughed.

"Don't you have somewhere you need to be?" she asked again, nodding to the ladies-in-waiting who were pretending not to look her way. No, not her way—his. It didn't matter where

Charles was—he always directed attention. When she was younger, Louise assumed it was because of his good looks, but now she surmised it was more than that. Charles was easy. Fun. Charismatic. He was the kind of person that made you feel better. Not her, of course. But others.

Like Lady Charlotte, the daughter of the Duke of Wembley. Charles had already denied that he was going to marry Charlotte. He'd said he wanted *Louise*, but she couldn't allow herself to believe something so far-fetched.

Surreptitiously, she eyed the woman who was surreptitiously eyeing Charles. Jane Seymour might be the Queen of Beauty, but everyone knew the real lady of the tournament was Charlotte. Not only was her lineage long and impeccable, but she held the kind of loveliness that could make a blind man see. The quintessential English rose, her skin as white as cream, her hair as yellow as the morning sun. She was the woman that men rode into battle for, wrote poetry for, fought wars for. She was the woman that men became knights for.

Charles followed Louise's line of sight to the group.

"I think they're doing well enough on their own," he said flippantly. "The last thing they need is my putting a halt to all their gossip."

Louise chuckled but was caught off guard at its bitterness. She cleared her throat. "I doubt it. The Knight of the Sun? Can't you see? They're all getting their favors ready in case you ask for them before the joust."

That appeared to amuse him. Charles lifted an eyebrow at the idea. "And what about you?"

"What about me?"

"What favor will you give me?"

Louise made an incredibly unladylike sound out of her nose. "I have no favors."

He screwed up his lips in disbelief. "Oh, come now. Of course you do. Do you think I don't know that your mother dressed you today? That entire ensemble was carefully curated by the marchioness, and she would *never* let you watch the joust without planting some favors somewhere just in case a dashing knight, such as myself, rode up to you before the tournament, tilting my lance to you in the stands for all to see and admire."

What a sight he conjured.

Charles moved closer, his fingers tripping up to the ruff around Louise's neck, giving it a little tug. "What do you have hidden in there? What will you give me out on the field?"

Outraged, Louise slapped his hand away, her face growing red. Why was he doing this? He knew as well as she that he would ask nothing from her. "Stop that!" she said. "Why do you always behave so badly?"

He chuckled. "I'm just trying to get you to laugh. Come now, we're old friends."

"We are *not* old friends."

"Then what are we?" he asked soberly. "Fiancés ... lovers ..."

"You're mad. We are ... we are ..." Louise couldn't find the words. And she was great with words. But it was Charles's turn for seriousness. The way he studied her made the words all jumble in her head like a bowl of trifle. His eyes, green and vibrant, burned darker and deeper the more he stared at her, as if her response *really* meant something, as if he *really* wanted to know the answer. What were they? Enemies? No, never.

But his being a friend was equally as off-putting ... equally pathetic.

Just like this tournament. Just like this procession.

The procession! Was it moving? In the right direction?

Louise woke from her stupor. "We're ... we're ... moving."

The lines around Charles's mouth constricted as if he was holding something in. "It would seem you are right," he replied in an even tone.

Through the haze of the excitement, Louise thought she heard someone call out Charles's name. His squire ready with his horse, ready for the knight of all knights to show the people what they'd been missing all these centuries.

The squire, decked out in crimson to match Charles, shoved

his way to them. "My lord," he said proudly, giving Louise a passing flicker of attention. "It's time to take your spot."

She didn't even have to ask where that was. It was near the front. Charles was always near the front. She, on the other hand, would trail behind the likes of Queen Jane Seymour and Lady Charlotte, smushed and corralled until she barely fit in their shadow.

And she would watch the show along with everyone else. Was that what Mr. Harvey had had in mind? Would her experience be any different than the other writers relegated to the outside? Harvey had chosen her. For better or for worse, he'd had faith that she could provide something more than the others, something different, something from *inside* the circle.

That was when it hit her. Louise's natural inclination was to say no to the preposterous idea, which was why she loved it. It was so insane that it was brilliant.

Charles began to follow his man but soon twisted back around, flashing Louise his pearly-white teeth. "Have your favor ready, just in case," he said, gesturing toward her chest. He secured his helmet over his head, and only his eyes were visible, a slash of green in the horizontal slit. "And try to stay awake, at least while I'm out there."

Louise laughed despite herself, a nervous giddiness running over. "I have a feeling I won't allow myself to miss a thing," she replied, the wheels in her brain turning.

"Will you cheer for me?"

"If you win."

"Then I shall win."

"Just because I asked you to?"

"Always. Because I want to give you something real, even if you are too much of a coward to believe we are."

Louise was anything but a coward. The world was full of people who were too afraid to reach for what they wanted. Louise wouldn't be like everyone else. She wouldn't be grateful just to orbit around the Knight of the Sun.

Today, she would take her place next to him.

CHAPTER NINE

LOUISE THOUGHT WOMEN had it bad. But knights had it infinitely worse.

It hadn't taken much to convince Royce to let her switch places for the day. In the end, the thoughts of an indignant Sir Pigceval had weighed too heavy on his conscience, and he acquiesced readily, meeting Louise in her room so they could make the grand exchange.

Thank the Lord the procession continued to rot at its standstill, because Louise needed all the time she could get to maneuver out of her convoluted costume and into Royce's armor. It was like a maze of fabrics and unyielding clasps and buttons, frills, and cold steel. Substituting her petticoat for chain mail, Louise awakened to the notion that men were slaves to fashion too—they just didn't talk about it.

Somewhere in all that changing and fussing, she became aware that there was still time to come to her senses, but she refused to let that cowardly notion take root. Men took risks. Men made things happen—male writers even more so. Charles Dickens didn't just sit around all day, dreaming up stories of urchins. No! He hit the grimy London streets searching for stories in the darkest parts of the city. He lived the tale, just as Louise was doing now. Mr. Harvey wanted to know what it was like to be a knight at the Eglinton Tournament, and she was just the woman to tell him.

"How do I look?" she asked, spinning away from the full-length mirror.

Royce studied her, cupping his chin before a smile split his face wide. "Marvelous," he said, adding a round of applause.

Louise walked a couple of laps around the room, instantly concluding that armor was even more cumbersome than it looked. She acclimated to the complexities of the attire, finding a way to move without looking like a baby deer just fallen from the womb. The months of exercise and extra eating worked in her favor, and it didn't take long for her to stomp from wall to wall with masculine swagger.

Royce had purchased the suit in France and spent the extra money to have it adapted to his body. Even so, it fit Louise better than she'd hoped. She was used to feeling caged by the corset she wore every day. At least with the armor, her legs had the range to bend and charge; there was a sense of motility she'd never experienced before. A sense that she could do anything, be anything, take anything she wanted.

Apparently, the old adage was true. The clothes really did make the man.

If Louise had been forced to complain, she might have mentioned the lack of room in the chest area, but that was a minor inconvenience. What mattered was that she looked like a real knight, not a woman playing dress-up.

Royce stepped in front of her, holding the one missing piece. "Just remember what I told you," he said sternly, keeping the froglike helmet just out of reach of her outstretched hands. "Just drop. Bertie, my squire, has been informed of everything. He'll keep the lance and shield for you until it's your turn to compete. You will only have to hold them for a few seconds after the flag is waved, and then you can collapse on the ground, crying hurt. You won't have to go anywhere near your opponent."

Louise worried at her bottom lip. "Won't that look suspicious? Shouldn't I charge for a few seconds before I take the fall?"

"Oh, my dear," he said in exasperation. "There's no need to act the hero. You're playing me, remember? Everyone out there already knows I have no talent for this sort of thing. They all assume I'm only doing it because my mother forced me to—and they're not wrong."

Royce tucked his hand inside his jacket pocket and pulled out a small flask before unscrewing it without ceremony. It seemed now that they had changed in front of each other, all polite considerations were also thrown out the window. Louise's nose tickled at the harsh smell freed from the container as Royce threw his head back and took a long gulp.

She wanted to ask him if it was a little early for that kind of drinking but decided to hold her tongue. He was doing her a monumental favor. She didn't want to offend him into taking it all back.

"You're right, there's no need to play the hero. Playing a man will be heroic enough," she teased, but Royce didn't laugh. He was too busy, in the middle of another drink.

Finding the opportunity, Louise snatched the helmet away, smacking herself with the bright blue feathers spouting from the top. Royce's helmet was festooned with so many, she felt like a rooster. A very manly rooster.

She slid the helmet over her head, where it hid her mischievous smile. It was snug thanks to her hair, which she'd piled on the top of her crown, though it rubbed awkwardly against her ears. *How did men fight in these things?* It was like being encased in a tomb. A narrow slit across her eyes was the only way she could see, and the vantage it provided was paltry at best. Still … if she couldn't see out, that meant people couldn't see in.

Royce flicked up the visor of the helmet, revealing her face. Louise took a deep breath. The air holes in the helmet also left much to be desired.

He slanted toward her, lifting a white eyebrow. "You will be careful, won't you?"

She returned a confident grin. "Don't worry, Royce. I will

take every precaution. I'm just doing this for the experience. Thank you for being concerned for my welfare. You are a true friend."

Royce huffed and slammed down the visor. "I'm not only worried about you getting hurt; I'm worried you will get caught. If the men find out I let you do this, they'll murder me."

"Oh, come now. It can't be any worse than running off with me to the Sandwich Islands?" Louise remarked through the cavernous mouthpiece.

Taking another drink, Royce shrugged and muttered something under his breath. Louise couldn't hear his response. It was probably for the best.

THE PROCESSION WOUND toward the lists with the ungainly grace of a teenage boy in the full flush of a growth spurt.

Louise joined near the back. Her squire, Bertie, kept her horse contained, holding the animal tight as he walked in front, hoisting Royce's standard high. A snow-white falcon stretched its wings majestically against a royal-blue background. It was the same falcon that was engraved on her breastplate. Even though it wasn't hers, Louise raised her chin proudly. Royce had told her not to play the hero, but there was something so enticing about her current environment. They could have all been marching to battle, the level of importance pulsing from the crowd was so high. Men sang, bagpipes played, feet stomped, children giggled, and all were addicted to the spectacle—even Louise.

The only issue that soured her spirits was the increasing rain. A storm had developed while she'd been perfecting her armor inside the castle, and had climbed to manic levels by the time the procession arrived at the grandstand.

Even though it dripped through the eye slit, pooling at her lower lids, Louise could still make out the gargantuan crowd waiting for them. She'd heard the crowds would be big, but she didn't think anyone had any idea it would be like this. Rows of people, ten or fifteen deep, lined the road to the grandstand where the two thousand people who had paid for tickets sat in annoyed anticipation. It was where her seat waited for her, near the center under the awning for the Queen of Beauty. That seat would remain empty today.

Bertie towed the horse toward the tent bearing Royce's colors, along with the colors of several other knights. Louise didn't stop to inspect; she was too busy dismounting in the most competent way she could manage. She'd gotten this far. She hated the idea of arousing suspicion before the event even started.

Leaving Bertie with the equipment, she entered her allocated tent and took up sentry at the far side, where she could see everyone and was close enough to hear most of the conversations. The other knights had taken off their helmets, and she dearly hoped they wouldn't make a fuss over hers.

She recognized the others easily enough as Lord Beresford, Lord Alfred, Sir Hopkins, and Lord Albright—all older men with children roughly her age or younger. A rush of relief hit her at being in their fatherly care. They were distinguished members of the *ton* who had never uttered an unkind or unsavory word in her company. They were gentlemen through and through.

They were also the most disgusting humans she'd ever witnessed.

Louise's girlhood innocence officially died a swift death in that space while the men wiled away the time, waiting for the event to begin.

Lord Beresford struck first in the obscene proceedings. He shuffled to the center of the tent, pressed one nostril flat with a finger, and blew a stream of snot out the other. In front of everyone! And no one said a word! Louise gagged as a long, wet green stream of ooze shot like a bullet from his nose.

"That looked like a good one," Lord Alfred called out jovially while the others laughed.

Lord Beresford blew one more time, getting a little more gunk out before responding, "This damn Scottish weather. My nose is running like a sieve."

"At least it's not your arse." Lord Albright chortled, shifting his wide bottom on his seat. "I don't know what I ate last night, but it went right through me. How the hell can I ride when I'm worried that I might shit my pants with all the bouncing?"

"Just ask Royce," Sir Hopkins said, nodding to Louise. She stiffened under her armor. They'd given no indication they'd seen her before; she'd prayed they'd just go on ignoring her. "Hey there, young man. We know you have lots of experience with this. How do you keep from shitting those guinea pigs out of your arse whenever you're scared?"

The fellows broke out in rapacious guffaws. Not wanting to attempt anything resembling a sound, Louise lifted her shoulders in a pathetic shrug. The men only cackled more, each responding with a quip as foul and immature as the last.

It was almost as if there was a competition to see who could behave the most disreputably. Was this what men did in private? Were they truly no better than uncouth boys?

Not that they were completely without manners. There were invisible rules at play. Each man had the opportunity to cut the other; no one was above the harsh, nonsensical jabs. And when they became bored with childishly heckling one another, they moved on to those outside the tent. Gossiping like mother hens, they entertained themselves with stories of their sexual prowess. Louise wasn't *that* naïve; thanks to her father's many exploits, she understood the seedier aspects of the world, but she'd had no idea men spoke about it so flippantly. Mistresses, scullery maids—dear God, even mothers-in-law—were ripe for the plucking and the fodder.

Shame was something Louise was well acquainted with. Being a female, it had been spoon-fed during breakfast along with her porridge for as long as she could remember. But these men had none of it. Not a tiny drop.

If anything, they reveled in their depravity—and their privacy. Without women around, they acted with complete abandon, scratching themselves in every open orifice their armor allowed. They belched and hiccupped, farted and yawned. They stretched and spread their arms, as free and careless as vultures. In essence, they were allowed to be unapologetically themselves in all their disgusting and wondrous glory.

Which also meant exposing their fears and insecurities—though that was less intentional.

With a bluster of breath, Beresford lifted himself from his chair, his knees cracking from the effort, and strolled over to the mouth of the tent. Louise readied for another round of snot. Instead, Beresford craned his neck outside and unleashed a laborious snort.

"Ugh, any chance he might reschedule?" he asked with a hangdog expression. "Not the safest environment for a joust, is it? Mistakes can be made. I, for one, am not looking forward to being convicted of manslaughter."

The men chuckled uncomfortably at the notion, all eyes avoiding the others.

The municipalities had informed Lord Eglinton on numerous occasions that if any of the knights left the event deader than they came in, arrests would be made—despite all the good intentions. This was why the lances had been blunted and the knights had practiced aiming for their opponent's shield. Everything had to go to plan. Risks could not be taken.

Unfortunately, no one had informed the prickly Scottish weather of that fact.

"Eglinton's in too deep," Lord Alfred said, picking at his teeth with a thin stick. He opened his maw so deep and wide that Louise noticed he was missing half his teeth in the back. No wonder the lord rarely smiled, and when he did, he did it with a closed mouth.

Alfred's efforts were rewarded, and he stared at what he'd dug from his teeth for a few seconds before flicking it on the ground and continuing. "The poor bastard has lost half his fortune from this venture. Maybe more. Have you seen all the people out there? If he doesn't pull this off, I'm sure those miserable plebians will tear this place apart. And don't get me started on the newspapers. They'll burn him alive."

"That's his problem. Not ours," Hopkins replied, combing his hands over his mustache. His voice was as light as fresh whipped cream, but Louise noticed his fingers shook as they played with his snowy facial hair, twisting the ends round and round.

Beresford made a harsh sound. "I only wanted to impress that little opera singer I've been chasing for the last month, and she already gave me a taste last night. My work here is done."

Alfred twisted up his mouth. "Josephine Gallas?"

Beresford puffed out his chest as much as his armor would allow. "The very one."

"Is she …" Alfred inspected his dirty stick. "Is she looking for a new protector?"

"I'll ask her tonight when she's on top of me."

"Ugh." Alfred sniffed. "That's not the vision I want at the moment." He paused. "But yes, thank you, that would be most appreciated."

Louise's knees shook. It was all so revolting and positively riveting. These were the same men that cried that the natives of the Sandwich Islands were savage and feral. These men who couldn't take a step without fidgeting with their private parts! Harvey had been correct. Louise could use them as practice for her travel writing. They were as foreign—and loathsomely entertaining—to her as people could get. She could have listened to their vile stories all day.

But not everyone had the patience for it.

The tent flaps were yanked back in a flurry and Charles came charging through. Though much older than him, the men stifled their laughter and stood to attention. Even Louise bolted from her corner.

Charles's long blond hair was drenched and dripping over his shoulders. His green eyes were dark with an intensity that Louise had only witnessed after he'd kissed her. Her insides warmed, putting her on edge.

"Are you ready?" he asked. It was a rhetorical question, meant more to inspire than to ascertain their feelings, but it didn't have the effect Charles had been looking for.

The four oafs took their sweet time, shuffling their muddy boots on the floor. They peered at one another from under heavy brows, giving speaking glances in a language Louise couldn't comprehend. Beresford must have been the one to draw the proverbial short straw, because he stepped forward. "Are you sure this is such a smart idea?" he asked, scratching his neck. "Eglinton couldn't have thought this through."

The muscles around Charles's jaw leapt. "He has."

Beresford stepped back, only replying, "Ah."

"The people are waiting," Charles said, his voice a distinct challenge. "Eglinton wishes for us to line up and salute the crowds. He's sick of you all hiding in here."

Alfred's face paled. "I don't know, Charles …" he said, taking the smallest steps possible to the opening. "It's the devil out there. A messy business, that."

"What's the matter, Alfred?" Charles sneered. "Afraid of a little mud?"

Alfred raised his bulbous nose. "Afraid of taking a lance in the throat." He threw Charles a beseeching look. "We're not really knights, you know. We're not trained for this. Most of the others can barely ride the lists in perfect conditions. Go speak to Eglinton; he'll listen to you. Tell him to call the whole thing off."

Charles nodded sympathetically, seeming to be swayed. Alfred's anxiety visibly released as Charles wrapped a long arm around his shoulders. "I understand. I truly do. You liked pretending to be a knight in London, impressing all the women and the newspapers, boasting to all your friends, and now that the time has come, you've lost your nerve."

The color ran back to Alfred's face. "I am not a coward. How dare you—"

"It's nothing to be embarrassed about," Charles interrupted, exhibiting more force to get the poor man near the tent opening. He paused at the flaps. "Do you see all those people out there? They are tired and bored and cold and wet. And angry. So fucking angry because we took too long preening and showboating to get our arses down here. And now they want a show, and we—*you*—are going to give it to them." He swatted Alfred's back with a hefty pat. "Be the man you've always dreamed of being. I know you don't have much heroism, and you certainly don't have any honor, but for this one moment in your life, finish what you started. Do something you said you were actually going to do. This isn't Oxford. Your father can't buy your way through. Earn this day. Be a man. Be a knight."

Louise cringed. As far as rousing speeches, it left much to be desired. Accompanying every stirring word were two stabbing Alfred straight in the back. But the other men must have been too dumb or too scared to detect it, because they all started cheering Alfred on, hooting and whistling until the lord collected his gumption and stepped into the rain.

Fools, all of them. Gullible fools.

Nonetheless, Louise must be a gullible fool as well, because she'd been ready to trip Alfred in the mud and be the first one out the moment Charles began to speak.

"When the time comes, I'd like to go first in the joust," she said, marching to the center of the tent where the men regarded her as if a statue had just spoken. She cleared her throat, trying for a deeper, more virile sound. "Um … my lord."

Charles's icy stare was so deep and so prolonged that Louise was certain that he could see right through the armor into her deceiving, womanly heart. Teeth clenched, she waited for him to tear the helmet from her head, exposing her perfidy. It never came. Instead, he flashed that Charles charm.

His golden face opened into a rugged smile that didn't reach in his eyes. "There now, you see," he said to the men, his hands on his hips. "Royce isn't afraid. He's ready to ride out there and show everyone what he's really made of."

The knights exchanged chagrined, put-out expressions that Louise couldn't help but take offense to, even if they were directed at Royce. Did they really think him to be such a weakling?

She lifted her head as high as she could. "Lord Charles, I am serious. Let me go first. I can do it."

"Oh, I'm sure you can, lad. I'm sure you can," Charles said with such condescension that Louise clenched her fists. Why did he have to be such an ass? "But the people are hoping for a little drama, a little bit of dazzle. Excuse me for saying you lacked much of that in practice. Let the real men go first."

That was the final straw. Louise might not be Royce, but she was more than familiar with being told to step aside for a man. "These *knights*," she said, "do not wish to go. They are afraid."

"Now hold on there, son," Beresford said, stalking forward, literally throwing his weight around like a bear asserting his dominance. "No need to be so crude and lie about us now. We never said anything of the sort. Of course we want to participate. Champing at the bit, we are."

Louise had no idea how her helmet stayed on. Her eyes felt like they were tripping out of their sockets. Crude? *Her?* After all the disgusting nonsense those man-children had just spewed!

Beresford held up both hands in a defensive position, as if he were talking a crazy person off a ledge. Louise was confused. Was *she* the crazy person? Because she actually wanted to follow through with what these paragons of virtue had started?

"No one is acting cowardly," Beresford went on. "We're just being cautious, that's all. No need for rudeness. As we're all gentlemen here, I think it's important that you give us apologies before we go out."

Charles raised his eyebrows. "*Are* you going out?"

Glumly, all four men nodded before turning to Louise for her apology.

But her lips stayed as impenetrable as her armor. The only apology she would be giving was to Royce later that night. Because she had no intention of taking a fall. Not in front of these craven imbeciles.

CHAPTER TEN

WHAT THE HELL had he gotten himself into?

Charles wiped the rain out of his eyes for the umpteenth time. This was not what he'd signed up for. Despite all the months of training and planning, nothing had gone the way it was supposed to.

If the procession had started on time, then perhaps the knights could have had a few hours to perform for the crowds without the deluge, but the party had moped its way to the lists four hours late, and by that time, the storm had already made its mark.

The pomp and ceremony that Eglinton promised had been quickly thrown to the wayside. No master of ceremony came to the forefront to introduce the knights; no gauntlet was thrown to signal the start of the event. Hell, even the Queen of Beauty skipped out on her duties. In an effort to keep dry, she and her ladies had been driven to their seats in a carriage so most of the spectators didn't even get a chance to admire her. It was all so anticlimactic. The opposite of romantic.

Not that Eglinton hadn't tried. In an act reminiscent of pulling teeth, he had forced the knights to line up in front of the grandstand at the beginning to create some semblance of courtesy and formality, but the majority of the men only lasted a scant minute before scurrying back to their dry enclaves. The feckless youth, Royce, remained the longest, waving his sword around like a boy who'd found his father's weapons. What a fool. Charles had to admit, though, that Royce's overzealous antics had done the trick. The long-suffering crowd had quickly forgiven the knights' lateness and cheered mightily.

The exuberance lit a fire under the knights as well. Determined to give the crowd a decent performance, the men rallied, dismissing the rain as if it was nothing more than an irritating nuisance. But like an ill-treated mistress, the storm didn't appreciate being ignored, and soaked any and all with its unremitting displeasure.

After thirty minutes, the lists had officially turned to soupy mud. The horses could barely lift their feet as they galloped, and the knights couldn't see through the rain well enough to strike one another. Five pairs of jousters had already concluded, and no one had landed a single blow. Incompetence was on full display.

It was a mess. It was discombobulated. But, most importantly, it was embarrassing. And Lord Charles, Earl of Somerset, hated being embarrassed.

As he bided his time to compete, he could hear the crowd growing angry and restless. Boos and colorful phrases were being thrown out into the gales as the shoddy event wore on. Charles couldn't fault them. These people had paid good money and traveled long distances to be here. And the entertainment wasn't the only disappointment. The venue was simply not accommodating to such a disaster.

The misery wasn't relegated to the lower classes, either. One solitary roof had been built for the grandstand, and it was only made to cover the Queen of Beauty's section. The wind had made short work of it. The slats had been poorly constructed, and the sheets of rain were running through them as if there was no covering at all, leaving the ladies and their expensive fabrics to the mercy of the elements. The weather didn't care who you were or how much you'd paid to be there. Everyone would suffer.

But not while he was out there. Charles rejected giving up

that easily. These people came to see a knight, so he would give them a knight.

He gathered his helmet and was just about to put it on and exit his tent when he saw his squire come up beside him. Jeffrey, a distant cousin, was currently attending Oxford. When he heard about Eglinton's idea, he'd practically begged Charles for a chance to participate. Since he hadn't the money—or the athleticism—to come as a knight, Jeffrey figured being the squire to one was the next best thing.

The young man had done his best to hide his jealousy while he attended to his more fortunate cousin, and Charles had appreciated that. And as the sodden squire now looked at him with his wide brown eyes, there wasn't a hint of resentment to be found.

"I don't think it's a good idea, my lord," Jeffrey said dolefully, grimacing as two more knights limped in from the rain, sprayed in so much mud one couldn't see the armor. The shine had most definitely worn off.

"What are you talking about?" Charles demanded. "It's my time. *Finally.*"

With his signature stride, he marched to the entrance, but Jeffrey, growing bolder, reached out for his arm. "My lord—"

"Jeffrey, I told you to stop calling me that. We're cousins, for Christ's sake."

The younger man ducked his head. "Sorry, Charles. I … it's just … it's getting bad out there. This all seems rather reckless."

Charles furrowed his brow. He peeked out of the tent flaps toward the pavilion situated next to theirs. Lord Eglinton was standing under a striped awning that was doing next to nothing. For all the chaos going on around him, the earl appeared as calm as ever, as if the storm was just another light Scottish shower. Who knows? Maybe to a Scotsman, it was.

Charles shook Jeffrey's hand from his arm. "It's not that bad."

"Not that bad?" Jeffrey repeated, incredulous. "Charles … the visibility is terrible. I know the lances are blunted, but there's a chance you could really get hurt out there."

Charles answered with a scoff. Hurt? With all this armor? Hardly.

Jeffrey would not be deterred. "Fine, then. If you're not worried about yourself, at least think of your horse. It's almost a certainty he will break an ankle in all this muck."

Now, that did give him pause. Charles considered his cousin's warning. Putting down an animal was torture. Was a mere day of play worth that? His resolve softening, he sighed, glancing around the tent. Glenlyon—no bagpiping bodyguard in sight—was hunched on a chair in a corner, pathetic as a drowned cat, nursing a wound on his arm. It wasn't even a respectable cut, gained in battle. He'd slipped and sliced himself on a knife that someone had dropped in the mud. Jacobson slumped next to him, equally as pitiful. Charles couldn't stand the pompous son of a bitch, but Jacobson had had the misfortune to be out in the open preparing to mount when a piece of wood flew off the grandstand and knocked him in the head. He was lucky he was still conscious. Hell, he was lucky he was still alive.

The others weren't faring any better.

The boos became louder. To give the knights a few minutes to recuperate, two performers had taken to the field to provide some one-on-one combat for the audience. Charles deduced that if he were a paying spectator, he would have been equally disgusted. Even though the swords were clearly props, they were still too heavy for the knights under the current conditions. Each swing looked like it was being made at half speed, each step a slog of effort. They only managed to clank swords twice before one of the men slipped and fell right on his face. When the "victor" tried to help him up, they both landed arse-down in the slop.

Halfheartedly Jeffrey chuckled at the dismal scene. "Perhaps we should stop while we're ahead. It's all becoming a bit too real out there."

The hair on Charles's arms stood up. He gave his cousin a baleful glare. "There's nothing wrong with something being too real."

Charles escaped from the tent, mounting his horse with little fanfare. The animal snorted, shaking its head a few times, giving his master no doubt on how it felt about the day, but the noble steed didn't balk as Charles led him onto the field.

He wasn't going to deny it—the applause was a little disheartening. Most of it was drowned out by the rain; however, this meager welcome wasn't how he'd envisioned his glorious moment. He'd expected cheers and tears, flowers thrown by little children, kisses thrown by grown women.

Charles gestured to Jeffrey for his standard, and, raising it high above him, he rode around the field, encouraging his horse into an elegant, careful prance.

Yes, this is the way. The crowd seemed to wake up from its trance, clapping and yelling for the knight who wasn't afraid of a little rain. Charles couldn't even feel it anymore. Like water on a duck's back, it slid off him as he pandered to the people. For this one slice of time, he felt like a hero among men, a warrior for his people, a dream for women.

Speaking of women ...

Charles signaled to Jeffrey to take the standard and give him his lance. He directed the horse to the front of the grandstand. Charles had prepared all those months to joust, not to play the romantic; however, a knight's job was more than fighting. A knight was an idea. A hope. A symbol of all that was chivalrous and honorable in the world.

He was also a lover.

The horse stopped in the center, opposite the queen and her ladies. Lady Jane was doing marginally better than the others. Her brother had taken it upon himself to stand behind her with an umbrella. The miserable thing wasn't doing much, but it was something. The bedraggled and cold other ladies weren't quite so lucky, with all their luscious ermines and furs plastered and heavy against their tiny bodies. Charles thought he was losing consciousness; the entire section appeared to vibrate in front of him, but he soon realized they weren't vibrating—they were shivering in unison.

It was time to put some blood on their cheeks. On one set of cheeks in particular.

The crowd held its breath, waiting to see chivalry in action, expecting Charles to lower his lance in front of Lady Jane, or even Lady Charlotte. However, his eyes continued to wander.

To the seat on the end. Louise's seat.

The empty seat.

She hadn't come! A hot flash of anger erupted in the pit of his stomach. All the rain soaking into his body couldn't seem to squelch it. Charles told himself Louise was smart. This was no place for her. He told himself she was probably reclining on her bed right now, with a good book in her hand and a fire roasting the room.

But how dare she be so warm? How dare she be so comfortable?

And more importantly, how dare she not be there to witness his bravery, his valor!

Not that he was doing this for her ... but it was the point of the matter.

The ladies began to fidget even more. Charles couldn't leave now; he had to do something, even if it was with the wrong woman. He shifted his attention to Charlotte. Good Charlotte. Lovely Charlotte. Proper and feminine Charlotte. With much aplomb, he lowered his lance, and she sweetly, and most femininely, tied an embroidered pink linen around the tip. Most likely she'd embroidered the thing herself. Charles wasn't even sure if Louise knew how to embroider. Probably not.

He shook his head. Why did he care? He didn't. Then why did he suddenly wish to know so badly? Because Louise was his, dammit! And he should have known. He wanted to know everything about her.

The crowd ruptured in exaltation, and Charles raised his horse into the air, balancing the animal on its back feet before directing it to the far side of the lists. His opponent, Lord Craven, was waiting for him on the opposite end.

No, wait. It wasn't Craven.

Charles squinted through his worthless eye slit. Who the hell was it?

Jeffrey arrived at his side, patting the horse on the head, cooing words like it was a baby. He handed Charles his shield.

"Who is that?" Charles asked.

Using his hands as a visor, Jeffrey peered through the pounding rain. "Lord Royce. Craven must have turned chicken."

"Lord Royce?" Charles's heart sank. Lord Royce was an unskilled child. Poor sod, he didn't have a chance. Case in point: Royce's lance was waving back and forth in the air as if he was having a hard time keeping a grip on it. He'd probably drop it before they even met in the middle.

Charles should go easy on him. The crowd was already behind him; there was no need to be a bad sport. On the other hand, Royce needed to fall. A hit had to be made. The people needed to see a real knight in action. Even if it was just this once, only for today. Charles could strike without hurting him. A simple tap would take Royce from his seat.

The signal was made, and they took off. Charles kicked his horse into action, getting more speed than he'd anticipated. Balancing the lance at his side, he held it in the crook of his arm, squeezing it with all his might to keep it from slipping. Words would never express how alive he felt at that moment. The crowd chanted his name. This might be Eglinton's tournament, but this was Charles's field. In this crazed moment, he let himself believe his hype; he let himself agree with all the newspapers and admirers. He was born for this. The armor on his back was his birthright; this life was made for him.

Royce was straight ahead, picking up momentum the closer he came. The young man could barely mount his horse months before, and now he was raging down the field as if the spirit of the falcon he wore on his armor had finally decided to show up.

Charles had expected Royce to intentionally fall off the horse by then, to save face. He found some fledging respect for the eccentric lord. Royce possessed a spine after all.

Charles lowered his chin, aiming his lance in the middle of Royce's breastplate.

Water showered down his helmet, blocking his vision. Charles leveled his breath, holding steady.

But his horse couldn't do the same. The animal rocked off kilter, losing its feet. It was just the advantage Royce needed. As Charles's mount was crippling beneath him, Royce's lance came forward, though much too high. All the knights had been taught to aim for the chest. It was the safest hit.

But Royce, for all his speed, had misjudged the angle. When Charles's horse fell, Royce's lance stayed elevated. It skimmed the outer edge of Charles's helmet, shooting him straight out of his seat. It wasn't a direct hit, but it was enough.

Charles had no inkling of how long he stayed in the air. Could have been seconds. Could have been hours. All he knew was that he'd never felt so weightless before. So completely unfettered.

He landed with an immense splat.

Royce and Jeffrey were at his side in seconds. They flipped Charles onto his back, checking him for any damage. Gingerly, they slipped off his helmet, being careful with his neck. The rain felt delicious on his face. It meant he was still alive. When Charles began to twitch, Royce and Jeffrey let out matching sighs of relief.

Royce ripped off his gloves and held Charles's head in his hands. Such soft skin for a man, Charles thought before remembering that he was probably not supposed to enjoy it as much as he did.

A long red tendril fell out from beneath Royce's helmet. Charles stared at the piece of hair, disbelieving everything that was running through his addled brain. It couldn't be. *How? When? Why?* Charles tried to speak, but his mouth wouldn't work; his tongue was too stunned.

"Royce" broke out into sobbing onslaughts of high-pitched

apologies that Charles didn't even pretend to listen to.

He couldn't.

The crowd was too wild. Because it had finally seen some action. It had finally seen a real knight. Unfortunately for Charles, it hadn't been him.

CHAPTER ELEVEN

LOUISE HAD NEVER written a story so fast in her life. Once the first sentence came to her, the rest flew out of pen like magic.

I first suspected we were off on the wrong foot when Lord Craven, our Knight of the Griffin, couldn't even throw his own heavy extremities over his saddle.

There wasn't a doubt in her mind that it was exactly what Mr. Harvey wanted from her. Brutal honesty. Unflinching realness. All for the tournament that never was.

Not long after Louise's triumph on the lists, Lord Eglinton had decided enough was enough. Like a dog with its tail beneath its legs, he'd ventured out in front of the grandstand and informed the crowd that the conditions were too dangerous. The knights were calling it quits for the day with the hope they would be able to try again the next. Wishful thinking, if ever Louise heard it.

The downpour had reduced the lists into a swamp and the surrounding fields into a shallow pond. She'd been lucky enough to get back to the castle none the worse for wear. In fact, even muddy and soaking wet, Louise felt better than she'd ever felt in her life.

"How much longer are you going to be?" Royce asked from the bed. He'd been stretched out over the duvet ever since Louise returned to his room to take off all the armor. She'd wanted to start writing as soon as possible, and he'd been generous enough to recommend his desk. It wasn't like he was using it. Since he'd been drinking all day, all Royce was in the mood for was more drinking ... and toying with his guinea pigs. Five skittered over him, using his prone body as an obstacle course. Louise couldn't watch and resorted to breathing through her mouth. She didn't have time to itch.

"Just a few more seconds," she said, head down over her work. She took one more pass over the story, checking for any mistakes. She would give Harvey no reason to doubt her professionalism.

Finally, Louise put the pen down. Harvey had set up a messenger that would meet her later that night to hand over the story. Then it would be quite literally out of her hands, and the first phase of her grand plan would be at an end. It scared her to believe it had all gone so perfectly thus far.

"Oh, Royce, it was extraordinary." Louise breathed from deep in her stomach, hooking an elbow over the back of the chair as she twisted toward him. "I still can't believe I did it."

Crossing his arms behind his head, Royce pulled his attention from his pigs, amusement and annoyance equally apparent on his cherubic face. "I can't believe it either, especially since I specifically asked you not to."

Louise attempted to curb her smile and show some contrition. It was terribly hard; her body continued to mutiny against her kinder instincts.

Her arm still vibrated from the contraction of her forearm muscles. Her lance had become something of a phantom limb. She'd held the long stretch of wood tight for so long that she could still feel it in her grasp, still feel the pain as she'd used every reserve of her body to project the ten-pound pole out in front of her. It was excruciatingly heavy, but when Louise had made the final strike ... it could have been a cloud.

This was why men didn't want women exercising. Muscles

put them closer to an equal playing field.

She'd done it. Louise had been a knight. And she'd knocked Charles off his mount and his proverbial pedestal. Life couldn't possibly get any better than this. His shocked expression while prone in the mud had been priceless. He hadn't thought she'd been strong enough to do it. Well … to be fair, he hadn't thought *Royce* would be strong enough.

After she'd ascertained that the only thing marring Charles was his pride, Louise had ridden around the lists in a victory lap, reveling in the adoration of the people. The experience had been beyond surreal and over much too quickly.

Power was a strange and remote fruit, but after tasting it once, Louise was a glutton for more.

"I'm sorry," she replied. "I know you wanted me to fall, but the crowd was so ready for something amazing. They'd sat through so much—" Louise glanced at the dark window where the rain pummeled the glass. It had not let up for one minute since she'd returned, and the constant battering was a nag on her conscience that she should have done more for the people who'd come to the event.

That morning, most of the spectators had sent their carriages and conveyances away, assuming that they wouldn't be returning home until late in the night. By the time Eglinton canceled the jousts, the majority of people were stranded without any hope of getting back to their homes and hotels by horse. They would simply have to walk. The closest village was two miles away— not a staggering distance in fine weather, but, of course, it was not fine. Appropriate lodgings were few and far between. She'd heard grumblings that the village couldn't house a small fraction of the gathering that had journeyed to Scotland. Where would they all go?

"Royce …" she said slowly. "Do you think we should go out and check for any stragglers? Don't we have a responsibility to help the people? After all, they are here because of us."

Louise didn't know when the knights became "us" instead of

"them," but she loved the shiver that shot up her spine when she said it.

Royce's attention was back on his rodents, and he took turns tickling each one's furry belly. His expression clouded over. "Are you mad? Go out in this? Are you sure you didn't take a hit on the head today along with Lord Charles?"

Louise frowned. "There are families out there … children. Someone could die."

"I doubt it. Don't be so dramatic," he scoffed.

Louise's eyes narrowed at her friend's lack of empathy. Then she watched as he took another swig from his trusty flask.

She wasn't ready to give up. Her victory was still fresh and coursing through her veins. She felt invincible. Her time at the lists had compelled her to believe that everything she said was important and worthy of being listened to. "Royce, please. We are knights—"

"No, Louise, *we* are not," he replied acerbically, sliding the guinea pigs off him so he could hobble up from the bed. "We are people, just people, who have the advantage of a warm room and a roof over our heads—and, hopefully, a good dinner soon. Don't carry on about it. Just be grateful that you had your fun today and now can relax with me."

His smile did little to calm the sickening roll in her stomach. What was the point of being a knight if you weren't there to help others? Was it all just for show? She'd always known it wasn't real, but for a smidgeon of time that day, Louise had believed in the magic of the tournament. Had she been as gullible as the others?

She mirrored his stance. "I can't relax. Not when people might still be out there."

"Stop it, Louise, that's enough," he said, raising his voice. She flinched as if he'd slapped her. Royce had never spoken to her like that before, and she wasn't sure how to react. Louise reminded herself to address it with him the next time he was sober. She couldn't allow him to talk to her that way. She was going to be his partner, not just his wife.

For now, though, she made excuses for his brutish behavior.

The second part of her master plan was soon to take effect. She and Royce had initially decided to run off together the night of the tournament, when everyone would be too busy at the medieval dinner and ball to notice their disappearance. But thanks to the rain, those events were now postponed indefinitely. Perhaps Royce's short temper was the result of the uncertainty. They were so close to the end; it made sense for nerves to be frayed.

Seeing her distress, Royce calmed himself, painting a grin over the tension, but it did little to quell Louise's unease. "Listen, my friend," he said, hanging an arm around her shoulders. She cringed. One of the pigs had pooed on Royce's shirt, and he hadn't cleaned it off. "You wanted to know what it felt like to be a man today, didn't you? Well, this is a part of the lesson."

Louise tilted her head up to him, even more confused. Royce's white teeth gleamed while he continued his instruction. "Women have husbands and fathers, people to look out for them and keep them safe. Men, on the other hand, well … we only have ourselves."

Turning Louise square to him, Royce held both of her shoulders in his hands, making her wince from the fresh pair of bruises left behind by the armor. He didn't notice and went on. "A man must always remember to take care of himself—first and foremost. Heroes die. Ordinary men live long, content lives, and they are the ones who write history." He chucked her chin lightly with his knuckles. "Don't you see how lucky you are to have me taking care of you? You should congratulate yourself every day for picking me to be your husband." He hiccupped, smiling at his pigs on the bed. "We *really are* going to be so happy together."

CHAPTER TWELVE

W HISKEY MADE EVERYTHING better.

Charles reached for the half-filled bottle and topped up his glass again. He rarely let himself imbibe this much, but then, he rarely got rammed in the head with a lance and thrown off his horse. And rarely by a woman he was infatuated with. Desperate times, and all that …

Charles took a long pull of the sharp drink. An hour ago, he'd started out merely sipping; he had a feeling he'd be gulping it in no time.

A gurgle of laughter escaped him. *What a fucking day.* Jeffrey had warned him not to go into the maelstrom… But Charles hadn't listened. No. He hadn't *wanted* to listen. The event had been going so demonstrably wrong. He and the other men had worked so hard for so long, and he just wanted to perform, to do what came so easily to him, to live up to the standards they all held him to, the standards he'd perpetuated.

Charles could only be grateful he wouldn't be in London this week. Lord only knew what all those newspapers would write about him. He'd been the darling of the tournament to all the journalists in the months leading up to the big day, and he'd taken that goodwill for granted. If he had learned anything, it was that the writers loved tearing a person down from their pedestal even more than they liked placing him on it. Charles had risen too high. It was his time to fall, and he had done so in a spectacular fashion.

And Louise had had a front-row seat. What was wrong with the bloody woman? Why did she have to be so … different … hardheaded and … *different*? Had she thought at all about the consequences of someone recognizing her? She could have lost everything—she could have lost her life!

Stupid fucking Royce.

He was the real reason Charles was still sitting in Eglinton's library, even though it was long past midnight and the house was fast asleep. His fellow beleaguered knights hadn't been in the mood for celebrating. One by one they'd retreated to their rooms, licking their proverbial—and not-so-proverbial—wounds. Charles didn't trust himself to climb the stairs just yet. If he did, he would head straight to Royce and kill him for going along with Louise's little game. Then he'd handle Louise, though what that meant, he wasn't sure. He was coiled too tight, too swallowed by his feelings. The smartest thing Louise had done all day was stay out of his line of sight. She was probably hiding with her idiotic partner.

What kind of a man was Royce, allowing a woman to take his armor and participate in a joust? Did he think it was funny? The idiot must be so under Louise's spell to let her get away with doing whatever she wanted all the time. No, that was puppy love. A real man took care of what was his; he didn't let it ride off into danger to placate some childish fantasy.

The resolute pitter-patter of feet outside the library dragged Charles from his rambling thoughts. Damn, who was still awake? He'd forgotten to close the door, and he wanted to talk like he a wanted a hole in his head.

The fire had gone out in the hearth. The moon, which had only recently broken through the thick clouds and trickling rain, provided the only paltry light in the room. Maybe if he stayed perfectly still, whoever it was would walk right past, thinking no one was there.

He tensed, his fingers tight around his glass as he blended into the shadows. He watched a figure pause outside the doorway. Back and forth, back and forth the person paced, their lovely red hair undulating down their sides.

Charles found his first smile that evening. Perhaps his luck hadn't completely run out after all. He hadn't been ready to confront Louise before, but thanks to the liquor, he was more than willing now.

Tucked away in his corner, he spied on her as she wore out the marble floor for a few more minutes.

What the hell was she up to?

Charles couldn't possibly believe she could commit more mischief, but this was Louise, after all. With her, he was learning that anything was possible.

Once more, he castigated himself for not recognizing her in the tent before the joust. He scowled, remembering everything that she'd been privy to, the gross, utter maleness that gentlemen usually took such pains to hide from their feminine counterparts. He should have known something was amiss when she hadn't taken off her helmet like the others. But Charles had been too engrossed, too single-minded on the day at hand, too ready to impress the crowds. His ego had allowed her to slip right through the cracks. Perhaps Royce wasn't the only one who needed a sound beating.

A shiver crept up Charles's spine. *I could have lost her.* And he'd only just grasped how much he wanted her. All the heat drained from his body and an odd thought ran through his muddled head. Would he be warmer if she turned to him now? Would her fiery nature bring him back to life?

Forgetting himself, Charles shook his head at the ridiculous notion, and his seat creaked. Louise's shoulders jerked at the sound, but before she could investigate, another figure approached. Not just another person—another man.

It all happened too quickly. Charles was launching himself from his seat to find out just who thought it appropriate to meet with a woman—*his woman*—this late at night when the exchange ended in a wisp of movement that, if one blinked, one might have missed entirely. A brushing of hands, a passing of an item. A quick "thank you" and that was it. No furtive kiss or hasty embrace. Nothing. Just Louise alone again, and a man charging back up the long staircase.

That didn't stop Charles or reduce his anger. He continued for the corridor, permitting the coward to flee. He only had one person on his mind anyway.

Louise whirled just in time to catch him coming upon her. Her eyes took up her entire face as he snatched her by the waist and pulled her into the library, kicking the door shut after her skirts cleared the threshold. Charles's grip was solid.

Louise didn't fight him. Instead, she laid her head back against the wood and rolled her eyes. "What are you doing awake?" she intoned like she was asking the heavens instead of him.

It turned out that standing wasn't Charles's best idea, and he instantly thought better of it. Whiskey was all well and good when it came to making headaches and inhibitions disappear; however, it tended to stymie all other faculties. Walking—hell, standing—was not in the cards for the time being.

He reached back for a chair and slid it over. Sinking back in the seat, he crossed his long legs at the ankles with a devil-may-care attitude, stability and composure regained.

"I could ask you the same thing," he replied casually.

Louise cocked her head, her hair showering over her front like she were a Botticelli painting. His very own Venus. "Sharing a bed with my mother is not conducive to sleep. Her snores are louder than the thunder."

She was such a liar. Charles let it go; he decided to give her so much rope she could hang herself. "Do *you* snore?"

"Of course not!"

"How do you know?"

Her innocent expression created a rightness in Charles's body that he hadn't felt in days. Not since he'd last been with her.

"I just know," she replied adamantly.

Charles shrugged, reaching for his drink but realizing that he'd left it on the table in the corner. "Lots of people snore; it's nothing to be so outraged about."

"I'm not outraged," Louise said, looking very much outraged. "I just don't snore, and I don't want you thinking that I do."

"I won't mind … when we eventually start sharing a bed. Just so you aren't self-conscious about it."

Color infused her cheeks. "Thank you for your concern, but I won't be self-conscious about it because we won't be sharing a bed." She gripped her words like a sword, slashing at Charles with vicious intent. Nothing could wipe away his grin. Sex was inevitable. And he was almost sure she knew it too.

Louise darted her eyes at him critically, so much so that he found himself swiping his hair off his forehead. "It doesn't look like you even *tried* to find your bed tonight."

Charles's grin turned wolfish. "Care to help me with that?"

"Ugh. You are a drunk pig."

"You called me a pig earlier today when I wasn't drunk. Do you have a fascination with those animals?"

"Only when they're in front of me," she shot back wickedly. Her lips curled. She was so proud of that tongue of hers. "So, tell me. Why are you still so wet? Have you been sitting here since you've returned?"

"Would you even care?"

Louise frowned. She searched for a seat and pulled one up to his. It was all very civilized. "You might not believe me, but I am sorry the event was called off."

He snorted. "Stop lying. You never cared about the tournament."

"You're right, but I …" Louise gulped as if she was trying to get down medicine. "I care about you. You've worked hard for this; it's a shame it ended as it did."

His eyes like slits, Charles regarded her, reading her words between their lines and finding no guile. "You care about me? It's about time you admitted it."

"God's teeth, Charles, I'm trying to say something nice to you, and you have to take it there."

"I didn't take it anywhere." He chuckled. "You did."

Louise slapped her hands on her upper thighs, pitching her torso forward to get to her feet, but Charles reached out, capturing her wrists. With one fluid pull, he had her sitting over his lap.

"You're not going anywhere until we talk," he said, arranging her legs so they draped over his. She was tucked into his elbow, the side of her breast pressing enticingly into his chest. Charles knew her to be courageous and hardheaded, but he was surprised by the visceral strength he felt under all the layers of clothes. He could sense the long, sinewy muscle, the youthful athleticism beneath the velvety skin. He'd always considered Louise an "inside" type of girl, not very sporty. She could ride with the best of them but had never shown much interest in hunting or other male-dominated activities. Where had this power come from?

"We don't need to talk," she stated, wiggling so much that Charles had to clench his jaw to stop from yelling out.

"Yes, we do," he growled. "Why don't we start with why *you* are awake now? Who were you meeting in the corridor? And you better not say Royce."

Louise sucked in a breath, anger turning her eyes into shards of deep blue sea glass. "You ..." she stammered. "You should not spy on people."

"And you shouldn't be meeting a man late at night unless that man is me."

She slammed a palm into his chest. "Oh, Charles—"

He seized her palm, holding it strong and steady over his racing heart. Let her know what her touch did to him. "I mean it," he said again, keeping her gaze. "Now tell me who that was."

"It was no one. A servant. I was just sending a letter. To my brother."

"At this time of night?"

Louise bit at her bottom lip sourly, like a child miffed at being caught. "I didn't want to forget."

Charles's mouth formed a grim line. Pointing out the falsehood was worthless. They both knew it was a lie.

"Now your turn," she continued before he could probe any further. "Why are you still up and so wet?" She squirmed over him, and Charles almost apologized for soaking her petticoats. He'd been cold and soaked for so much of the day that he'd stopped registering it.

"I was helping some of the spectators find shelter."

Louise's fingertips curled into his chest. He must have had too much whiskey, because it felt like she was trying to cup his heart.

"You mean you went back out?"

"Back out? Hell, I never left. No one was helping the poor bastards. It was the least I could do after falling and ruining their fun."

"You would have helped them even if you hadn't fallen."

The words were like a caress to his broken spirit. Charles could almost feel it piecing itself back together. His reply came out low and utterly wrecked. "Be careful, Louise. That sounded almost like a compliment."

She *humphed.*

Charles laughed. "Why is it so hard to admit that I'm the man of your dreams?"

Louise's hand slipped out from under his. She held it primly in her lap. "Because I stopped allowing myself to dream about knights a long time ago."

"No one can control who they dream about."

"That's true," Louise said. She met his gaze squarely. "But when they wake up, they can choose to forget. And I forgot you, Charles. Out of sight. Out of mind."

His soul cracked into pieces again. Louise's admission was so vital, so hurt, that he wanted to pick her up and carry her to his room. Charles yearned to peel off her clothes and place her on the bed. Then he would lie behind her, folding his arms and legs over her so she would be forever warm. He needed her to feel his heartbeat through the skin of her back. Let the shouting of his blood tell her what he, infuriatingly, could not. That he would always take care of her, that she didn't have to be wary of his intentions, that he was no longer the callow, selfish boy who couldn't see past his own nose. That the rest of his life would be performed in her honor.

But that authentic eloquence was difficult for Charles. He was known in their world for smooth words and an even smoother smile, but none of that was real. It was performative. His true side usually only found its release through his paintings, and even that was a solitary endeavor.

"I wish I was strong as you, because I don't think I can ever forget what I saw today," he began tentatively. His fingers skipped from her wrist all the way to her shoulder. "Despite the rain and the mud and the flags and the plumes, I saw red. Fiery, scorching red riding toward me. Right before everything turned to shit. Oh, don't think about leaving now. There's nowhere to go anyway. You're right where you belong."

Like she was an animal resigned to slaughter, Louise's skin turned icy in his arms. Her expression fell at Charles's little slip. She'd been outed.

"What are you going to do to me?" she said, right to the point.

"What do you want me to do?"

Louise's focus was directed to his lips. "I suppose you want me to kiss you again?" Such lack of passion, such businesslike calm, almost made Charles's balls shrivel to dust.

A chuff of air came from his nose. "We're bargaining now? Fine, but I think we're well beyond kissing, aren't we?"

"I don't understand."

"Tell me the truth, Louise," Charles continued, irritated with her callousness. Why couldn't the woman just fall in love with him like everyone else? Why was she making this so damned difficult? His pride kept him from asking those pertinent questions. "Why did you do it? Why did you ride out there today?"

She blinked as if she knew he had more on his mind. "I've resolved to say yes to things. An opportunity came to me. Saying no wasn't an option."

"Was it worth it?"

"It was the single greatest moment of my life."

Charles didn't have to like that response, but he could respect it.

"What do you want?" Louise asked once more, her voice barely above a whisper. He had no trouble hearing her. In the darkness of the room, the moon high, it felt like they were the only two people on the earth. It was this privacy, this solitude, that finally gave him the courage to speak from the soul that continued to crack and splinter within.

"Say yes to me," he pleaded softly.

"Forever? You know I won't do that. *Can't* do that."

Charles leaned his forehead against hers, wrapping his arm around the nape of her neck. Not pressing. Not pulling. Just holding. "Fine. I'll settle for right now."

CHAPTER THIRTEEN

*S*AY YES TO *me.*

Those words were equal parts a blessing and a curse. Charles was waiting for Louise to make the first move. He wanted that. He wanted her to take action, so she couldn't say that it was all his decision. He laid that at her feet. He laid himself at her feet.

It was a beautiful gift.

Louise couldn't lie to herself about that. Sitting in Charles's lap was like reclining on marble, hard and cool, but remarkably smooth and luxurious, honed and manipulated to create opulent comfort. These were the reasons people were hypnotized by him, wrote about him, sang his praises. Charles was the rock people broke themselves against. He was the hero of every play; he was the slayer of the fiercest dragons. He was the north star that led them to the best versions of themselves. He wasn't real. He was pure fantasy.

And he'd given Louise the choice. Charles had asked her to say yes, and she would take it. Because this was her life now, one of potential and capability, one of taking chances and risks, one of savoring life's pleasures. And no one promised more pleasure than the Knight of the Sun. Louise told herself that she could take this risk because she knew it would lead to nothing. Her heart couldn't break if she refused to use it.

When her lips met his, it was unlike their last kiss. Gone was the anger, the need to prove himself, the insatiable emotion, and in its place was a pureness Louise found hard to identify. Coming together was almost like eating a strawberry in its perfect state of ripeness, earth-shattering in its natural sweetness.

They stayed that way for a few seconds, letting their lips press against one another's, allowing their breaths to mingle, to become one. Louise's heart pounded in her ears as her body was electrified under the muted action. Everything in her wanted to burst and swell, ebb and flow, flicker and shine.

She mirrored his position, placing her hand behind his neck, nudging him closer. Charles's lips curled over hers in a smile, but he didn't break contact. Louise used that moment to deepen the kiss, licking inside his opening, tasting the bitter alcohol and succulent thrill that awaited her. Charles wasted little time catching on. His tongue filled her mouth, playing with her lips, capturing all her senses until she felt as limp as her resolve. She didn't know where this was going, wasn't exactly sure what she'd said yes to, but she also knew she wasn't about to stop it anytime soon.

Charles's hand kept her guessing. As they continued to lose each other in their kiss, his palm started at her ankle and seductively moved its way up her leg, hiding underneath her skirts like a genius thief. He skimmed her inner highs like a musician strumming the strings of a harp, or even an artist caressing the dried oils of a painting, lost in wonder at the brush strokes needed to accomplish the effect.

Louise's stupor broke as he came closer to the apex of her legs. He grabbed a handful of her inner thigh and squeezed, drawing a hiss from her lips.

Charles chuckled into her mouth. "Sore, are we?" he said silkily. "Have you ever ridden astride before? Ever felt the animal between your legs?"

He massaged her skin harder as he spoke, and the torment was the exquisite kind that left Louise confused. She shook her head, grasping for words.

"Not since I was a child."

His hand skated over her thighs to her bare behind, squeezing and stroking the skin in what felt like admiration. "Is this sore too?" he asked.

"Y-yes."

"Well, we should do something about that, shouldn't we?"

Louise was too adrift to find any meaning; she kept trying to capture his mouth, but the cursed man continued talking about being sore. Yes, she was sore. Of course she was! But his touch was making everything better—more than better. Couldn't he just keep kissing her and keep doing what he was doing?

Charles had other ideas. In one swoop, he picked Louise up and carried her to the chaise. He placed her facedown, on her stomach, her hips and legs off the end with her knees planted on the floor.

"Charles!" she yelped, but her cries were useless. He knelt behind her, placing his large hands on the base of her back.

"Shh," he said as tremors twitched from deep within her body down her limbs. Her greed overwhelmed her as she waited for Charles's next act.

"I just want to see the damage that your willfulness created today, my love," Charles purred behind her. He caressed a lazy path down her spine over her round backside. When he lifted her skirt, a startling coolness covered her innocent skin.

Louise squeezed her eyes shut. Charles was looking at her behind! Her *bare* behind. And then he was touching it again. Cuddling and molding the flesh, causing her to bite at her lips and drop her forehead into the cushions. She could not scream. She could not scream. Not when someone might come and put a stop to this heavenly experience.

Charles's palms were calloused and rough against her skin, but nothing could have prepared her for the slap that followed. *Clap!* Her bottom rippled and sizzled with the surprise of his slight strike. Louise gnawed at her fist. The electricity of the slap swam all the way to the center of her legs, pulsing there as if her heart had moved.

"Tell me if that's too much," he said, tilting his torso over her body. "I don't want to hurt you."

Louise's chest rumbled, her voice heavy with embarrassment … and eagerness. "Then why did you spank me?"

"Because you deserved it," he said, rocking his pelvis into hers. "You scared me to death. Don't ever do that again."

"You don't control me," Louise panted. "And you never will."

He spanked her again, harder this time, and Louise once more felt something foreign and delicious spark inside her lower belly.

"You can spank me all you want, but it won't make me yield," she warned.

"I don't want to spank you."

She smiled against the cushion. "Oh, yes you do. You want to control me."

His palm spread over her smarting skin. "No," he said. "I want to make you come. You're wet right now. I can see it. And you're even wetter now that I spanked you again. Do you want me to stop?"

Louise couldn't understand her reaction. "No," she said.

"Too bad," Charles responded. "I want something more."

Louise was so hot, throbbing so intensely, that when his mouth covered her sex, she jerked forward on the chaise, creating a stimulation even more glorious. She gasped, and Charles's head popped up.

"Do that again," he ordered her.

"What?"

He pushed her pelvis onto the curve of the chaise, and Louise was filled with that inner flare once more. "That," he said. "Grind for me. Show me that you can take what you want."

"What do I want?" she asked, genuinely. With all her reading and her father's debauchery, she still didn't have the vocabulary for what he was introducing.

In answer, Charles licked her sex, and she automatically strained forward ... *grinded* forward. "You want to spend. You want to come. You want to break apart inside. You want to throb and blossom until you lose all feeling."

"I do?"

"You do."

He didn't speak again. Not for long minutes, while he stayed true to his word, inviting Louise to lose herself in the titillation of the moment. He relished his time, lapping at her lips, encouraging the languid moments of her body. Together they rocked and twisted, bucked and jerked, until the friction from the chaise and his mouth became unbearable. When it had completely taken over, when the storm was crested high at the precipice with nothing left to do but break, Louise reached back. Charles found her hand and entangled their fingers as Louise was showered with all that he'd spoken of and more. A rush of energy, of delight, a beginning, middle, and end of time, all wrapped up into a few mind-altering seconds of utter transcendence, infused her body.

Charles's panting returned Louise to the mortal plane. He smoothed her skirts and came to sit on the ground next to her head. He looked pleased and youthful, flushed, with the whites of his eyes bright and expectant. It warmed her heart ... and reminded Louise of when he was younger, how easy and fun he was, how lovely it was to watch his body in motion.

"Was that it?" she asked.

Charles's laughter exploded, his face pained in defeat. "I'm afraid so."

"Good," she said, offering him a conciliatory kiss. He tasted different now with her on his lips. "I don't think I could live through anything more."

He played with a long red tendril, wrapping it tight around his finger so Louise couldn't retreat. His lips stayed light on hers. "But you will, my love. I will make sure of it."

Even through her passion-filled fog, Louise was reminded of

the words that had started this lovely escape. She was about to remind Charles that she hadn't promised forever, but a twinkle of light under the door sucked up all her attention.

In a blind panic, she only had enough time to push Charles away before the door flew open and a forbidding shadow loomed large in the library's entrance.

Lady Delilah's voice hit with the force of a sniper. "I can't say I'm not surprised."

Louise scrambled up to standing, knocking Charles on his behind in her haste. "Mother," she said, guiltily out of breath. "This isn't what you think it is."

Lady Delilah's lips pinched. Into a smile? The light from the candle she held flickered along her face, creating shaded emotions Louise couldn't read.

"It doesn't matter what I think this is, darling," her mother began, stepping soundlessly into the room, clicking the door closed behind her. "It only matters what I see, and I see two unmarried people who have no right to be together."

Raking his hands through his hair, Charles climbed to his feet, issuing a ragged sigh. Louise stepped in front of him, believing in her frazzled mind that if she stood in front of him then her mother would forget he was in the room. No chance.

"No, Mother," Louise said. She captured her mother's gaze, silently pleading. "You saw two people innocently talking, nothing more. Truly. There's nothing to read into here. I promise you."

Lady Delilah ventured closer. She wore her nightgown and robe, her hair plaited in one long braid that ran down her sharp shoulder. Her features were somber, and yet Louise could make out hesitation, an effort to believe what her daughter desperately wanted her to.

An eyebrow arched as Lady Delilah raised her chin to Charles. "Is that what I saw?" She spoke slowly, full of effort, punctuating every word, giving each a weight of its own. "Did I see nothing? I know I'm old and my eyesight might be going, but

I would have sworn I saw my daughter's honor being compromised."

Louise's head hung like a dead flower. This was beyond mortifying. Charles would have to do his best to convince her mother, but if anyone could do it, it was him. Lady Delilah had never hidden her love for the cad. He was like a second son to her.

"I'm afraid that's exactly what you saw," Charles said, his intention plain.

Louise's neck snapped up. She spun on the bloody horrible liar and shoved him in the chest. "She saw nothing of the sort. What are you doing?"

Charles swiped his hair off his face. His chest puffed out, his color high; he looked like a Viking who'd just finished vanquishing a boatload of foes. "I'm telling her the truth. I besmirched your honor."

Besmirched. Good Lord. It was official. She was in the middle of an awful play.

Louise covered his mouth with her hands. "Stop talking. You're ruining everything."

His stalwart expression told her he wasn't going to abide by her rules. Panic set in. How had everything gone left so quickly?

"Mother," Louise cried, twirling back around. "Don't listen to him. He's teasing me like he always does. My honor is intact. Everything was as it was."

"Nothing is intact anymore," Charles announced jovially over her shoulder.

She groaned, holding her face. "Shut up!" she said into her fingers.

"Louise?" her mother said gently. Helpfully. *Hopefully.*

Louise opened her fingers just enough to glimpse her mother. "Darling, look at me."

"I am looking at you."

Lady Delilah lowered her chin. "Take your hands down."

Louise did as she was told. She'd been behaving so well up

until now. She only had a few more days until she was free. Why had she put herself in this position? She'd been able to withstand Charles's charm for the last ten years; why had she succumbed now, and in such a disastrous fashion?

Lady Delilah's forehead furrowed in apparent pity. Louise wasn't fooled. One didn't become the Marchioness of Marlborough by not snatching the advantage when it was handed to you.

"I'm doing this for your own good," her mother said.

"Don't pretend this wasn't what you wanted all along," Louise replied bitterly. "It was always your goal to marry me off."

"I won't deny it," her mother said, "though I would have preferred more circumspect behavior on your part. This isn't like you. And that leads me to believe you wanted this to happen."

Louise stared at the floor, the pattern of the rug whirling in her mind until the reds and oranges and yellows all blurred together with her tears. "We were alone," she said, wiping at her nose.

"And now you aren't," Lady Delilah said. "I'm sorry, my dear. I hate to be the bearer of bad news. But you made your bed tonight. Now you must sleep in it."

Chapter Fourteen

"Royce! Royce, it's me. Get up! Answer the door. Please, Royce!"

Louise banged on the wood as loudly as she dared. She shoved her head next to the knob, hoping he could hear her better through the keyhole. Had he had too much to drink? Louise pounded a little harder. "Royce!" she hissed. "It's an emergency, please!"

Footsteps vibrated on the other side of the door, and Louise finally allowed herself to breathe. Her heart had been beating outside of her chest ever since she followed her mother back to their room. Lady Delilah had told Charles they would finalize the marriage in the morning over tea. Ever the good daughter, Louise had stood glumly to the side, her tongue paralyzed. She'd only been biding her time.

She had waited for her mother's even snoring to commence before she slipped out of the room—straight to Royce's. Things had changed. The plan couldn't wait. If they were going to flee, it had to be now.

The door swung open. "What the hell is going on?" Royce asked, hair mussed, creases in his left cheek from his pillow. As he took in her hysteria, his face went white. "Did they find out about you? Are they after me?"

Louise stormed into his room, knocking him back on his

heels. "This has nothing to do with you! We have to leave," she said. "Now." Anything that looked like his—signet ring, stockings, combs, wallets—Louise scooped up and tossed in the middle of the bed. "Just pack what you need. Leave the rest with Bertie. I'm sorry, but we have to go. We don't have time." She stamped her feet. "As we agreed before, I will allow two guinea pigs, but no more."

That got his attention. Royce's mouth dropped open. "Allow? *Allow?* Two guineas? You were serious about that?"

Louise kept on packing. "Royce, we've talked about this. I'm only thinking of the guinea pigs. Do you know how long we might be on the ship? It might take us six months to reach the Sandwich Islands, and sailors are notoriously hungry for fresh meat. There's no way you'll be able to watch over them all the time."

Royce padded back to the bed, sitting on the edge while rubbing at his bloodshot eyes. "Louise, I have a headache, and you're clearly delusional to think I would ever let a seaman eat one of my babies. Stop, please. Explain what is going on." When Louise wouldn't listen, he reached for her skirt, halting her frantic movement. "Tell me what happened."

Like a levee breaking, the tears poured out of her. Louise told him everything. Meeting Harvey's courier in the hallway, getting pulled into the library by Charles, all his questions, his wet clothes, his empty whiskey glass, being caught by her mother … everything except the kissing bit. Royce didn't need to know about that. No one ever needed to know about that.

His hand slipped from her skirt, and his expression turned murderous. "Marriage? Do you think it will result in that?"

Louise tore at her hair. "Have you been listening to me? It's my mother! And she thinks she's got the Earl of Somerset by the nape of his neck. Of course this will result in marriage! Who knows when? If it were up to her, probably tomorrow!"

"Tomorrow? But what of Charles? I thought he was meant for Lady Charlotte. He wouldn't want to give all that up for you."

Louise flinched. "That's rather harsh."

"I didn't mean to offend you."

"Well, what did you mean?"

"Nothing! I just …" Royce flashed her a rueful half-smile. "You're not exactly his type, are you? Look, forget I said anything. I just woke up and I'm not thinking clearly. You're mine already. We have a plan, and we will see it through."

The slow, warm tickle of relief awakened Louise's spirit. "Yes! You're right. On to Gretna Green. If we leave now, we'll be there in no time. So what if we're early for the boat in London? We can spend a few extra days there, hiding and gathering what we need."

"London, yes," Royce added, lacking her enthusiasm.

Louise needed to move; it didn't matter what she was doing or if it amounted to anything—she just needed to pretend that her actions mattered. She'd even pack the damned guinea pigs if Royce asked her—but only two of them. She was not budging from that number.

"Um, Louise, what time is it?"

She frowned, folding up one of his linen shirts into a ridiculously small square. Louise didn't have much experience with folding and couldn't get it right. Oh well, she'd have plenty of time on the *Clementine* to learn new things. How exciting! "A little after three, I think."

She heard Royce stand and begin rustling around the room. Good, finally, he was moving!

"And where is Lord Charles now?"

Louise balled the shirt up in her fist. With a puff of frustration, she threw the unwieldy linen into one of Royce's handbags. She faced him, hands on her hips. "He went to bed, I suppose."

"And your mother?"

"Snoring like a steam train," she answered. "We have hours until anyone notices we're gone."

Royce rewarded her with a smile, but it lacked warmth. Perhaps it was her frazzled state, but it made her feel slightly disjointed.

"What is it?" she asked.

"Nothing," he said. "Nothing at all. I just can't believe it's time."

Louise wiped her sweaty palms on the back of her skirt. "You're still with me, right?"

He studied her curiously. "Louise, do you really think so badly of me? To desert you at your lowest? I may not be a knight, but I'm not such a blackguard as that."

Louise tried for a smile. She inhaled, containing herself. "I'm sorry, Royce. I shouldn't have doubted you—you, who have been my one constant confidant through all of this. Please, forgive me. I'm just beside myself."

"I know, dear girl. I know. Don't worry. I'm here now." Royce enveloped her in a deep hug, but the moment Louise was ready to rest her head on his shoulder, he pulled away. "You're right. No time to dawdle. Would you be a dear and grab my signet ring on top of the bureau? I can't forget that. I'd hate to encounter the natives without looking my very best."

She frowned. "Oh, yes, yes. I thought I packed it already. Yes, let me look."

She turned to walk to the bureau. The top was empty. Standing on her tiptoes, Louise swiped a palm over the glossy surface. "Are you sure I didn't grab it before? I don't see anything, Royce. Royce?"

The air *whooshed* behind her, and then there was nothing left to see.

A STABBING ACHE pounded between Louise's ears as if someone was taking an ax to her temple. Groggy, she opened her eyes, and a blinding light confounded her, making the pain worse. Blinking a few times, Louise found her head smashed up against a glass window with the curtains pulled just enough to allow sunlight to slide through. Crusted drool formed over her mouth, gluing her to the pane. Her jaw stung when she closed her lips and straightened herself in her seat, resting her head back against the cushion.

Royce sat across from her, dressed in his traveling jacket and trousers. They were in a carriage—his, presumably—and the herky-jerky motion only compounded the confusion rambling through her exhausted and bruised body. Like a butterfly caught in a glass jar, Louise's mind couldn't settle as she attempted to recount the last few hours and why she'd been drooling for most of them.

"You fell," Royce said in answer, reading her perplexed state. "In my room. On your head, no less. You were too worked up in your alarm and lost your footing. Poor Bertie had to help me get you into the carriage. You're not that light, you know."

Louise reached behind her head and, sure enough, found a bump the size of an egg near her crown. "I suppose I was worked up," she said slowly, wincing as the carriage bumped and the seat cushion pushed into her bruise. "I'm usually not so clumsy."

Royce responded with a sorrowful, patronizing smile. "You haven't been yourself." He crossed his legs, folding his hands on his top knee. "And I'm not just talking about this weekend, which was proof enough. I mean the last six months. To be honest, I hardly recognize you. And I'm not just talking about the"—he lowered his voice—"extra weight."

It wasn't *that* much extra.

Louise pushed her hair off her face. Even that small action was an effort. She'd only fallen. Had Bertie and Royce dropped her a few times before placing her in the carriage? They certainly weren't the most coordinated of men.

"I can understand that," she replied diplomatically. Her mouth felt odd, coppery and dry. She ran her tongue over her teeth, trying to ascertain where the foul taste was coming from. When her tongue hit on a small cut at the corner of her mouth, she realized her lip was split and she'd swallowed blood.

"You hit your face on a corner on your way to the floor. Bad luck, I'm afraid," Royce said, answering another unspoken question. He added a little chuff of laughter, as if this occurrence had been a silly lark, a hilarious hitch from the plan.

"How long have we been in the carriage?" she asked. Louise felt terrible enough as it was, and discussing any deviations to the plan was only going to make it worse.

Royce pulled back the curtain, letting in just enough light to check his timepiece. When he noticed Louise grimace, he politely let the space fall back into middling darkness. There. That was the good-natured Royce she knew.

"Almost six," he replied. "You've been out for a few hours. To be honest, I hoped you'd stay asleep for the whole journey. Nevertheless"—he sighed—"you're awake now. We'll stop soon and get you something to eat in Moffat. That will make everything better. We've got quite a way to go. I don't know about you, but I can't wait to go home. A week in Scotland is long enough, thank you very much."

Louise nodded dumbly, trying to let the confident tenor of Royce's speech put her at ease. But something continued to nag at her. And then it struck her. *Home.* There was no going home, not for a very, very long time.

Louise pushed her dread to the base of her stomach. Royce must have tripped over his words. There was no reason to jump to the worst possible conclusion. Still … she asked him anyway.

"We're making good time," she said, making conversation. "We can reach Gretna Green by nightfall, then. I think we should get married right away. Why wait? Best to just get it over with so we can move on to London, don't you agree?"

Royce's features brightened, but his patronizing undercurrent was never far away. He reached out and patted her hand as if Louise were a dimwitted child, slow on the uptake. "You have no idea how it warms my heart to know how much you want to be my viscountess. All in good time, though. You really must work on your patience, Louise."

The alarm she was squelching started to rise like a wave. Still, she kept her tone casual. "What do you mean *all in good time?* Gretna Green isn't that far. That was the plan, was it not?"

Royce sighed. Was he annoyed? *With her?* What was she not understanding?

"Plans change, dearest."

"My plans don't. That's why I made them in the first place."

His grin was so condescending, Louise wanted to scream. "It's like I said, you haven't been yourself. Someone had to see reason. Be rational."

Royce was speaking in riddles, and Louise's throbbing head didn't have the luxury of dealing with them calmly. She clawed the seat with her nails, stopping herself from lunging out and scratching Royce's face. The back of her throat was constrained and narrow. Words flowed out but lacked the politeness of before. "How *exactly* did *my* plans change?"

Finally, that smug confidence vanished from his face. Taking his time, he unlatched the cage next to him and took out a fat tan-and-white guinea pig, snuggling it in the crook under his chin. He rubbed the fur back and forth, back and forth, driving Louise mad with every silent second. "You know I love you, right?" He didn't wait for a response. "And because I love you so much, I'm taking matters into my own hands. You see … I'm a viscount now, soon to be an earl. I can't go galivanting off to the Sandwich Islands. Not when I have my father's attention for the first time ever! He's finally acknowledging me, teaching me! He told me he was proud of me! Well … not in so many words, but I felt it. I really did!"

Dumbstruck, Louise searched for the correct way to respond. *You bloody, filthy liar!* didn't seem like the best path to take at the present, especially since she was still in his carriage and continued to need his help. But she wanted to say it. No … she wanted to say much worse things.

Louise's mouth was drier than the desert. "You should have told me this before. At least then I could have made changes. Found someone else to accompany me."

Royce had taken a biscuit out of his pocket and was now feeding it to the pig. Louise almost retched in her mouth as he placed the biscuit between his lips and offered it to the rodent as if he was its overly attentive mother. "There's no need to find someone else," he said once the biscuit had been accepted. "We have a splendid relationship, and I mean to keep it. Keep you."

Louise shook her head. Had she bumped her ear too? She wasn't hearing him right. "You can't *keep* me, Royce. If you're staying behind then that's fine, but I still have a boat to catch. If you drop me off in Moffat, I can arrange for some sort of transportation to London." Louise was amazed by how steady and relaxed that admission came to her. The next six months wouldn't be easy. She would have to rely on the kindness of strangers and her own wits to stay safe, but that was the way it would have to be. No one was going to stop her.

"I'm going to have to stop you there, dearest."

"Stop calling me dearest."

Chagrined, Royce lowered his chin. "You're overwrought. Your head hurts. Why don't you take another nap? I'll wake you when we get to the inn."

"I'm done sleeping," she seethed. "You're the last person I'm going to close my eyes around. I can't trust you. And you can't keep me!"

Royce went on as if he hadn't heard her. "Someone had to stop you from hurting yourself—what was left of your reputation—and Lord knows your brother wasn't going to do it. He's too busy making a mockery of your family as it is. I let you play with the idea of the Sandwich Islands because I thought you would grow out of it. I thought you were filling your head with that nonsense because no titled man wanted you due to Marlborough's financial difficulties. But look at us now," he said jubilantly, raising one arm. "I'm no longer a second son, and your family—though embarrassing—boasts a long bloodline. My father may not be overjoyed by the match, but he'll approve of my decisive actions. It is *your* family that will be the most thankful.

I'm nothing like your degenerate father, and I'm certainly not some good-for-nothing like Somerset who would ruin a woman in a library."

"Did you forget you're stealing me?"

Royce rolled his eyes. Louise must really be incensed, because she thought she saw the guinea pig roll its beady eyes as well. "I'm not stealing you. I'm rescuing you, and you've let yourself become so mired in fantasy that you can't tell the difference. Do you honestly believe a lady—a marquis's daughter—can travel to the Sandwich Islands? Even with a husband, it's positively ludicrous—barbaric! The place is filled with savages, cannibals, lust-craved heathens. I would never forgive myself if I let you go!"

"Stop the carriage," she stated firmly.

"What? No, we're in the middle of nowhere."

Louise's hands balled into fists. "Stop the carriage. Now. I'm getting out."

Royce raised a blond eyebrow. His blatant show of masculinity and control was marred by daintily returning the pig to its cage. "Out of the question," he replied haughtily. "We will stop soon enough, and then we will continue on to my home, where we will get married in the family chapel, just like all the other viscounts before me."

Slowly, Louise leaned forward in her seat. From under heavy lids, she offered her words with deadly warning. "If you don't stop this carriage right now, I will throw those guinea pigs out the window. How long do you think they'll last, Royce? How long until some hungry animal, just waking up with an empty morning belly, gobbles them up? Is that Sir Pigceval? Or Lady Guinea-vere? They aren't very heavy, are they? Both could fit in the palm of my hand ..."

"Louise ..." Royce's voice trembled. She'd hit the right chord. She could have told the stupid man she was going to slit his mother's throat and not gotten the same reaction. "Try to remember that you're a lady ... and a decent, God-fearing human being."

She could smell the fear on him—or maybe it was just the guinea pig droppings. "Don't tell me what I am. No one gets to do that anymore. I'm not a lady. I'm a writer. I'm an adventurer. And I'm a goddamned knight and a woman of my word. If you don't stop this carriage, their bodies will be on your conscience—not mine."

Royce's Adam's apple bobbed under his cravat.

"Do you really want to test me?" he asked, finding a spine Louise didn't think was there. She'd underestimated him. But he'd underestimated her as well. Because Royce forgot that her new motto meant everything to her—even her pride.

Louise answered with a resounding *yes*.

CHAPTER FIFTEEN

THE MOMENT HE woke up, Charles knew he'd made a mistake. He never should have gone back to his room last night. He'd seen the look on Louise's face when her mother dictated all that would be done. Mouth closed and expression impassive, Louise hadn't uttered one rebuke while Lady Delilah took complete control of the reckless situation.

Charles should have done what everything inside him screamed to do—throw down a blanket outside Louise's bedroom and camp out all night so she couldn't get any wild ideas. He knew Louise well enough. She always got ideas, and wild ones tended to be her favorites.

As he rubbed the sleep from his eyes, an unpleasant warning sensation in his gut signaled that all was not right.

Lady Delilah confirmed it by pounding on his door. Too refined, it wasn't the kind of knock that woke the castle, but it was one you didn't ignore.

When Charles pulled her inside, he only half listened to her agitated explanation. He was too busy barking orders to his valet, throwing on his clothes, and making a list in his head of what he had to do and the minutes needed to do it. Every second counted. Any other time, Charles would have gladly sat down with Lady Delilah and been a voice of reason, a shoulder to cry on, but that gentlemanly politeness wasn't available in their predicament. She didn't need a priest to confess her sins; she needed a man of action. Despite all of his recent failings, Charles knew he was that.

All signs pointed to Gretna Green. Known for hasty, ill-advised weddings, the town was the only logical option open to the couple. Louise had found her back up against the wall, angry at Charles, disappointed in her mother. It was a bad mix of feelings, the kind that could drive someone to make a drastic mistake.

Like marrying Lord fucking Royce.

The selfish man-child who was so far removed from reality he had to create a fantasyland of guinea pigs just so he could fit in somewhere. Men like him were the supreme argument against primogeniture—and marrying cousins.

What the hell could Louise be thinking? She wasn't thinking. She couldn't be.

Charles was out of the castle and on his horse in under thirty minutes. It would have been sooner, but Louise's mother was beside herself and wouldn't let him leave until he'd granted her one very important promise.

Holding the reins of his horse, Lady Delilah blocked his path out of the stables. Her voice plagued with anguish, she stated, "You created this problem, Charles. Now fix it. Bring my daughter back safe … and married."

He didn't understand. "Married? To anyone?" *To Lord Royce?*

Lady Delilah's haunting stare was difficult to hold, cutting him to the quick. She swallowed hard, and the skin of her neck strained from the effort. "I once thought Royce could be a sound option but … the more I watched him …" She trailed off. "Louise is a determined woman, willful and independent. Men like Royce would never know how to handle her. In their frustration and incompetence, they will always regress to force." She glanced away, her shaking hand covering her mouth. "My daughter thinks that just because I've never left this island that I have no worldly experience. But trust me when I say I know this. I know it all too well. Stop her from making the biggest mistake of her life."

AFTER THREE HOURS in the saddle, Charles conceded that he had to stop. *He* didn't need it. His arse might be numb, his face weather-beaten, but none of that registered. But his poor horse. The sweet thing needed water and a rest. If his memory served, Moffat, a decent-sized town, would be coming up soon with a respectable inn that could be of assistance. It was a logical place to break, and Royce and Louise had probably stopped there not that long ago.

Charles was keeping a decent, steady pace. If the road's muddy conditions were forcing him to tread cautiously, then the carriage must be moving like a snail. Wheels got caught in better situations than this all the time.

Like the poor sods in front of him.

Squinting against the late-morning sun, Charles could just make out a carriage half a mile up the road. Speeding up, he quickly realized a wheel was stuck in a hole in the road, but it was no longer connected to anything. The carriage had completely flipped on its side and lay alone in the tall, marshy grass several yards away.

Standing on his stirrups, Charles scanned the area for the horses that might have gotten loose, but he was only met by rambling hills. The riders must have taken the horses into Moffat, he concluded, sitting back in his saddle. For an optimistic moment, he thought he was lucky enough to have stumbled upon Royce's carriage, but there was nothing exceptional about the black vehicle. Charles couldn't make out any crest or sign that would announce that this was a viscount's conveyance.

But then he heard the screams, and his heart and hope picked up once more. Because the shrill sounds were coming from a male.

Charles was at the carriage just as Royce climbed out of the broken window, tripping over the door and landing on his face in the mud. "They're gone!" he wailed, beating his fists into the ground. "I can't believe you did it, you stupid bitch! I'm going to kill you. I'm going to kill you!"

Hauling himself to his feet, Royce hobbled back to the carriage. He yanked on the door, but it wouldn't budge. "Get out, you bitch!" he yelled. He was just about to climb back in through the window when Charles jumped off his horse. He grabbed Royce by the shoulder, spinning the crazed man around. Scratch marks and blood covered his filthy face. Royce's expression was glazed over, and Charles didn't think the man recognized him, so lost was he in his hysteria. "She did it!" he babbled, clinging to Charles's jacket. "I never thought she'd do it. What kind of a woman is she?"

"Where's Louise?"

"I'm going to kill that murderous cunt. Snap her until all her bones break—"

Royce never saw the punch coming. Charles shut off his delirium with one swing, knocking the man to the ground. He stayed down.

"Louise?" Charles called. With a firm pull, he yanked the carriage door open and leaned forward to stick his torso inside. Everything he'd feared crashed into him at once. Louise lay there at the bottom, crammed against the opposite door, her arms tangled haphazardly around her head.

Charles lifted himself into the tiny space, making sure not to harm Louise any more than she already was. At first glance, he couldn't ascertain her injuries, though he could see her lip was slightly swollen and crusted with blood. Gingerly, he picked her up, cradling her in his arms, not taking one breath until he realized that she was still taking her own.

Cautiously, Charles carried her out. Louise rewarded him by fluttering her eyelids as the sun covered her rag-doll figure.

"That's it, darling girl. Wake up for me," he said, naked emotion warbling his voice. His fingers shook as he held the side of her cheek, caressing the skin into life. "Come on, Louise. You can do it. There you go. That's my strong girl. Yes. Thank God."

Forgetting himself—forgetting anything other than the pure bliss of relief—he hastily kissed her forehead.

"Ow!" she cried, immediately forcing Charles to fall back on his heels.

"I'm sorry. I'm so sorry," he said, laughing through his panic.

She opened her eyes, and Charles declared that for the rest of his life, he would never witness a shade of blue that was as beautiful. "You don't have to apologize. It's not you," she replied gruffly, clutching the back of her skull. "It's my head. I have a bump. It hurts."

Charles muttered a curse, monitoring the spot she held. "I should have known. Is that the only place? The carriage looks horrible. We'll be lucky if only your head is hurting."

She replied with a bland chuckle, but closed her eyes again as if the action had troubled her. "It wasn't the carriage that did it." She placed her palm over her forehead. "Oh, Charles, I don't know how you're here, but thank you. Royce hit me on the back of the head at the castle and forced me into the carriage."

Fury stormed in his chest. "He did what?"

"He kidnapped me," Louise said, almost to herself, getting more peeved as she continued. "That wasn't the plan. We were supposed to run away together, but in the end, the stupid man decided that he would *change* the plan. Well, that didn't work out for him very well, did it?"

Charles didn't think the ferocity he felt would ever dissipate, though the odd tone of her voice actually helped. It was almost as though Louise was more upset over Royce not following the plan than the fact that he'd rendered her unconscious.

"Louise," Charles said gently. "You weren't really going to marry that fool, were you?"

Her expression turned viperish. "That was the plan, but he just had to foul it up."

"Why?"

Finally, Louise looked at him. "Why did he foul it up? The

same reason all men foul things up—ego and vanity and control."

"No, sweetheart. Why did you want to marry him?"

Anxiety leaked through her furor. Louise's mouth began to tremble, and a glassy film formed over those blue eyes, making them look even more like the ocean during a gale. "We'd made a deal. He was supposed to protect me. Or at least provide the semblance of protection," she added as an afterthought.

"But Louise—"

"That's why I got so furious," she went on. "I do not take promises lightly. We'd struck a bargain, and I thought he was gentleman enough to stick with it. But no, he had to get his own ideas. So bloody undisciplined."

"Yes, sweetheart, but—"

"He's the one who left me in a predicament. A bad way indeed."

Charles froze, zeroing in on Louise's midsection. "A predicament?"

She followed his gaze and laughed. "Good Lord, Charles, not that—something way more important. Please follow along. This isn't difficult. You see, I didn't mean to crash the carriage, *or* murder the guinea pigs. All I did was hold them out the window. I had no intention of dropping them; I just wanted to scare him. I am perfectly capable of holding two guinea pigs in my hands, but Royce panicked. He flew into this rage. I have *never* seen a man get that look in his eyes before. It was demonic. Such a tantrum."

Charles's head was spinning as if *he* had been in the crash. "Get to the point. You dropped his rats?"

"No! I didn't drop them. Not really. He lunged at me. All I could do was defend myself, but it was difficult because, as I said, I was holding two guinea pigs out the window, and the carriage was jostling so terribly. I never would have dropped them if he hadn't bitten my shoulder. I think I saw them land on their feet. Guinea pigs always land on their feet, right? Like cats?"

"He did *what*?" Charles roared.

Louise frowned, taken aback by his outburst. "It didn't hurt; it just surprised me. And then I ... And the driver couldn't control the carriage any longer ..." She looked down at her palm and its empty contents. Her eyes filled up with tears again. "I love animals, Charles. You have to believe me. I would never hurt one on purpose, even if their owner did go back on his word."

Charles held his head in his hands. He needed to think. None of this was making any sense, and the more she explained, the more insane it sounded. Maybe her head *was* damaged more than she thought.

Louise patted his hand. "You came for me. Thank you for stopping him, Charles. Now I don't have to rely on that stupid man anymore, and you can help deliver me to London."

London? "I'm not taking you anywhere near London. I'm taking you to my home." He stood up and back-pedaled to his horse. "Well, first we'll go to Gretna Green, and then we'll go home. I'll send your mother a letter when the deed is done—Fuck!"

Louise propped herself up on her elbows. "What?

Charles punched the air as he watched Royce tearing away. "That bastard stole my horse—and our only mode of transportation." He took a deep breath. "Fine, nothing I can do about that now. Moffat isn't that far. If you're well enough, we can walk—or I can carry you. I'm sure someone will come by shortly to offer us a ride, and then we can hire horses for Gretna Green." His pulse relaxed as the plan formed in front of him. He would make this work. There was nothing he couldn't do with the correct mindset.

Unfortunately, Louise didn't share that mindset. "All right, I've had enough," she began, her voice rising. "Listen, Charles. I have had a very, *very* taxing day, and I don't think I can take any more. I am going to London, and that is final. Again, thank you for all your help, but all I need you to do is drop me off in Moffat and point me in the right direction."

"What's in London?"

"A ship."

"What ship?"

"The *Clementine*."

"And where, pray tell, is the *Clementine* sailing?"

"Lots of places."

"But which place do you think you'll be getting off at?"

"The Sandwich Islands. I'm not sure which island yet. I thought I'd wait until I got there, let them speak to me."

Of all the bloody … "What the hell is in the Sandwich Islands?"

The absurd woman smiled. "My future."

CHAPTER SIXTEEN

"No. No. No. No," Charles repeated, marching ahead of Louise. She hoped he would choose another word soon—not only for her sake. She was worried the disgruntled man was on the precipice of a seizure. Even with all the effort and time Louise had put into her new muscular physique, carrying an unconscious Charles was not in the cards that afternoon.

Besides, she was hungry, and her feet were starting to pinch in her shoes. She'd worn her slippers to Royce's room the night before. Had she known he was going to knock her out and throw her into his carriage, she might have opted for more sensible leather boots. At least she wasn't in her nightgown. Thank the Lord for small mercies.

The town had to be close, she reassured herself. The pair had been walking for nearly two hours with only the sun and sheep as company. As hard as Louise tried, the sheep wouldn't speak back to her. Still … the wooly animals were better conversationalists than Charles, who held on to one word like a drowning man to a flimsy raft.

"No. No. No," he muttered.

"I can hear you," she called out from behind. Somewhere along the journey, Charles had peeled off his coat and waistcoat and was down to his linen shirt. A line of sweat formed from the nape of his neck to his trousers, soaking through the thin material, making it cling to his broad back. There was nothing decent about it, Louise concluded. That didn't stop her from appreciating the view, though.

"Good," he snapped. "I *want* you to hear me. Then maybe you'll get it into your head that your little plan is ridiculous."

Louise swallowed her ire. She was too tired and hungry to fight.

On second thought, no, she wasn't.

"Your opinion on the subject doesn't matter. I don't care if you think my trip is ridiculous. I've worked too hard to get here, and I'm still going."

That did it. Charles launched into another round of "No. No. No," which made Louise want to run for the hills bracketing the road. On any other day, her adventurer's spirit would have adored the heather-covered mounds and the rippling stream following them through the valley, but the steam rising off Charles was enough to cloud the bucolic visions.

"You're not going anywhere," she heard him spit. "Such a foolish, pigheaded, selfish—"

"Selfish!" Louise gaped, stumbling to a stop. Blisters were beginning to form on her soles. "I'm taking control of my own life. How in the world is that selfish?"

"Stupid," he rasped, continuing on his march.

Louise had to yell to be heard—which she had no problem doing. "I am not stupid! How dare you say that to me?"

Without skipping a beat, Charles spun on his heel and advanced on her. He'd tucked his hair behind his ears, and all Louise saw was the vicious glint in his eye, the malicious purpose spearing out from those green orbs. He didn't open his mouth until he was directly in front of her. He must have felt like yelling too.

"I didn't say you were stupid," he replied, blowing the hair away from her face with his vehemence. "I called your decision stupid—which it is—*and* selfish. You have a duty. You may not like it, *Lady* Louise, but it is your duty and destiny all the same.

You were brought up to be a lady, to marry a lord like me and live happily fucking ever after, *which we will*. Flying off to God knows where, putting yourself in danger, worrying your entire fucking family, is selfish, and certainly not part of that destiny."

Charles's face was red, his features battered and drained. The veins at his temple twitched and his nostrils flared as he attempted to regain his composure.

"Who says that's my destiny? Was it written somewhere?" Louise replied, countering his passion with a voice just over a whisper. It was worth a shot; Charles refused to listen to her shouts. "Who?" she asked again when he continued to stare at her, growing more bewildered. "Some person long ago, years, centuries before I was born. That hardly seems fair."

"It's just the way it's done," he said. A dying man clinging to his last breath. A dog with a bone. A man who had everything, assuring himself that he should be content.

"Who told you that?" she went on. "Or better yet, why do you have to listen?"

Louise saw it then, something she'd never considered before. Charles always played every situation so coolly, so aloof. Nothing ever bothered him. Why should it? He was the person who every man wanted to be, and every woman wanted to be with.

But he was scared.

Scared that it would never be enough.

Louise watched him blink, fast and irritated, as if she'd hidden a pebble in his shoe that he couldn't find. The cords of his neck labored against his tanned, glowing skin, and he widened his stance like he was readying himself to carry a heavier load.

Slowly, Louise reached out and traced the light blue vein on the side of Charles's forehead. Sweat marked her finger as she followed the length of the staccato beats. She heard him hiss in a breath. His eyes bored into her, but Louise couldn't hold his gaze. Her attention stayed on the light blue line as it slowed and relaxed, calmed under her faint touch.

Charles remained still. And when Louise eventually let her

hand fall back to her side, he didn't try to stop her. A blush colored her cheeks. "I'm tired of obeying those ancient rules, playing those archaic games. I am so, so tired."

It was subtle, but the corner of his mouth inched up. "You? The woman who only yesterday was bearing down on me from the other side of a lance?"

The remark was meant to be funny, maybe even break up the stiff and claustrophobic situation they'd manufactured around themselves, but neither laughed, nor did they choose to move away.

Because it was the kind of intimacy that deserved honesty. And intimacy—in any of its forms—never felt wrong when Charles was near her.

"Some days I feel like I'm ninety years old," Louise began. "And other days I think I could be ten again. I have this burning inside me, this unrelenting desire to do something with my life. To see and taste and feel and experience everything this world has to offer. We only have this one life, isn't that so? That's what they preach at the pulpit. Well, I can feel mine running out like every single grain in the hourglass cuts into my body before it falls. And that exhausts me. Because I feel like I can run to the top of that hill over there without stopping, but no one will let me. Do you know what that feels like? To have so much to give and have nothing asked of you? Or worse, to have so much to give and have someone tell you that what you have to offer isn't good enough? That is why I'm tired, Charles. And that is also why I cannot rest."

They stayed that way for countless heartbeats, letting the Scottish wind swirl around them, the ripple of the heather and the high, piping songs of the meadow pipit providing the only sounds. Louise's heart thumped against her rib cage, and the muscles of her stomach constricted to such a degree that it no longer skimmed her corset.

Charles's gaze was so all-encompassing and absolute that Louise wondered if he could see her heart pounding inside her, see how vulnerable she'd made it by opening up to him.

"This is what you meant before, then?" he asked quietly, his focus narrowing—not in scrutiny but in genuine interest. "About saying yes to life."

Louise smiled shyly, kicking the pebbles at her feet, all thoughts of blisters completely vanished. "It's become a sort of motto."

Charles released a giant exhale and followed it with a forlorn chuckle. "I wish you would have chosen another."

"Do you really?"

"You know ... I don't know."

Good answer.

Louise was hindered from saying any more when the clunking rumble of wheels caught her attention. She tore away from Charles's enigmatic—*and adorable*—expression to spot a cart coming down the road toward them.

"People," she announced breathlessly.

Charles frowned but reluctantly turned toward the fortuitous development. Louise allowed the distraction to energize her, filled her lungs with cool air, and released the pent-up emotion that had developed. What was it about Charles that always unsettled her so? Handsome men weren't that hard to come by, and if most of them weren't as fit, then some of them were close. But none of them touched a nerve like Charles. Was it because she'd once been infatuated? Was that the source of her sensibility? Other than that, Louise couldn't make heads nor tails of it. The Knight of the Sun was just another person in an already long list of people who expected her to not only fall into line but also toe it.

And yet Louise still had tried to plead her case. Perhaps that was the difference. Charles might not agree, but at least he would listen. For a woman who'd been told her whole life she should be seen and not heard, that characteristic was worth its weight in gold.

"Hello there," a man yelled from the cart. Solidly built, with a thick neck and even thicker forearms, the stranger wore a cap and a friendly smile as he sat next to a pretty woman with curly black hair and a lovely, plump face. "You're the first we've seen in a long while. Haven't had any trouble, have you?"

Charles sidled next to Louise, draping a heavy arm over her shoulder. She thought the invasion of privacy, not to mention his sweat, would turn her nose, but it was quite the contrary. She found herself leaning into the cushion of his warmth, angling her nose to take in more of his salty, earthy smell.

Charles smiled grandly like the people's knight that he was. Always performing. "Had a bit of bad luck, I'm afraid," he explained. "Wheel got stuck in the mud a ways back, and when I was trying to fix it"—he scratched at his head, eyes cast low—"the horse spooked and bolted. I should have known better. You haven't seen her, have you?"

The woman covered her mouth with her hand, sharing a distressed look with the man. He took the hand in his own and held it against his thigh in a loving gesture. "Afraid we haven't," he answered. "That is bad luck—sorry to hear about it. We just came from Moffat; it's another hour's walk, I gather." He shared a weighted look with the woman, and she nodded. "My wife and I would be happy to take you there if you wouldn't mind accompanying us first. We're here, enjoying some time together. Clara heard about the spring waters and ... well ... thought it might be useful, since we're trying to start a family. But there's only so much soaking you can do in one day."

Louise and Charles returned a cordial laugh as the man went on.

"We heard there's a waterfall not far from here, one of the prettiest in these parts. Thought we'd take a leisurely Scottish stroll. You're welcome to come with us. We won't be too long; then we'll drive you to the town and get you all sorted out."

"That would be fine—"

"I'm sorry, I don't think so."

Charles and Louise faced one another, their responses smashing together.

"I figured you were married," the stranger said, nodding to his woman. "That just sounded like the most married thing I've ever heard."

Louise issued a tight, polite smile and had opened her mouth to decline the offer once more when she felt Charles envelop her hand. Unlike the other times when he'd yanked and pulled her in annoyance, he simply brought her into his chest, where her forehead skimmed against his chin. "Are you really in such a hurry to get back to walking?" he asked pleasantly, which Louise concluded was more for the couple's benefit than hers. "A sightseeing tour sounds like just the thing for you."

She shook her head and was again inundated with the freshness of his smell, the pure masculinity that only encouraged her to want to be closer. A room at the inn sounded like the smartest decision—a single room. "I don't have time for this, Charles. I told you. I need to get to London," she whispered sweetly.

"We have plenty of time to do what we have to do," he answered. "Or was all that talk about saying yes to life mere prattle? This sounds like an opportunity. Life is beckoning. Surely you must answer the call."

Louise scowled, forgetting her audience. Her détente with Charles was obviously at an end. She had no idea what he was up to, but being wary and obstinate seemed like the best play. Scotland was Scotland. It had already been traveled and written about by countless men and would still be here when she returned from her journey. Being a slave to her plan was the only way she would be able to make up for all the missteps that had occurred in the past few days.

The woman's lyrical voice caught at the periphery of Louise's deliberations. "We brought a picnic with some lovely wine and cheese. We have more than enough. I daresay I packed more than we could eat in a lifetime."

And just like that, Louise's obstinance shattered. Not letting go of Charles's hand, she towed him behind her to the cart.

"Picnic, you say? Yes, that would be lovely, thank you."

She had to give him credit. When Charles climbed into the back of the cart next to her, he didn't utter a word.

But as the ride began, he glued himself to her side. "I think I'm beginning to like your motto after all."

CHAPTER SEVENTEEN

WERE THEY THERE yet?

Charles didn't want to ponder how many times that question had run through his mind in the hour since they'd stopped the cart and started the trek on the winding stone path through the gorge. Sam and Clara, the endearing Samaritans, had led the way, calling over their shoulders every few minutes that they "could feel we're getting close."

Not bloody likely! Charles had wanted to shout the tenth time they made that wrong assumption. But Louise would have snapped at him—and then teased him. And he was not in the mood for teasing.

But ... Charles had trained to be a knight for an entire year. His armor alone was nearly fifty pounds, and he could run, jump, dance, and even do handstands in it if necessary. These hills, on the other hand, were taking the piss out of him. His thighs burned, his calves knotted, and his capacity to take a deep breath without coughing was nonexistent. This "leisurely Scottish stroll" was nothing of the sort.

To make matters worse, Louise didn't seem to be suffering from the same affliction. Like an animal in its native habitat, she took the constant dips and rises with ease, an ebullient smile on her face whenever she thought Charles wasn't looking. She was a goddess roaming these ancient hills, her red hair flowing like a mantle behind her, her face sun-kissed and brimming with vitality. It made the interminable journey worth it. But only just.

Sam stabbed the walking stick he'd brought with him into the soft ground and glanced back at them again, his grin irritatingly blithe. "We have to be close," he said, not even a hint of desperation or irony in his tone. "I can hear the water. Can you?"

Charles unhunched his shoulders and granted the optimistic nature lover a nod. Sam was daft, misguided and—Charles was almost positive—lying about there being a waterfall.

Clara beamed at her husband before turning back to the path, beating her own walking stick along with the dexterous aplomb of a mother mountain goat.

Charles cursed under his breath, ripping off his hat to wipe the sweat from his brow. Top hats had no place on a hike. The wind threatened to blow it away at every corner. Soon, he would let it.

"Ooh, ow!" he heard Louise mutter as she fell back behind him. Charles twisted to see her hop on one foot over to a large stone off the path, taking a seat on its sleek surface. Discreetly, she pushed up her skirts and rubbed an ankle, her brow wrinkled in irritation.

"Are you all right?" Charles asked, sending a quick thanks up to the heavens that she'd been the one to stop first.

She nodded, continuing her ministrations, her discomfort obvious. With no bonnet to shield her and her hair a glorious mess, Charles was reminded of all that had happened.

The woman's unceasing capability had thrown him off balance. He'd considered her endurance untouchable and simply overlooked everything she'd been through in the last twenty-four hours. Louise had been kidnapped, in a carriage accident, had to verbally spar with him, and now she was hiking through the heather. Her bruised lip had tempered, but Charles was certain the bump on the back of her head still bothered her. He was a selfish fool. He shouldn't have pressed the trek. Only ... he hadn't wanted to arrive in Moffat so soon, not when they were still at such a stalemate over her future.

"Let's go back," Charles ordered her. "You've had enough." He reached down to scoop Louise into his arms, but she pushed him away.

"Absolutely not," she replied adamantly. "We've come this far. I'm not stopping now. If *you* need to go back, then be my guest. Don't think I haven't heard your huffing and puffing."

Indignation roared its evil head. "It's the elevation," he countered. "The air is thinner than I'm used to."

Louise snorted, her suffering feet holding her full concentration.

Charles decided on another tack and planted his hands on his hips. "Your slippers are failing. You'll be covered in blisters soon and won't be able to walk for a week. It's not worth it."

"It is," she grumbled, switching legs. It wasn't the time—and Charles felt like nothing less than a lecher, considering the woman was nothing less than a stubborn wench—but he couldn't help but admire the shape of her calf, the luscious fullness of her thighs that shaped the drape of her skirts. Charles recalled how it had felt to hold them, massage them, grip the plush flesh in his palms, the creamy richness of her skin.

He dropped to his knees, swatting her hands out of the way.

"What are you—?"

"Oh, be quiet," Charles said, cupping her foot and placing it on his thigh. He slipped off the abused green slipper and scrutinized the damage. Louise's thin silk stockings were stained and dirty and offered no protection against the rub of her slipper. These stockings were meant for *real* leisurely pursuits—*not* the Clara and Sam kind.

"Stop that," she barked, trying to yank her foot out of his grasp. Charles's hold was too tight.

"No," he countered. "I am more than aware that your opinions of me aren't the highest, but trust that I know how to keep from getting blisters."

Louise hesitated but nevertheless asked, "How?"

"Wear shoes and stockings that prohibit you from getting blisters."

"Genius," she replied tartly. "I'll remember that the next time I'm kidnapped."

Charles chuckled, squeezing her heel, manipulating the long, tight muscles of her sole. Conversation stalled on his tongue. He hesitated, not wanting to break the tranquility, but the words came out in a rush. "Why Royce, of all people? Did you really think *he* would be of use to you?"

To his relief, Louise accepted his question easily, not recoiling at his invasion. Perhaps she could hear his genuine curiosity. "I thought he could be managed," she said with a shrug. As he continued to knead her foot, Louise settled her palms back on the rock and lifted her face to the sun, closing her eyes. "In my defense, six months ago he wasn't the heir. His life was rather uneventful, and his mother was hounding him to marry. I thought an arrangement would work."

Charles lifted a brow. "Just an *arrangement?*" he asked.

Louise frowned. Her eyes stayed shut, though two pink marks rose high on her cheeks. "Of … course," she stammered. "We had no enthusiasm for that sort of marriage."

"We or you?"

She peeked one eye open. "I think you already know the answer to that. Royce has only one love in his life, and it is much furrier than me."

"I'm not too sure about that," Charles joked, sliding a palm up her prickly calf.

Louise jolted to sitting, tossing her skirts back over her ankles. "Such a child."

"Relax. I'm just playing with you. You used to play, remember?"

"How would you know?" she answered testily. "You and Edward never played with me. What in the world are you doing now?"

Charles ignored the question, sitting back on his behind. He thumbed off his boots and gray merino stockings before slipping his boots back on. It wasn't the most comfortable arrangement, but he would deal with it.

Next, he grabbed her legs again and layered his stockings over her own before she could kick him away. He regarded his handiwork. The stockings were ridiculously big on Louise, but they would do the trick. The extra padding would guard against any new blisters for the rest of the hike and provide the comfort she needed to get through the remainder of the day.

She wiggled her toes inside the thick material. That was why Charles loved his valet so much. The man knew how to pack for summer in Scotland.

"That's … very …" Louise paused. "Thank you. For being kind."

Charles reacted with a rueful smile. "It isn't the worst thing to travel with a knight."

Her lips twisted to the side. "I suppose it's not."

"You know … I hate to pat myself on the back today, but I also saved you from a carriage wreck. Why is it that you are more gracious about this small action?"

She cocked her head, taking her time studying him. With infinitesimal smoothness, Charles widened his shoulders, giving her a better picture to admire. "I don't know how to explain it," she said. "I just am. Any knight would save a woman from a carriage, but I have doubts about many giving up their thick socks."

Charles left it at that. He returned Louise's slippers and offered her his hand. She took it at once, hopping off the rock and back on the trail. They were far behind their leaders now, but neither seemed to care to make up the difference. They settled into an ambling pace, lost in peaceful camaraderie.

"So why the Sandwich Islands? You said it's your future, but I need you to explain it to me," Charles eventually said, no longer afraid to broach the question. He still assumed the answer would be ridiculous; however, that didn't diminish his legitimate interest.

Louise hesitated. "Have you ever heard of Ephraim Eveleth and his book, *History of the Sandwich Islands?*"

"Of course. I read it along with everyone else."

"Really?"

"Don't sound so surprised."

"I'm not. I mean … I am, but … good. Never mind, that's beside the point." Nervously, she brushed her hair off her face. "Anyway, so then you know he called the native people 'wretched creatures' and 'savages.' He said missionaries like him were saving their culture. I've read that book more times than I can count, and my anger never subsides because he was telling me what to think. He wasn't describing the native people for what they were; he was judging them from his own prejudices. And that's not the worst of it," she declared, waving her arms in front of her.

Charles appreciated this animation that Society would deem woefully unladylike. He valued that she'd become comfortable enough around him to exhibit this side of her.

"Eveleth brought his wife with him on his missionary trip—Sarah Stickney Ellis," Louise went on, her timbre sharpening. "And she released a book of her own—*The Women of England, and their Social Duties, and Domestic Habits.*"

"Quite the mouthful." Charles laughed.

Louise *did not* laugh. "Indeed. Even though this woman had had the luxury to travel all over the world and explore new cultures, she advised us ladies to stay home and suffer through domesticity. Her contention is that women have a moral duty to maintain the home and that should be our reward and joy in life. Our families—nay, the nation—depend on our selflessness. The gall!"

Charles was on shaky ground. He thought he understood Louise's disenchantment but was unsure of how to empathize. Cognizant of the current mood they were enjoying, he was prudent with his response. "You don't think a woman could be content in the home?"

She bit her bottom lip. "No, no, that's not what I'm saying at all. I'm sure many women are content and overjoyed with that life. My concern is not for them; it's for the women like me who don't want that to be our only option. We should have a choice, yes? Just like men."

A choice. Even with all his independence, Charles didn't think he'd been given one. As the only child of an earl, his future had been determined the moment he emerged from the womb. For all his years, he'd followed the path set before him, the benefits of his position always outweighing the negatives. Charles had bumped into barriers occasionally, like when his father had denied his wish to study art in Paris after Eton (and it had rankled him greatly at the time), but for the most part, everything had been open to him. Louise had lived a very different existence.

"So that incited your ambition to leave?"

"Yes, absolutely," she replied, punctuating her answer with a vehement nod. There was nothing subtle about this woman. "Sarah Stickney Ellis stayed with me for a long while. I should truly write her a letter in thanks, because she made me think. How could I disagree with her so elementally, down to the marrow of my bones, and then still value her or her husband's opinion on the islands? Why would I trust them, of all people, to inform me about these places? That's when I realized that another point of view was needed."

Charles faced her with a teasing smile. "And you thought it should be yours?"

Louise blushed, shrugging through her awkwardness. "Why shouldn't I share myself with the world? Isn't it mine as much as anyone's?"

CHAPTER EIGHTEEN

"I FOUND IT! We're here!" Sam yelled from somewhere up the path.

Louise sent up an inner thanks. The conversation with Charles was getting a bit *too* intimate for her taste, though the real problem was that she was enjoying it. He was a talker. A convivial fellow that could get along with anyone. Everyone liked him … including her.

But that was something she couldn't afford to do. She'd seen firsthand how men like Charles treated their wives and all the other women dumb enough to fall in love with them. Louise wasn't interested in a one-sided relationship; she needed a partner, someone who wouldn't desert her each time the grass on the other side of the road appeared greener. Her father had been a slick-talking devil too, and he could barely spend a week with his family before dreaming about those emerald pastures. Louise adored her mother, but she would never become her.

Louise rambled up the path toward Sam's excited voice, following the winding trail until the world appeared to open up in front of her.

A waterfall avalanched down the rocks in a blinding rush. Never before had Louise seen nature in such abundant magnificence, the kind that inspired equal parts fear and reverence, like God's will could be read in the rapids.

Sam and Clara joined her, wearing identical expressions of esteem and wonder. "Sir Walter Scott wrote about this waterfall," Sam said, lowering his head bashfully. Clara smiled at her husband, squeezing his hand. "That's another reason why we came," he explained. "Clara—and me too, I have to admit—have a special love for his novels. People say he's a little too romantic for their tastes, but I don't know ... I like a little romance now and again. When I see pictures like this, those flowery words of his make sense." Flicking up his cap, Sam scratched at his temple. "I'm trying to remember the poem now ... how did it go?" he asked Clara.

Charles's voice rose from behind their group, rich and resonant against the falls. "*Where deep, deep down, and far within toils with the rocks the roaring linn; Then issuing forth one foamy wave, and wheeling round the giant's grave, white as the snowy charger's tail, drives down the pass of Moffatdale.*"

Louise blinked, rounding on Charles, trying to work the many differing pieces of him into something she could understand. He stared at the falls, his back straight, his profile strong and fierce along the cliff. Blond hair blowing behind him, he could have been a hero in any of Sir Walter Scott's books. But Charles wasn't a caricature spouting sonnets. His chivalry and valiancy weren't exaggerated and showy. Unlike the other men at the Eglinton Tournament, Charles hadn't wanted to impress; he'd only yearned to inspire. He had a depth to him, and though Louise kept trying, she had yet to discover its limit.

That was what made him different than her father, and that realization frightened her. She'd been so confident she could handle her feelings—the ones she'd held for Charles most of her life. She could tread easily with shallow men, but how could she resist swimming in the deep end with a man like Charles? The temptation pulled like a strong current.

Clara and Sam clapped, overjoyed at the performance. "That's it," Sam said. "Down to the very last word."

Uncomfortable with the sentiments welling up inside her,

Louise eased to Charles's side, nudging him with her elbow. "How did you know that?"

His lips stayed closed as he smiled, albeit a little sadly. "Oh, every knight can offer a pretty line now and again. If the mood is right and the inspiration is there."

"Like it is right now?" she asked.

Charles caressed the top of her hand with his thumb. When had he taken her hand? When had she let him?

"Yes," he said.

Yes.

⋙✦⋘

Not content with the view, Sam located a lane leading to the base of the falls, and the two couples stepped gingerly down the narrow track. Once there, Louise helped Clara spread out a thin blanket for the couples to sit on, and they enjoyed the picnic in relative ease. Conversations weren't forced, but they weren't encouraged either; everyone seemed content to let the thunder of the water saturate the blissful occasion.

After they finished the wine and packed away the extra food (Louise had asked for seconds but was too flustered to be the only person to ask for thirds), the pairs split up naturally, allowing each other space to experience the idyllic scene in private.

Sam chose a spot just on the pool's edge, his muscular legs lengthened in front of him on a rock poking out from the water. Clara perched on his lap, one arm spread wide along his burly back, cupping his opposite shoulder. The atmosphere had shaken something loose in the group, resulting in this lack of propriety. Louise told herself not to watch the affectionate husband and wife, but she was amazed by the way Clara's hand would leave Sam's shoulder to trail up and down his back in a loving manner. Their relationship was so real and effortless. What might that be like, to encounter the world with someone at her side, with someone who was just as curious and eager? A partner but also a lover. Louise wondered.

Unable to sit, she skipped over the rocks in the shallow end of the pool, making a game of balancing on one leg as long as she could before hopping to the next stone. It was silly and childish and plain fun. Her lungs stung with the chill of the breeze, and the spray from the falls had soaked half of her hair; nevertheless, she was all air and bubbles inside, buoyed by the graciousness of what she'd been fortunate enough to encounter.

Charles continued to pull at her curiosity, though. He sat alone, away from the water. With his back against a boulder, he bent his long legs close to him as if he was hiding something from prying eyes. Slowly, Louise ventured near and spotted a stubby pencil and small journal in his lap. Her shadow fell over him before Charles realized she was there. The pencil stopped moving, and he lifted his head.

"More pretty poetry for the knight?" she asked, craning her neck. A second passed, and she wondered if he was going to shove the journal in his pocket without letting her see it.

Charles did the opposite. Without saying a word, he handed Louise the book.

It wasn't poetry at all. It was a drawing. Of two people sitting in front of a waterfall. Her brows pinched together. She twisted toward Clara and Sam, who were deep in conversation, heads abutting, two people almost one—exactly like the charming scene in Charles's picture.

Louise's throat tightened. "So you haven't given it up."

Charles trained his focus on the couple while he answered. "It's just a hobby."

She skimmed the lines on the page with her fingertips, feeling the effort, attention, and talent that went into every mark. "This is more than a hobby, Charles. This is art."

"You think so?" He ended the question with a halfhearted chuckle, but Louise sensed more in his words. She'd been a proponent of hope for so long that she could always hear it in others.

"I know so."

He hooked his arms around his knees. "The Royal Academy didn't agree this year. Or the year before. Or the year before that." He met her with an abashed smile. "It seems my idea of good art differs from theirs."

Louise groaned, taking a seat next to him. "What do those old curmudgeons know about art?"

Charles sniffed. "Quite a lot, I'm afraid." He picked up a handful of pebbles and took turns, dropping them one by one. When he was finished, he did it all over again. "I must have lost my mind, because I actually waited for the president to leave his office one afternoon to ask him why I hadn't been chosen for the Summer Exhibition."

"There's nothing wrong with that."

Charles gave her a side glance. "I felt so pathetic and desperate. The poor man almost looked more embarrassed than I was. He said my drawing lacked a point of view. And then all he wanted to do was talk about the tournament. It seems that once you put on the armor and pick up a lance, it's difficult for people to see you as anything else."

"No," Louise said, poking at his side. "It's because you're good at it. You've always been good at everything you do … being a knight, being an earl … being a friend to my brother." She paused, bringing the paper up between them. "But you might be best at this. You shouldn't stop."

"No?"

"No."

"Thank you," Charles said, taking the picture from her. He folded it into neat squares and put it in his pocket.

"For what it's worth," she continued, "you have a point of view. It just happens to be different than the Royal Academy's. And that's not a bad thing."

SAM AND CLARA made good on their promise. Just as the sun was setting, casting an orange glow on Moffat's tree-lined main street, the foursome arrived at the Sheep's Head Inn and Tavern.

Charles followed Sam inside to rent their rooms for the night while Louise held back on the street with Clara, partaking in the town's bustling late-afternoon energy. This was no sleepy village, as Louise had expected. The appeal of the mineral waters had created a bustling avenue for commerce. The high street was crowded with inns and taverns, each highlighting the benefits of "taking the waters."

"Do you think it worked?" she asked Clara as they watched an older woman pass them on the street, her three younger daughters marching in line behind her. Clara sent her a questioning look. "The waters?" Louise added, blushing slightly while nodding at Clara's slender midsection. "That's why you came, correct? You are trying to start a family?"

Clara wrestled with a smile. She placed her hands over her stomach. "We've been trying for over a year," she said. "Some of the women in our village told us the waters would do the trick."

"Have you always wanted children?" Louise expected a ready response but was thrown off when Clara took her time, a pensive expression on her face.

"Not particularly," she replied. "I'm the oldest of eight, and by the time I was ten, I'd had my share of crying babies." They laughed, and Clara turned to where the men had gone into the inn, giving the door a wistful, secret smile. "Oh, but then I met Sam … and everything changed. Men have an annoying way of doing that to you, don't they?"

Though not married, Louise decided that she'd gained enough recent experience to respond in the affirmative. Before she could get the words out to explain, the men returned. Charles's stony demeanor instantly put her on edge.

"What's wrong?" she asked. Charles squeezed her hand. It was meant to be comforting but also served as a warning.

Instead of answering her, he faced Sam and said, "We cannot

thank you enough for what you've done for us today."

"Not at all," Sam replied, swinging his arm around his wife. "We should be thanking you. We were lucky to have such wonderful company." Clara snuggled into his side, exhaling as if she could only relax now that they were touching once more. Again, something tugged at Louise's chest.

"Will you share supper with us tonight?" Clara asked.

Louise had already assumed that they would; however, Charles had other ideas. "I'm afraid not," he said regretfully, laying a palm at the base of Louise's back. The soft touch snatched her sanity. She would have thought that after a day of playing husband and wife with little brushes given here and there, she would be used to it. But there was something about that touch, the way it wasn't meant for the other couple's eyes. It wasn't part of a façade; Charles had wanted to do it and made it seem so utterly natural. As Louise crawled back to reality, she pondered whether she wanted it to be natural or not.

"It's been a long day," he explained. "I'm afraid if I sit down at the table, I might fall asleep in my food."

Clara and Sam didn't hide their disappointment. For the next few minutes, they tried to convince Charles to change his mind, but he wouldn't budge. Louise didn't attempt to persuade him. Once he mentioned sleep, she'd realized that she wanted nothing more than to lay her head down and close her eyes—for days if possible. Food could wait, which was saying something coming from her.

She clasped Clara's hands and planted a kiss on her soft cheek. "If you're ever in London, please come and visit. You can stay with us for however long you like." What in the world was she talking about? Louise wouldn't be in London for long, and she had no idea whom she was referring to when she said "us." Regardless, the satisfaction she received when delivering the parting message was staggering.

Charles's hand on her back increased in pressure. He gave Sam his card. "Anytime," he added. "We'd be overjoyed."

The men shook hands before the foursome entered the inn together. They broke off when Sam and Clara followed the corridor toward the tavern and Charles led Louise to their rooms. They were halfway up the stairs when Clara's boisterous gasp reached them. "The Earl of Somerset!"

Louise giggled, jostling Charles's hand playfully. "The Knight of the Sun strikes again. You certainly have an effect on people, don't you?"

CHAPTER NINETEEN

THE ROOM WAS small, tidy, and, most importantly, clean. Charles had ordered a bath, and the maids were already coming into the room with their pails of water as he and Louise entered. Even with the splashing and scurrying of feet, it felt claustrophobically quiet now that Sam and Clara were no longer there to provide a point for their interactions. Pretending to be man and wife had given everything they'd done and said that day a free pass from wondering intentions. Now that Charles and Louise were alone, every action, every pause, every twitch, was open for interpretation.

Hands knotted behind his back, Charles watched Louise wander to the bureau. She picked up the hand mirror and grimaced when she caught her reflection, promptly placing it back down.

"I ordered the bath for you," he said. "Not because I think you need it … I just thought you'd want it after … after … you know."

They stared at the water, at the steam rising along with their discomfort.

"Thank you," she said stiffly. "I take it there weren't two rooms? Is that why you were upset when you first came out of the inn with Sam?"

"I was worried you would blame me," he said.

Louise nodded. "I'm sorry," she said quietly. "I'm not always fair to you, am I?"

"After how your brother and I treated you when we were younger, I can understand why."

"Good." She laughed. "You were terrible."

"We were boys. And yes, we were terrible."

The last servant girl poured her bucket into the tub and bobbed to Charles before leaving the room, closing the door behind her. The silence intensified so greatly that he could feel the pressure building along his temples, like he'd dove too deep into the sea. For a man who always knew what to say, how to alleviate a thorny moment, the atmosphere was oppressive. He simply didn't know what to talk about. The problem was, Charles didn't want *to talk*.

Louise swiveled her head around the space. "There's no screen."

"No."

Her amber brows crept up to her hairline. "So … would you mind … turning around, or …?"

"Oh, oh, of course!" he stammered, spinning so quickly he became dizzy. *Stupid!* Louise wanted to bathe without a lust-crazed man watching her!

She didn't move right away, most likely because she was waiting for him to leave, but Charles wasn't about to do that. He would never leave a woman alone in an inn. And, in addition to that very chivalrous reason, he just didn't want to go. He wouldn't look, but that didn't mean he couldn't listen as she washed herself, imagining what was going on behind him. Was that scandalous? Unknightly? Caddish? Charles didn't care.

He used his time readying for bed, washing his face and neck with the water that had been provided in the ewer on the bureau. Charles contemplated sleeping in all his clothes but dispelled the notion. He would be comfortable, and that was that. Louise would have to get used to men wearing less clothing if she was going to the Sandwich Islands.

Was she still going to the Sandwich Islands? No. Louise wasn't going anywhere without him. But Charles wasn't sure if that answered the question. Regardless, she would have to get used to *him* wearing less clothing.

He stripped off his coat and waistcoat. Toeing off his shoes, he found two fresh blisters on his heels, but they didn't sting badly. How could they when the memory of holding her foot in his lap was still fresh in his mind?

Louise stood from the tub, and Charles heard the water sprinkle down her body. Night had descended, and the room boasted a sultry glow thanks to two lonely candles on either side of the bed, along with an anemic fire in the hearth. They had one window that looked onto the high street. All Charles had to do was peer at that window and he would catch the reflection of Louise's naked body. Instead, he squeezed his lids shut. His imagination would have to be enough for tonight.

She stepped from the tub, rubbing her body with the linen provided. Charles heard her clothes rustle on the floor before the bed dipped and creaked. "Thank you," she said. "You can turn around now."

Charles didn't want to seem as eager as he was. He turned casually, finding Louise situating herself in bed, hugging the very end, using as little space as possible. The covers were pulled up all the way to her chin, but he could tell she only wore her shift underneath. Her hair was wet and hung in stringy waves on either side of her scrubbed-pink face. It struck Charles how innocent she looked, stripped of the tough façade of armor she routinely applied to herself in his presence. Despite that, he still felt powerless in this cramped space.

Louise nodded to the opposite side of the bed, her eyes cast down to her lap. "You don't have to sleep on the floor."

"I didn't expect to," Charles teased.

She answered with a calculating smile then spread out her arms, issuing a gigantic yawn. "On second thought," she said, stretching her legs over the entire mattress, "maybe, sir knight, it's best if you stay on the floor. For my honor's sake, that is."

Charles huffed. Two sure strides and he was at the bed, whipping the covers away. A brilliant flash of pale legs startled his composure before he crawled in.

"Ahh, that's better," he said, arranging himself on his side, his hands clasped together under his cheek as he waited for her next move.

Disgruntled, Louise resettled herself, sticking to the farthest reaches, making sure not one piece of skin, or one tendril of hair, would have the misfortune of touching him. She gave him her back, but that wasn't enough. Louise curled her legs into her chest like a roly-poly, one ball of exhausted anxiety.

Charles longed to reach for her, to slip his arms around her body and hold her all night long. He wanted to drown his nose in her hair, cradle her behind with his pelvis and feel her breath tickle his forearms. He wanted to give Louise all the security and assurance in the world, and wouldn't mind accepting some in return. But she wasn't ready for that. Charles wasn't sure *what* she wanted. She desired him—that was obvious—but she continued to hold herself back as if he was a simmering fire she was afraid would burn her if she wasn't constantly on alert.

Her thoughts were as loud as the waterfall from earlier.

"I don't bite, you know," he said. "I'd hate for you to fall off the bed. You can move closer to me."

Louise's shoulders shuddered. He didn't know if she was laughing or huffing. "You might not bite, but you slap."

Huffing. She'd definitely been huffing.

"I promise I won't slap tonight. And you asked me to do it!"

"I have no idea why."

"Yes, you do. You got wetter—"

Louise groaned. "Please, not tonight!"

"Just admit that you liked it and I'll stop."

"Fine, I liked it. Are you happy now?"

Charles had to lean in to hear the last bit, since she'd covered her face with her hands. "Very," he said, smiling. It was encouraging that she wasn't lying to herself. It was a start in the right direction—the direction to him. "I'll be here all night. Just let me know if you want me to do it again—"

"No, thank you," Louise cut in. "Good night, Lord Charles." She blew out the candle on the table next to her.

Lord Charles, eh? He did the same to his candle. "Good night, Louise."

The room fell stagnant with only the noise from the tavern leaching up from downstairs. Louise didn't shift, not one muscle. Was she worried that he would continue to speak to her if she did?

Charles had resolved to sleep, burrowing his head into the lackluster pillow, when Louise broke their peace one final time.

"What is going to happen in the morning?" she asked, killing him with her timidity. It didn't suit her.

He gave her as much of the truth as he was willing to spare. "I am going to send a letter to your mother."

"What will you tell her?"

"That you are safe and whole and that I am doing what she asked, and that everything will be fine."

"What does that mean?"

Charles glanced up at the ceiling, doling out more truth. "That the next time she sees you, you will be the Countess of Somerset."

CHARLES WAS BOILING hot. He peeked open an eye. The fire had petered out hours ago. Clearly, it wasn't the source of his feverishness.

Louise was curved along him, her back wedged deliciously along his front. Charles's arms were wrapped around her, with his hands tucked snugly into the crevice of her thighs. He had no idea how they had ended up in this position, but he wouldn't fight it—it was the right one.

His nose in her hair, Charles inhaled, appreciating the fresh, minty soap she'd used. Louise's tresses were still damp, much like they'd been when she hopped along the stones near the waterfall. At the memory, Charles opened his hands on her thighs, palming the skin through her flimsy shift. Magnificent torment—it was all Charles would allow. She had earned her sleep.

But then she moved.

Louise shifted her pelvis, arching her hips, increasing their pressure against his lower stomach. It was a subtle movement—infinitesimal, really. If Charles hadn't been awake, it might not even have registered. But he *was* awake, and he felt every glorious inch.

She did it again before rounding her hips forward to their original position, rocking slightly into his hands. Charles gritted his teeth at the exquisite pleasure the tiny action imposed. His cock came to the ready, lengthening and swelling at the un-schooled invitation.

Was this an invitation? *No.*

Louise was asleep; these were artless stirrings. And Charles would bear them. Or he could untangle himself and reposition on the edge of the bed.

Fat chance.

No, he would bear them. Besides, she might get cold if he left her; it was a sacrifice Charles was willing to make for her greater good.

He had to repeat that mantra to himself three more times as Louise continued to rock. If he'd been hot before, he was positively sweltering now. Sweat dotted his hairline and he could feel it pool at the base of his spine. Why had he left his shirt on? Oh, right, because of Louise's tender sensibilities. Well, what about *his* damn tender sensibilities?

Enough was enough. Charles had to take action before he spilled in his pants. Snuggling nearer, he pressed his hips into her backside and increased his hold on her inner thighs. That should mitigate Louise's torturous teetering.

Only, it didn't. Not enough.

She stirred against his hands. The apex of her thighs angled toward his wrist. Once more, Charles had to examine if this was an invitation. Did Louise want him to touch her? Outspoken as she was, he still doubted she would come out and say it. Was this her subtle version of asking?

There was only one way to find out.

Charles moved one hand, twisting it so he could reach the hidden core between Louise's legs. Mirroring the clandestine motions she'd used, he traced her seam with the tip of his thumb in an easy rhythm one couldn't mistake. He held his breath, waiting for her reaction. Louise could rebuff him now and they could both go back to pretending to be asleep, or the night could take on a life of its own. Coward that he was, Charles wasn't sure what he wanted her to choose.

When her body began to mimic the leisurely tempo, Charles's stomach jumped up into his throat. *And* his cock bucked with excitement. He'd been lying to himself before; he wanted her to choose this. He wanted her to choose him.

Charles retreated from her center, sliding his hand down Louise's legs to lift up her shift. All pretenses gone, she stretched out her limbs like a cat waking from a glorious nap. Her backside jutted into him even more, and he pushed back, grinding himself on her, allowing one momentary gift to his shaft. The pleasure he experienced zapped through his body like a bolt of lightning. He was positive if he took off his clothes, they would stand on their own for days.

Taking his clothes off sounded like a grand idea. Without overthinking the situation, he shimmied out of his trousers, breaking away from their cocoon long enough to tear his shirt off as well. Louise didn't twist around to watch—she did something infinitely better. She removed her shift. And when Charles returned to their spooning position, their bare skin sizzled at the contact, heat against heat, spark against spark.

Charles twined his arms around her, just holding them in the provocative position. He thought to say something. Anything. Nothing came to mind. They'd been doing so well so far without words, so why start now?

He searched back between her legs, cupping her core with more determination. Louise was more than ready for him. Her folds were wet and primed for his touch. Her tiny bud was pointed and insistent, and he took care to give it the attention it desired. Her breathing quickened, her hips undulating against him once more. Even though she didn't need it, Charles brought his fingers to his lips and licked them before placing them at her entrance. Really, all he wanted was a taste of her essence, the exotic piquancy that had driven him mad in the library.

A sound finally shot out from Louise when Charles entered her with his finger, curving it slightly along her narrow walls. She gasped at the action, instantly grabbing his wrist and tensing her thighs, keeping him exactly where he was.

He rocked her on both sides, sandwiching her between his hand and his pelvis. When Louise came, she arched her back and clutched one breast, tilting her head to the headboard. Charles unleashed a ragged curse. He couldn't see anything! He wanted to fill her scream with his tongue, kiss the cords of her neck, pinch her swollen nipples with his teeth.

After Louise's initial tremors died down on his finger, Charles flipped her onto her back and loomed over her. He cradled his shaft in between her thighs and rubbed his length in her wetness, coating himself so he was nice and smooth.

Louise's smile was contented, but there was determination in those steely blue eyes, and when she met his gaze, Charles knew they weren't done. Not even close.

She cupped the back of his neck and captured his mouth with a searing kiss, amplifying that thought. Their tongues groped madly as they took from one another, unleashing a savage desire that had been building for weeks. Charles had thought nothing could be better than his head between her thighs, but his cock mightily disagreed. This was where he belonged, forever and always.

Louise pushed him away. Charles balanced himself on his hands as she explored his chest, kissing his nipples playfully, massaging the skin and hair to the point of pain. Her grip was proprietary; her examination was personal. All the while his cock pulsed avidly against her swollen nether lips, waiting, just waiting, for what she did next.

"Would you believe me if I said I'd wanted to do this for most of my life?" she asked, using one nail to tickle a light path down the center of his chest.

Charles's laugh was deep, husky, and pathetically off-kilter. He felt like an untried lad again, just waiting for his more experienced partner to show him the way to paradise. "I'm not sure. You had a funny way of showing it."

She caught one of his nipples between her teeth and tugged, causing Charles to emit a strangled moan. Her eyes sparkled. "Because I never thought I could have you," she said.

He swayed into her thighs. "You have me. What do you want?"

She bit her bottom lip, all amusement vanishing. "I want you to say yes to me."

They were the same words he'd spoken to her in the library. But it meant something infinitely different.

"Forever?"

Louise's lips thinned, and she shook her head.

Charles rocked into her again, harder. "Forever, Louise?"

"Will you settle for right now?"

Jesus Christ, he was about to explode. Why was the woman being so obstinate? An agreement had to be made quickly. Charles glanced down at his shaft, poised and rigid at her entrance. Louise followed his gaze. The long, round muscles of her belly undulated as she tipped her pelvis toward him, taking his tip into her entrance. He managed to string a sentence together. "As ... as long as you understand what this means," he rasped. "Then I can settle for right now."

Louise grinned. She was a cat again, but this time, one that had the cream. Her hand moved around his hips to settle on his arse. "Right this minute?" she asked.

Charles lowered himself to his elbows. Her lovely breasts crushed against him, and she took a little more of him inside her. His whole body felt like it was going up in flames—in the best way possible, like a saint being burned at the stake before being assumed into heaven. He fisted a bunch of her beautiful red hair, locking her head in place. "Right this second?" he said, holding her stare.

Louise's arrogance fled. She lowered her chin in a barely there nod.

And Charles surged. One stroke and he was planted inside her, overwhelmingly held by her tight walls, the taut squeeze of her body. Louise went rigid underneath him, her legs bent on either side of his hips, her feet flat on the bed. Grappling for breaths, Charles lifted his head to find her staring down at where they were connected, her eyes big, her mouth open.

"Is it ... too much?" he asked.

"No, Charles, you are not too much for me." She laughed, though he could tell it took effort. Louise was a virgin. He'd assumed she would be, though she'd never mentioned it. For his benefit—or for both of theirs—she was trying to act casual, but Charles didn't want her casual. There was nothing casual about this act, and never would be for them.

He pulled out of her slowly, flexing his hips to fill her again. She was impossibly narrow and small, and he could feel her take every blessed inch.

"Do you want me to be too much for you?" he asked, lifting her legs so that they wrapped around his lower back. She was fully open to him now, and her expression showed it. Gone was the flippancy and in its place was uncertain fascination.

"I ... I'm not sure."

Charles thrust home again, and this time she thrust back. She continued to frown, though, still not convinced. "I think you should say yes," he said.

"Yes?"

"Yes," he repeated, plunging once more, causing their skin to slap from the force. Fuck, he loved that sound.

Louise had heard it too, and her smile returned. "Yes," she panted. "Be too much for me. And I'll try to handle you."

Charles dipped his head into the valley of her breasts and sucked on the skin. "I know you will," he murmured silkily. "I know you will."

With that, he was done talking. Charles's brain was at the end of the line; his body needed to take over.

Louise was as good as her word. She tried to handle him. And she succeeded beautifully. Once she realized that she could be as active in the lovemaking as he was, she created a crushing speed and intensity that left them both witless. Charles had thought to go easy and slow for her first time, show her how the sensations could build and flourish under the slightest touch, but Louise was having none of that. She was determined to grasp her fulfillment.

Charles deepened his strokes, all finesse gone. A fever had taken hold, and the only thing left to do was ride it out. And Louise did just that. She rode him in a way that made him think he would go blind. They took from each other with ruthless abandon, like this was the first and only chance to get it right.

The crescendo was almost upon him. Charles panicked. He'd wanted to try four more positions by this point, but as usual, Louise had all the control. "Slow down, love. I'm going to spill," he said, to hell with his pride.

She arched her breasts into him, clinging to his shoulders. "Oh, God, I'm almost … It's happening again … Shh …" she said, eyes closed tight.

Charles's balls pulled up into his body. He increased his speed, charging into Louise, going deeper than he ever thought possible.

Her fingers clawed into his skin, walking their way up his

neck. Before she screamed her pleasure, she grabbed hold of his hair and yanked with impossible strength.

Charles came instantly.

CHAPTER TWENTY

CHARLES WAS A deep sleeper.

Louise rested on her side, one leg hooked over him as he lay supine on the bed. She took advantage of what little light she had to feast on her childhood love. *They don't make them like this anymore.* He was tall and broad, iron-like and formidable—it was no wonder she'd fallen for him so effortlessly when she was a little girl.

She grazed pieces of his hair out of his face. Charles slept with his mouth closed, and his chest rose high and strong with every breath. He was so unapologetically a man, and Louise had never felt more like a woman than when he held her in his arms.

She'd often worried about that. Despite her young crush, Louise had never felt one way or another for other members of the opposite sex. The girls in her circle had whispered about hearts skipping beats and sleepless nights, but she had never come close to experiencing anything of that magnitude as she grew older. She'd worried that she was simply indifferent to men. When she entered Society, the only emotion that ever rose to the surface was anger whenever she encountered Charles as he waded his way through the *ton*, breaking and discarding hearts in his wake.

In those times they'd crossed paths in London, Charles had never behaved in any way untoward or disrespectful. On the contrary, he was only ever polite and nice to Louise and her mother.

Nice. It was that niceness that boiled Louise. It was that politeness that rankled her spirits. Because it was the same gentlemanly performance that he gave to everyone else. And Louise wanted more. She'd always wanted more.

But as she lay there, counting Charles's tawny eyelashes like a lovestruck fiend, she had to ask herself if there would ever be enough. Would she always want more of him? And would that insufferable want propel every other aspiration out of her life?

The answer to that question was what drove her from the bed, taking great pains not to make a sound. She padded around the room, gathering her things, constantly on alert, ready and waiting for him to stop her at every turn.

For years, Louise had blamed her mother for loving her father. Couldn't she see what the rest of the family saw? Louise's father was myopic and cruel, a true libertine, and Lady Delilah could never stop loving him. She would do anything to make his life better, make his comforts more enjoyable. And Louise had watched it all with malice and disenchantment in her heart.

She would never do that, she told herself—live for a man, dote on his every word and action. She would never let one take and take from her until there was nothing left.

Well ... the words people told themselves in the past had a way of coming back to bite them, because lying in the bed was the one person who could consume Louise entirely if she let him.

She knew herself well enough to know that.

So she wouldn't let him.

Though it was early, Louise was able to secure a mount and was on her way toward the next town before the sun tipped over the horizon. The owner at the inn had given her a hard, discerning look, and she'd worried that he might attempt to halt her progress, but money had a way of keeping men quiet, and the second Louise threw the coins down on the table, the owner's mouth shut firmly and completely.

She hadn't told Charles about the funds she kept sewn inside her petticoat. It wasn't his business. He would have tried to take them from her, limiting her options without him. Yes, it had been a smart decision to keep that information to herself. Charles already knew too much—like where her boat was leaving from. No doubt he would follow her to London and attempt to intercept her there. Her only hope was getting out ahead and hiding until the ship took sail. Then everything would finally be at an end, and Louise could relax, forgetting the nightmares of the last few days. Although, to be fair, there was nothing nightmarish about any of the time she'd spent in Charles's company.

Louise could ask herself a million times why she'd given herself to Charles and not come up with the same answer. Succumbing to their attraction was *definitely* not in the plan. And yet when the moment presented itself, she didn't falter, didn't question that being with him was exactly what she wanted. Although foreign and new, lying with Charles felt like the most natural thing in the world, and she couldn't drag up any regrets over it.

She was beyond tired this morning, her inner thighs stung, and her lips were dry and swollen, but she felt like she was floating in her saddle, light, as though an old skin had been shed. A new Louise had been born, clean and scrubbed raw.

Their time together would be a lovely memory to keep her warm on the journey. Louise would remember Charles fondly as a good person, an old family friend—nothing more.

However, none of that explained away the tears on her cheeks on that chilly morning. Nor did it curb the relentless ache in the bottom of her stomach. Her skin might have been shed, but it left a cold feeling in its wake, a loss.

LOUISE DIDN'T STOP at the closest town, nor the one after that.

Hoping to maximize the distance, she waited until dusk approached before finishing for the night. She hadn't ridden hard, and had stopped numerous times to let her animal rest and drink in the river that trailed the road. Nevertheless, Louise's bones still creaked and cracked when she dismounted the final time, grimacing at the pain clawing through her limbs. She assumed it was cumulative. She wasn't used to riding astride, and in the past two days, she'd ridden in a tournament covered in armor and was now gallivanting across the country. Some might consider four to six months on a ship a small form of torture, but at this rate, Louise was looking forward to the limited confines of the *Clementine* where she could recuperate.

The town was much smaller than Moffat and lacked the variety of stylish inns that the spa destination advertised. That was fine with Louise; she didn't need the bother of choice. Eating and retiring were her only desires. She looked forward to the void of sleep, where she wouldn't dwell on the fact that she'd have to begin another long ride in the morning, though tomorrow she would speak to the innkeeper about hiring a coach for London. That would take some of the hardship off. Technically, she had the time to relax for a day or two. The *Clementine* didn't set sail until the end of the following week, but with Charles near, it made sense to keep moving at a decent clip. Damn him for getting involved! The man thought he had to keep saving her. Didn't he know by now that she was perfectly capable of handling herself? She'd gotten this far, hadn't she? All he did was make her think of—or *rethink*—her voyage.

The plan did not call for rethinking. The plan would stick, no matter what.

The inn included a small tavern that was filling with people when Louise hobbled in. The tiny room only held four tables, and she collapsed into the last empty one. She avoided all the strange looks lobbed at her and ordered a cider and *two* mince pies, ignoring her inner warning to be sparing with her money.

Minutes later, Louise was almost comatose in her seat.

When the chair across from her scratched back from the table, she jerked into life. A young woman hurried to sit, smiling apologetically. "You really shouldn't sleep here," the woman said softly. "It's not safe." She looked about Louise's age and seemed just as exhausted and lost. With her curly light brown hair and large brown eyes, there was a country sweetness to her, though her bearings hinted at an education.

Louise grunted. "It's safe enough. I'm sure a fork is coming soon along with my food."

The woman gave her a disbelieving smirk. "What would you do with a fork?"

"Find an appropriate place for the pointy end."

"Oh …" the woman replied. "I don't know that trick." She glanced around the room, no doubt searching for a better place to sit. When none could be found, she tried again. "I hope you don't mind if I share your table. I thought it would be better than sitting by myself; I'm glad I spotted you. Some of the men here can be … quite assertive when they find a woman traveling alone."

Assertive was one word for it. If Louise had to, she would guess that every male in the inn had their focus firmly locked on them.

She nodded, finding the sense in the comment, then rediscovered her manners and attempted to act presentable to her new acquaintance. Miss Margaret Stone was on her way to gain employment as a governess for the daughters of Mr. and Mrs. Joseph Wentworth. She'd answered an ad, and this would be her first time traveling away from her home.

"I can't say I'm not nervous," Margaret said anxiously, wringing her long fingers at the edge of the table—something Louise's governess had never done. "This is my first assignment; I want to make a good impression."

Louise smiled, warming to the conversation, her fatigue lifting. Wasn't Margaret just like her? Starting a new life away from home, grasping at independence? Perhaps divine intervention had thrust the two of them together! "I'm sure you'll do just fine," she replied enthusiastically. "The children will love you. My governess was one hundred years old and had a fondness for using long sticks whenever I talked back, which was a lot, unfortunately."

"I'm sorry to hear that," Margaret said, a short line forming in the center of her forehead. "But if you don't mind my saying … look at you now. An undeniably accomplished lady. I'm sure I have a lot to learn from you. Will you be on the coach tomorrow as well?"

Louise nodded. "To London."

"Oh good! Me too!" Margaret exclaimed, placing her hand over her heart. "Then I won't feel so alone."

"No, you won't be alone," Louise agreed. "We can take care of each other. That's what women are supposed to do!"

Margaret's eyes misted with a glassy sheen. She pulled a handkerchief from her reticule and patted at the offending tears. "You have no idea how much I value your saying that to me," she said, her voice choked. "I've been here all day. You see, I thought the coach left this morning, and, well …" A pink blotch stained her apple cheeks. "My funds are limited. I don't have enough to pay for a room."

"What will you do?" Louise asked.

Margaret's entire face burned scarlet. Her tone was woefully pathetic. "The innkeeper said I could stay in the stables. He said it would probably be safe there."

"Probably?"

Margaret nodded, her gaze drifting to the tabletop.

Probably didn't sound very convincing.

Blowing out the kind of breath that made her lips rumble, Louise shook her head. "You will do no such thing. You'll stay with me and be safe, and in the morning, we'll catch the coach together."

Margaret's head snapped up. "No," she cried. "I couldn't take advantage of you like that."

"You're not taking advantage of me. Let me remedy the

situation; I insist."

Margaret's perplexed expression made Louise laugh. Naturally, the young woman had been brought up to believe that only men could fix every problem. She had a lot to learn about life. Suddenly, Louise wasn't tired at all. Quite the opposite—she teemed with energy. She felt worldly and wise beyond her years. It was amazing what doling out advice to the less fortunate could do for one's self-esteem!

And Louise wasn't done yet. "Now, have you eaten?" she asked as the bar maiden placed two mince pies in front of her as well as a couple of forks.

Margaret didn't have to answer the question. She licked her lips at the meaty scent.

Louise pushed one pie across the table. "Take it."

Margaret didn't dawdle. She picked up a fork and gave it a strange look before shoving a heaping bite of pastry into her mouth. Her large eyes closed, and she hummed with satiated glee.

Louise grinned at the unfiltered antics. "Good?" she asked, taking her first bite as well.

"*So* good," Margaret agreed between chews—again, not something Louise's governess would have done. However, she had to allow that hunger tended to throw gentility out the window.

Margaret leaned back in her chair, her next spoonful hanging in midair. Cocking an eyebrow, she asked, "Were you really going to eat both of these?"

Louise stared at her one lonely dish. "Of course."

"All by yourself?"

"Of course," she repeated.

Margaret laughed. "I've never seen a woman eat that much before."

Louise considered being offended but changed her mind. The young governess was naïve; she only needed to be taught. "That's a shame," Louise said, tucking into her pie, "because I've never met a woman that wasn't hungry all the time."

EVEN WITH THREE younger sisters, Louise had never had to share a bedroom. Eugenie, Caroline, and Bess lived full-time at the family's country estate in Ipswich. The closest to Louise in age, Eugenie had only just turned twelve. A seven-year age gap was no small thing, especially since Eugenie was still playing with Louise's old dolls while Lady Delilah had Louise on the Marriage Mart in London.

Louise had never experienced late-night giggling sessions and secret conversations under shared covers with friends. Margaret provided all that and more. Even while exhaustion crept up on her, Louise kept the candles on the side tables burning in their cozy room that night. She told herself she could make up for the lack of sleep in the coach on the way to London. This experience was what she'd been hoping for.

When Louise had read and reread every book on the Sandwich Islands, she'd always been struck at the relationships of the women in the tribes. Community was first and foremost. It was nothing like the *ton*, where women were pitted against each other, all vying for the man with the biggest fortune and oldest title of the Season.

From her research, Louise learned that the women of the islands held an independence that was completely unfamiliar to her. Not only were they allowed to educate themselves about sexual relations—they were encouraged to speak on it and teach it to the younger girls. Communication was open, and sexual gratification was supported for both men and women. Lovemaking was to be enjoyed, and one could not enjoy it if one was left in the dark to its inner workings.

Not that Louise and Margaret broached such subjects that night—Louise's inhibitions were taking baby steps—but they did discuss just about everything else under the sun. From beaus to brothers to favorite books, the two women opened up and created a bond. By the time the final candle went out and Louise could no longer hold her eyelids open, she went to bed knowing that Margaret was a friend she would have for the rest of her life. She was a kindred spirit, a bosom friend of the first order. And Louise would never have found her—experienced this moment—if she'd stayed where everyone had told her to stay. If she'd done what everyone had told her to do.

Charles was not on her mind when Louise went to bed—not really. Her last thoughts were that she couldn't wait to tell him that she didn't need him. She had everything under control. She wondered what he would think about that.

CHAPTER TWENTY-ONE

CHARLES WAS TOO tired to think rationally. Obviously, that had to be the reason why the moment he spotted Louise arguing with the innkeeper, he wanted to grab her and kiss the wits out of her. That was wrong. What he should have wanted to do was throw her over his shoulder and tie her to his horse. That was more logical.

But again, he wasn't thinking. Charles hadn't slept a wink since the damn woman snuck out on him, and he vowed he wouldn't until she was lying next to him again—naked.

The noise didn't help things. Louise's voice had been at a shrieking pitch since Charles walked through the front door. Which was how he could sit back and listen to the whole debacle without detection. She was too incensed to notice anyone but the man dealing with her histrionics. The poor bastard, Charles thought. The innkeeper didn't look like he'd had his morning tea yet.

"I just don't understand," Louise screeched, placing her hands on her cheeks. "You said the coach hasn't left yet. Then where could she be?"

The innkeeper's expression was resigned, the lines on his face growing longer the more he repeated himself. "I told you, miss, I don't usually ask where our patrons go when they leave."

"But you saw her leave?" she asked. "Miss Margaret Stone?"

"I told you," he said. "I saw Margaret *Quarry* leave very early this morning with two men."

"No, no," Louise said, shaking her head like a wet dog. "You're not listening to me. You have the wrong woman. Margaret Stone didn't come with any men. Her father dropped her off yesterday, and she was taking the coach to London."

"I'm sorry, miss," the innkeeper said. For his part, the man really did seem apologetic. No doubt, he'd played this identical scene out countless times before. The only person that changed was Louise, but the outcome was always the same. Some poor, unsuspecting girl would exit the inn with substantially less money than she came in with.

"Look. You're not listening to me. She can't be gone. She's wearing my petticoat!"

The innkeeper grimaced. Discussing a lady's undergarments was decidedly not comfortable for him. "Don't ... don't ladies usually have more than one?"

"You don't understand!" she screamed, lurching for the man. She gripped his lapels and hauled him so close they almost bumped heads. "I need that petticoat. It's my future!"

"All right. All right. That's enough," Charles announced, coming to the innkeeper's rescue. He covered Louise's hands with his own, peeling away her ferocious hold. Stunned, she left her hands stuck in their clawed position as Charles led her out the front door. They needed air, then he would attempt to piece this horrendous puzzle together.

Louise let him drag her to the side of the building. Her eyes were frantic, flickering this way and that, not settling on anything, let alone Charles. He debated dunking her head in the horse trough, but her tears stopped him.

"I can't believe it," she cried, hiding her face in her hands. Charles gave Louise the time to cry; she needed it. Her wild, long hair fell down her shoulders, and she still wore the same yellow dress she'd been kidnapped in. It was a disgrace. Charles needed to get the woman home immediately. She was beginning to look like a crazy person. Or worse (if his suspicions were correct)—an easy mark for a thief.

Louise took a shuddering breath, but it did nothing to curb a fresh onslaught of tears. "How could I be so foolish!" she wailed. "She took everything. Everything! I have nothing anymore."

Charles placed his hands on her trembling shoulders, rubbing gently. "What did she take? What is everything?"

Louise dropped her hands, and her red, splotchy face tore at Charles's heart. He'd never seen her so utterly broken. "My money. All of it," she sobbed. "I had saved for six months. I sold everything I held dear, and kept all my pin money, all for my trip. And now it's … it's …" Her lips quivered. She couldn't finish her sentence; it was like if she tried then it would mean everything truly was lost—not just her money, but her dreams.

"Who?"

"Margaret Stone," Louise spat. "Or Margaret Quarry. Whoever she is! I let her stay in my room last night—I even let her have one of my pies! I was so hungry!"

"Why?"

She seemed so innocent, so young. Charles didn't have the heart to berate her for trusting a stranger at an inn in the middle of nowhere. "Never mind why," he went on. "Do you know where she went?"

Louise flung a noodle-like arm toward her right. "I don't know. That way."

He stood up straight. "What way?"

She made the motion again. "That way."

"Can you be more specific?"

"No, Charles, I'm afraid I can't. The innkeeper said she went that way, so that's the way she went."

He squinted past the morning sun in that direction. "Toward the lakes, then," he said to himself. That would make sense. Cumbria was known for its vast array of lakes and mountains. If *he'd* needed to lie low for a few days, that environment would provide the best cover.

The door to the inn opened, and the luscious, welcoming smell of sausage and eggs wafted around the corner. Christ, he was hungry. But that would just have to wait. Charles had to intercept the thieves before they made it to the sanctity of those hills; it was the only hope he had at retrieving the money. He shouldn't care. Louise had him now, and she didn't need the coins, but something inside him understood just how important the savings were to her. And what was important to Louise was important to him—especially her self-esteem. It crushed him to watch her berate herself so badly. Charles told himself he could abide anything, but that put him close to his limit.

"Go back to your room and stay there until I return," he said, backing away.

"I'm going with you," she hiccupped through her tears.

He hung his head. "No, you're not."

"It's my money—"

"That you lost because you are out of your element, Louise. I don't know where you got it into your head that you could handle the world on your own, but you can't. For God's sake, you let a woman get the better of you in Scotland; how are you going to cope with an island on the other side of the globe?"

She wiped the tears from her face. "You're just saying these nasty things to me because you're angry that I left you this morning."

"You're damn right I'm angry! I'm bloody furious with you. Why, Louise? Why would you do something so mean? So thoughtless?"

"I'm sorry," she said gently. "I'm sorry that I left you. I didn't want to ... if that makes you feel any better. But I had to."

"Why?"

"You wouldn't understand."

Charles sighed. It was like beating a horse when it was down. Louise was completely dejected—and not just about the money. He could see what sneaking from him had cost her, and it did something to curb his ire. Continuing this argument wouldn't solve anything, and it was only taking up time. He needed to get on the road before it was too late. But he would get his answers before the day was done.

"You're going to have to trust that I *will* understand," Charles said. "Can you do that? It's the only way I'll fetch your money." He rubbed his face, releasing a long sigh. "I haven't asked you for much, and you've given me even less. I don't know how much longer I can continue to be patient with you. Do you promise to tell me the truth later? The reason you left?"

Louise's answer didn't come quickly, but it did come. "Yes."

AFTER CONFERRING WITH the innkeeper, Charles learned that Margaret and her two men were most likely part of a gang that worked the Lake District, conning tourists and single women like Louise. It was a smart trade, since the Lake District had recently become a popular destination full of people eager to tramp the lovely grounds where the famous poet William Wordsworth "wandered lonely as a cloud."

In the end, Charles did allow Louise to accompany him. She told him that she didn't want to be alone, and he was of the same mind. Now that he had her again, leaving her didn't make any sense.

The ride was quiet and uneventful. Louise had stopped crying, but a heaviness plagued her features. Charles wondered if teasing would coax her from her irritability but thought better of it. It was a horrible feeling to be duped by another, to trust someone and have that trust thrown back in your face. He wouldn't make light of it.

But after a couple of hours, he couldn't abide her silence any longer and thought of the one thing that could get Louise to talk.

"Tell me something about your islands," Charles said, maneuvering his horse near hers so their shins grazed.

Unfortunately, the question didn't spark her to life as he had assumed it would.

Louise shrugged glumly. "You read the same books I did."

"Yes, but I only read each one once."

That brought out a flicker of life. "What do you want to know?" she asked softly.

"Anything," he said. "I always thought their ideas of marriage to be most … interesting."

Was she blushing? It was hard to tell with her newly tanned cheeks, but Charles surely hoped so. It was beyond endearing to know he could make her do it.

He watched with supreme satisfaction as Louise fiddled with the pommel of her saddle. "Well, I suppose it's important to know that they don't treat marriage as we do here, nor should they be chastised for that," she began earnestly. "The idea is completely different."

"Go on."

Her shoulders straightened and she stuck her nose in the air. The professor was ready to lecture. "From what I've learned, men and women stay together because they want to, not because of any obligation. There is rarely a wedding ceremony when one chooses to join with another, and they can decide to be monogamous or not."

"Or not?"

Louise gave him a quick look. "They can have other lovers—"

"Yes, I know what monogamy is."

"I wasn't sure."

Charles leaned toward her, hanging off the edge of his saddle. "And that appeals to you … that kind of open relationship?"

She directed her horse away. "It could have its advantages. Couples wouldn't have to continue the arrangement if the love is gone and they are miserable. Either side could leave and move on whenever they deemed it was time."

Charles hoped that he found the gang members soon. Louise thinking she could "move on" with another man put him in a *mood.* "You need to stop worrying about my leaving you," he said with a little too much force. "It's never going to happen."

"I'm not! And—"

Charles cut her off. "*And* you have to stop lumping all men in with your father. I am nothing like him."

"Who was talking about my father? I wasn't speaking about him, and I never said you were anything like him—"

Charles's horse's ears twitched.

"Be quiet," he ordered her, hopping from his mount. He scanned the hills. Smoke. A fire had been started, and Charles would bet all the money in Louise's petticoat that it had been started by their gang.

She scrambled off her horse and hugged his side. Her minty smell invaded him so quickly, Charles had to blink his senses back to life. "What is it?" she whispered. "I don't see anything."

He flicked his chin toward the plumes of smoke. "They must be breaking for the day."

She frowned at the midday sun. "It's too early."

"Not when they were up all night fleecing you," he remarked dryly. "Now stop talking. We'll need complete silence if I'm going to take them by surprise."

Louise grabbed his forearm. Charles stared at it longer than he cared to admit. "You will be careful, won't you?"

He cleared his throat, enjoying the weight of her palm, the way it felt like she owned him. "Of course I will," he said, flashing a wolfish grin. "The sooner I'm done with them, the sooner I can watch your sweet breasts when you're riding me later."

Her mouth dropped open. "What … You …"

Charles swooped in and kissed her. Witless. Just as he'd wanted to when he first saw her that morning. Palming the back of her neck, he deepened the kiss, filling her mouth with his desire and yearning. He didn't hold back and wouldn't allow her to either. When Louise's tongue slipped around his, he groaned, his knees weakening from the minor action. He was a puddle at her feet. When Charles pulled away, she gave him a bemused look, clearly not entirely sure of his intention. He kissed her again before she could figure it out.

"Why did you leave me?" he asked.

"What?"

"This morning," Charles said, gripping her supple waist. "Why did you flee? You apologized. You said you didn't want to do it … then why? Is it truly a race? Did you do it because you're worried that I am going to leave first?"

"No! And I didn't flee," Louise groused, lowering her head.

He tipped it back up with his finger. "You promised to tell me. The truth."

Her mouth screwed up, and Charles kissed her again to wipe that expression off her face.

"Stop that! I can't think when you do that!"

"Try harder," he said, laughing, "because I like doing it."

She gnawed on her bottom lip. "It hurts too much—"

"Making love to me? I tried to be gentle—"

Louise's face burned red, but she returned a tiny smile that made Charles want to strip her naked and do it all again right then and there. "No, no, you were wonderful; that's not what I meant."

Her voice cracked on the last word. Charles folded her into an embrace, holding her tight. "Then what did you mean?"

She took a deep breath against his chest. "It hurts too much to be with you, Charles. And the longer I stay, the more you make me feel. I can't risk it; there's too much at stake."

"What's at stake, sweetheart? Tell me."

She shook her head, on the verge of tears. "Me." She shrugged helplessly. "I'm strong, Charles. I know that about myself, and I've worked so hard for that strength, but whenever I'm with you … I just feel like it all deserts me in an instant. And you can't help it. You're the Knight of the Sun. You consume all in your path; it's just your nature."

Charles's body surged with euphoria. He cradled Louise's head in his hands, pulling her back to look at him. "You love me, just admit it."

Her lips pressed firmly in a line. The stubborn wench! "Maybe I did once … a long time ago."

A long time ago. That wasn't good enough.

Charles went on. "Feeling too much doesn't have to be a bad thing. And I'm going to keep reminding you of this fact until it sticks in that skull of yours—I'm not leaving."

"All men leave sooner or later," Louise said.

"Well, I'm not all men. I'm the Knight of the fucking Sun."

CHAPTER TWENTY-TWO

L OUISE HAD LIED.

Of course she was still in love, and would be for the rest of her life. She'd loved Charles her entire girlhood and was mature enough to know that that sweet, youthful love would never go away. It was the love that made old women sigh in remembrance, first love—the thrilling cliff that made all young girls jump into adulthood eagerly.

But it was getting worse, because Louise was coming to terms with the fact that she *liked* Charles as well. And liking him was something entirely different. Because Louise was no longer a girl with childish fantasies. Liking Charles said something about the woman she had become.

For instance, she shouldn't have liked the way he stormed into the thieves' camp, brandishing a small knife like a glorious King Arthur against his nephew, Mordred. Nor should her heart have skipped along with every fist he'd pounded into the two deplorable men's faces. The actions were barbaric, the blood positively savage. Yet Louise never turned away. She didn't even close one eye at the gruesome spectacle. This was no playacting, no pretend knights jousting against wooden dummies. With no armor to shield him, Charles was the epitome of a warrior as he conquered the makeshift camp, scaring off their horses and swiftly tying the two unconscious men with their backs together.

Charles had been right. The Knight of the Sun was no ordinary man. He was something to behold.

Margaret might have made a decent thief, but she didn't think fast on her feet. While Charles made short work of her partners, she'd frozen in place, watching everything with wide, shocked eyes. When she eventually came to life, she lunged for a knife that one of her men had dropped, but Charles slapped it out of her hand as if it was nothing more than a pesky flea.

"Sit down," he barked, pointing his weapon to an open patch of dirt. Margaret didn't argue. However, she did commence her begging.

"Please," she said, tucking her skirts tight around her legs. "Don't hurt me. We only have a little. Take it and leave us alone."

Charles crouched near her, the tip of his knife at the hem of her skirt. "Oh, I heard you had a little more than that."

Margaret's angelic brown eyes narrowed. She lifted her head and swiveled her neck to look around them. Louise knew exactly whom she was looking for, and stepped out into the open.

When Margaret saw her, she actually smiled. "You're cleverer than I thought," she called out over the distance.

"I wish I could say the same about you."

"Oh, I'm very clever," Margaret replied loftily. "If you didn't have your man here, I would have gotten away easy enough. So, what now? Are you two running away together?"

"Something like that," Charles said. "Now hand over the petticoat."

"You haven't even bought me a drink."

The cheek!

Charles's grin was merciless. "You can take it off or I can take it off for you."

"You promise?" Margaret asked coyly.

Oh, for pity's sake! Louise marched into the camp and snatched the knife that Charles had kicked. "He doesn't want you. Now take off the petticoat, and you better hope my money is still in there!"

Sullenly, Margaret glanced at Louise as if she'd just interrupted some romantic tête-à-tête. Was she trying to get under Louise's skin? Was it working?

When Margaret realized that Charles wasn't going to play along with her, she shimmied out of the petticoat and flung it at him. "It's all in there. I sewed it back up after I counted it like a good girl. I even left the little sketch you kept in there. Pretty picture. You were a cute little child. Skinny … not like now."

Louise's stomach dropped. She could feel Charles's heavy gaze switch to her, but she stared at the ground, her cheeks burning in mortification. Stupid Margaret and her stupid, big mouth!

Slowly, Charles opened the seam with the money. He took a long time inspecting, and Louise had no doubt what had caught his attention.

It was another lie. Louise had told him she couldn't remember what had happened to the sketch he'd made of her. Too mortified, she hadn't wanted to tell him that she kept it with her always, afraid to leave it anywhere in case she lost it. It was her most treasured possession.

And it outed her completely. How would Charles ever believe she no longer loved him when he held the evidence to the contrary in his hands? If she had felt powerless in his presence before, she felt utterly impotent now.

Gently, Charles handed the petticoat to her without saying a word.

Louise could usually tell how much money was in the pocket based on the weight. She'd held it for so long, she was certain she could feel if one pound was missing. However, now it felt more substantial and cumbersome with the sketch's implications. "What are we going to do with her?" she asked quietly, nodding to Margaret.

Charles cocked his head. "What do you want to do with her?"

His voice was so tender, it made Louise want to cry—and

torture the big-mouthed thief.

"Tie her up with the men, leave her for dead?"

The color drained from Margaret's face. *There.* That was payback for the sketch—and the flirting.

"You ... you don't want that on your conscience," she stammered.

Louise folded her arms. "You don't know what my conscience can handle."

"That's true," Charles cut in. "She can be rather heartless when she wants to be. In fact, just yesterday, I thought she was the most heartless woman in the world." His manner was wistful and mournful, and Louise almost believed them. Had she truly hurt him? Could it be possible that he wanted to be with her as much as he said he did?

Why did it matter?

"I am not heartless," Louise grumbled, feeling uncomfortably on display in front of the thief. More and more she felt like she was made of glass, desperately close to breaking.

"I'd like to hear more," Margaret said. She placed an elbow on her thigh and held her head in her hand as if she was a child waiting for story time. *The nerve of this woman!*

Charles had a playful smile on his lips that did not bode well. When he opened his mouth, Louise beat him to it. "Don't you dare tell her anything about our ... our—" She cut herself off, having a difficult time finding the best description ... for whatever she and Charles were. Lovers? The word made her knees tremble.

"Your what?" Margaret prodded. "Your scandalous involvement? Your ... arrangement?"

Louise rolled her eyes. "We don't have an arrangement—"

Charles slid in. "Yes, we do."

"No, we don't."

"We *are* getting married."

Margaret might look like a child sitting on the ground, but Louise was the one acting like one, stamping a petulant foot in the dirt. "No, we're not. We are ... we are..." She had never been so ineloquent.

"What?" Margaret asked, her eyes shining in mirth. "You are living in sin?"

"Of course not!" Louise said.

Margaret shrugged. Her smile was positively malicious. "It's nothing to be so offended about. Last night when you were droning on and on about those damn islands, didn't you say that's how the women behaved there? Marriage wasn't the done thing; women could take lovers at their leisure. You sounded awfully proud of those women and their liberties, but you're singing a different tune today. I hope you're not going to be just like those Bible beaters who sail over there and attempt to convert the heathens, make them even more English than the English."

"I'm not!" Louise objected. Why did she have to be so loquacious last night? Why did she tell a perfect stranger all her business? She shot a panicked look at Charles, who stood by quietly, studying her intently. He seemed as interested in her answer as Margaret. "I have nothing but respect for the islanders."

"But …?" Margaret asked.

Louise's jaw clenched. "*But* that's not what we are," she seethed, waving a hand between Charles and herself. "We are not living in sin, and we definitely do not have an arrangement. We are just two old family friends who know each other very, very well."

Margaret grinned. "Yes, in the biblical sense."

"Oh, will you be quiet!" Louise spun to Charles. "Can we tie her up now? We've wasted enough time here, don't you think?"

"So, he's going with you, then? To the island?" Margaret asked, losing what little fear she'd had. Apparently, Louise's convoluted life story was too entertaining to worry about being left for dead and eaten by wolves.

Charles still did not move. Louise would have to finish this herself. She flopped on the ground, tearing off her slippers. With irritated pulls and tugs, she ripped off both Charles's stockings that he'd loaned her and her own. His wool stockings were too valuable to Louise, but she figured she could use her battered silk ones to tie Margaret's hands together. Too bad she didn't have one more; she'd love to gag the insufferable woman in the process.

Margaret crinkled up her nose as Louise approached her. "Ugh, those smell horrible! When's the last time you changed your clothes?"

"It's been a while," Louise muttered, annoyed at her embarrassment. To be admonished on cleanliness by a low-down criminal! She knelt behind Margaret and yanked the thief's arms back, twisting the silk around and around before tying it off. Louise didn't know if she was doing it correctly but assumed she was on the right track when Margaret grunted in pain. *Good.*

She stood up, wiping her hands on her skirt, avoiding Margaret's gaze. She would not allow the woman's tears to persuade her, nor would she let any pleading alter her decision. Margaret wouldn't have thought twice about doing the same to her. Of that, Louise was positive.

But when no sniffles or pleas came, she relented and checked. Margaret continued to stare at her as if Louise had two heads and she couldn't decide which one to chop off.

"So, is he?" Margaret asked. "Going with you?"

Louise clawed at her hair. "No. He … he can't … He doesn't want to. He wants to keep me here." *Stop rambling, Louise! You don't owe this villain an explanation!*

"Huh. There seems more to it than that." Margaret arched a pretty eyebrow at Charles. "I'll stay with you. Anywhere you want."

Snorting, he turned to Louise. "When did I ever say I didn't want to go?"

Louise stopped short. "I … you …" She flopped her hands down by her sides. "Your life is here."

"My life is anywhere."

She couldn't speak. Charles's expression was so earnest and

guileless that she didn't know what to make of it, as it jumbled her agitated emotions together in one hopeful ball in her chest. So she ignored it, rounding on Margaret again. "Why do you want to know?" she asked.

"Just interested, I guess."

"Well, don't be! I am no concern of yours."

Margaret *tsked*, tossing her long brown hair over her shoulder with a flick of her head. Almost as if she'd been tied up before … which wasn't a stretch of the imagination for Louise. "Don't be so rude. We were fast friends last night, and I'm only looking out for you. You won't last, you know. Not without him. Look how easily I fooled you. You were much too easy, so willing and ready to trust. Face it, Louise, you don't have what it takes to make it in the big, bad world on your own."

"Please, can we go?" Louise asked Charles, dismissing Margaret. He didn't answer immediately and appeared to be lost in thought. After a few heartbeats, he nodded. But instead of following Louise across the field to their horses, he walked to Margaret, cutting her free.

Louise watched as Margaret rubbed her wrists, while Charles whispered in her ear. The thief nodded and began to gather her meager possessions. The incapacitated men did not garner any notice.

"Why did you do that?" Louise called out.

Charles waited until he was at her side until he answered. "She was right, Louise. You don't want her death on your conscience," he said, marching past her to his mount. "She was right about a few things."

"Oh, that's right," she replied hotly. His words burned her to the quick. It felt like a betrayal. Not only had Charles allowed the wench to judge her, but he also agreed with the verdict. "You've already said I won't make it on my own. Maybe you should have let Margaret stay with you; you have so much in common."

Leaning against his saddle, Charles sighed, rubbing his eyes. Louise hadn't registered how glassy and red they were, how utterly exhausted he looked. She wasn't being fair. Adequate, restorative sleep had been hard to come by for her over the past few days; she could only imagine how depleted *he* was. She wished she could take her venom back. He didn't deserve it now, not when he'd just come to her rescue yet again. Charles needed a hot bath and a bed, not to be battered by her.

But Louise was hurt. She understood people would have their doubts, but she wanted Charles to believe in her. His opinion held weight. It would always matter more than anyone else's.

"Never mind," she said quietly. "It doesn't matter. Let's go back to the inn. It wouldn't hurt either of us to take a day off from traveling. We can talk later."

"We will definitely talk later," Charles said, mounting his horse in one easy movement. Louise hurried to do the same and keep up with him. "But we are not going back to the inn. You got me out this way; now that I'm here, I have some more business to attend to."

"What business—"

Before Louise could finish her question, Charles moved his horse next to hers and leaned across his saddle. His mouth was on hers in an instant. She opened to him without thinking, her body knowing what it wanted before her mind could catch up. With long, seductive passes, they savored one another, thirsting for another kiss before the last one was complete. Louise twisted his hair around her fingers and smiled into his mouth when the action elicited a luxurious moan. That luscious sound made her breasts grow heavy and her nipples point against her corset. She adored the sounds he made. Charles hadn't talked much when they'd made love the night before, which surprised her. He always had so much to say. But the little sounds he made, the ragged breaths, the wrecked exhales, were enough to drive her crazy. More than that. They made her feel wanton.

With little effort, Charles picked Louise up out of her saddle and placed her in front of him. She sat on his hardness, twisting her legs around his back.

This was what she needed Charles for—*only this*. She could handle this much, she told herself. Just this much. Any more and she would never be able to leave him.

"Take me somewhere," Louise begged, angling her head so she didn't waste one inch of his precious mouth. Charles hadn't shaved that morning, and his whiskers rasped her cheeks, burning her skin, giving their act even more of a visceral sensation. The twinges of pain Louise had felt earlier between her legs were now gone and replaced with a different kind of ache, a desperate urge that yearned to be soothed.

Charles's countenance was somber when he pulled away, lightly tracing Louise's lips with his fingers. "I know you have what it takes to conquer the world," he said softly. "I think I always have. You can see it in the sketch. That little girl was fearsome. That's the real reason I don't want you to go to the islands. I don't want to keep you here in some cage." He skimmed his nose against hers. "I'm afraid if you leave, you won't come back. You'll meet some brilliant, swashbuckling adventurer and never think of home again. And then where would I be? Then whom would I draw?"

These were the pretty words that Louise guarded her heart against, but they tore down her walls as easily as a rainstorm would a straw roof.

"I'm terrified you'll say yes to the wrong man and the wrong future," Charles continued. "And I only have myself to blame, because I came to my senses too late."

Louise reached for his hand, holding it to her breast, urging him to physically caress her with the same sweetness of his words. "I ... I don't know what you're saying," she said, tugging at his bottom lip to kiss her again.

Charles rooted out her nipples underneath her gown and tweaked them between his fingers. "I'm saying that I'm here now."

"You're too late."

"I don't fucking care," he murmured, capturing her mouth

for a kiss that was meant to put a period on the conversation. Louise accepted him eagerly. Talking about their future was never safe; she was too raw and desperate for him. She would say anything to get his fingers to start moving under her skirts.

But there was a noise. An irritation. A rough and insistent "ah-hmm," as if someone was fighting the kind of phlegm Louise had woken up with after her drinking episode with Mr. Harvey.

Charles broke from their kiss, rolling his head to their rude audience.

Margaret was waiting a few yards away, her hip stuck out impetuously. "Sorry to break this *non-arrangement* up, but I'll be taking that horse now."

Charles nodded toward Louise's animal, the one he had just lifted her from. "Take it. It's yours."

Louise watched in horror as Margaret came to claim her prize. "I need that horse!"

He faced her again, lovingly brushing her hair off her face. She noticed that he did that a lot. Tactile and gentle, he touched her whenever he could, and it never stopped making her chest tingle. "No, you don't."

"Yes, I do."

"No, you don't," repeated.

Their argument was irrelevant at this point because Margaret had already mounted and taken off. She truly was an industrious woman, Louise concluded.

"I don't understand," she said, shaking her head.

Charles shifted in his seat, moving her so she wasn't cuddled between his legs anymore. The thief had struck again, stealing their moment. At least Charles seemed as put out as she. His jaw hardened, and, with an aggrieved exhale, he righted Louise in the saddle and flicked the horse into a walk.

"Where are we going now? What business do you have to finish?" she asked.

His gaze latched on to the road ahead. "To beat the bloody hell out of the man who thought he could take what was mine."

CHAPTER TWENTY-THREE

L OUISE WAS NEITHER naïve nor slow, and yet it took her far longer than Charles expected to figure out where they were headed.

In fact, it took a two-hour ride and the stately country home to be directly in front of her nose before she asked, "Who lives there?"

Surprised, Charles craned his head around her neck. "Have you truly never been here before?"

"Obviously."

He laughed. "And to think, you could have been mistress of all this, if only you hadn't shown your devious penchant for killing rodents."

Louise shot up in her saddle, knocking his chin with the top of her head. "This is Penrose?" she asked, naming the Merton family's country home.

Charles answered by starting up the long gravel drive. The Georgian pile was elegant and understated, with two rows of windows lining up against its façade. Sheep grazed on the field surrounding them and offered bored passing glances as Charles guided their horse toward the stables.

"Charles," she said. "What are we doing?"

"I already told you."

Louise paused. He could practically hear her mulling over

what he'd told her hours ago. Her head began to shake furiously, tickling his face. "No, no, no. Let's just leave. There's no reason to cause any more trouble."

"I didn't cause any trouble. Royce started it all, and I will never forgive him. He stole what was *mine*."

"Charles, please," Louise begged. She placed her hands over his on the pommel, and electricity jolted his body. As much as Charles loved riding with her snugly against his crotch, he couldn't wait to get her off. Not one minute had gone by where he hadn't thought about carrying her down from the horse and ravaging her in the high grass. The only reason why he hadn't was because of what he had in mind for later. The wait would be worth it.

Louise caressed the tops of his hands, her voice lovely and reassuring. "He didn't steal me. I'm fine. I'm whole, thanks to you."

They arrived at the stable, and with a quick scan, Charles easily found what he was looking for. "I meant my horse."

He meant his horse. Yes. Silly Louise. Honestly, she should have guessed it. A man and his horse. What greater love affair was there?

Charles dismounted and helped her down. They walked to his animal in the closest stall, checking for signs of distress and finding none. Only after he was satisfied did he bring his attention back to her.

"I won't be gone long," he said.

Louise threw up her hands. "Where are you going now? We have your horse. Let's just go before we see Royce."

He flashed a cocky grin. "Oh, but I *want* to see Royce."

"You aren't going to kill him, are you?" She understood that the question was ridiculous, but she was dealing with a man who'd had his prized horse stolen. Men were murdered for much less.

"Don't worry," he said over his shoulder, marching out of sight. "I just need a quick word."

Louise doubted that. Charles's idea of a quick word was much different from the normal person's. But there was nothing she could do about it now. As strong as she was, Louise was no match for a vengeful Charles. For once, she listened and stayed put. She had no wish to see Royce bloodied and mangled, despite the nasty way he'd treated her. She still felt horrible about the lost guinea pigs; in her opinion, they were even.

With no stable boy nearby, Louise used the time grooming and tacking Charles's horse, giving the attention and love it deserved after its kidnapping. "I know how you feel," she purred to the animal, scratching the soft pink spot of its nose.

The horse's ears twitched toward the stable entrance as clomping could be heard up the lane.

"Who's there?" a coarse voice called out, drowning his own horse's heavy steps.

Before Louise could answer or hide, Royce's father, the Earl of Merton, rode into the stables. As dark as his son was blond, the earl entered any space like he'd just conquered it. Louise had met him countless times through the years but had only spoken to him a handful of those. The old man was harsh and blunt, as cunning and sharp as the pointy nose on his haggard face.

He dismounted with little fanfare, like a man who was born in the saddle, and his harsh black eyes latched on to her. "I know you," he snapped. "Marlborough's sister, aren't you? The one my son was sniffing around. Don't tell me you've reconsidered his offer."

Louise gulped. "His offer?" she squeaked.

Merton huffed, getting to work removing his horse's tack. A young boy ran into the stable, red-faced and out of breath. He stood by the earl's side, taking all the equipment the older man threw at him to put away.

"I knew your family was desperate, but I didn't think you were *that* desperate," the earl went on as his hands worked fast over all the buckles and clasps. "Even with the title, my son isn't exactly a prized possession. I don't blame you at all for declining his proposal, even if your family is something of a joke. In fact, I think I respect you more for it."

Louise tried to keep up. Merton spoke ruthlessly fast. "He … ah … Royce told you that he proposed?"

"I just said as much, didn't I?" Merton yapped like a dog guarding his only bone. "Before he left for that ridiculous tournament. To this day, I still have no idea why his mother signed him up for it. That boy is a terrible horseman. I don't know if I even believe his story that he knocked Somerset to the ground."

Louise's eyes narrowed. "Actually, he did knock Somerset down in the joust." Royce really needed to thank her for helping with his reputation. "Everyone saw it."

Merton studied her curiously. "How about that," he said. "So, is that why you've reconsidered?"

"I haven't reconsidered," Louise replied. "I'm here with Somerset… I'm just … We need to …" She didn't have the slightest idea how to explain her current situation without sounding absolutely reckless and insane. Nor did she want to alert the earl that his son was probably gaining a couple of black eyes as they spoke. Though the more she came to know the old codger, the more Louise didn't think he would mind.

"Ah, so you've decided on Somerset. Good decision. Like I said," he went on, rolling over Louise's stammering, "I respect you more for saying no to the stupid boy. Maybe it will teach him that women want *men*, not crying babies as husbands. Did he tell you about the funeral? Of course he did. He's been moping ever since he returned, asking everyone to attend. As if I—an earl— would ever be present for a rodent's funeral!" Merton's face was as blazing as his words. Spittle collected on the corners of his mouth as his tirade went on. "What kind of a man spends all his time playing with those nasty creatures? He shows no interest in anything else. And he's my heir … my only son left. My God"—he lifted his head to heaven—"why did you take the wrong one? What have I done to deserve this?"

The earl laid his arms over the back of his horse as if the ignominy of his remaining son had stripped him of the strength to stand.

Louise remained immobilized, stunned into place. If the earl was waiting for her to comfort him, he would be waiting a long while. There was simply no empathy to be had from her—at least for Merton. She had enough experience with lousy, distant fathers to know the toll they took on their children. If Royce was odd, uninterested, and prone to drink, Louise had a hunch that his father did little to help matters. She couldn't blame the earl entirely for his son's faulty character, but she couldn't let him off the hook for it either.

"I should go," she said, inching out of the stables. An overwhelming desire to find Charles came over her. Stopping him from doing any real harm seemed vital.

The earl let her go without a word, too enthralled by his own misery, and Louise let herself into the house, where she was soon greeted by a butler. If the servant was shocked by another visitor for Royce—and one desperately in need of a change of clothes, at that—he didn't let on, and directed her toward the stairs. Royce's study was on the top floor, the butler informed her. Near the servants' quarters. It was best for everyone that way, he intoned.

Louise had a hunch the servants would not agree. The smell hit her like a bag of bricks. Wood chips and a rancid stench crowded her in like a low fog as they climbed, instantly bringing her back to visions of guinea pigs pooing on Royce's shirt while he scratched their fat bellies.

Louise wondered if she had it in her to confront the infamous guinea pig village Royce had boasted about, but as she reached the top floor, her fears were put on hold.

Charles stood down the corridor peering through a doorway,

arms crossed in front of him, his head cocked, as if trying to translate an ancient text. In such deep thought, he didn't notice Louise until her slippers rapped lightly on the wood floor. He put his finger to his lips, miming for her to stay quiet, and nodded at the doorway's opening, which wasn't as wide as she'd assumed.

Louise leaned closer, able to peek inside with one eye.

This was no mere village. Royce had created a metropolis to rival the greatest in Europe. Constructed of wood, the miniature city spanned the length and height of the room and came equipped with churches and homes—even a towering castle on the outskirts for the lucky, blue-blooded pig. The fluffy animals scampered about, enjoying the splendor along with the copious amounts of food scattered at various intervals.

Royce was seated in the middle of what Louise assumed was his ode to Hyde Park, a grassy, square patch that featured a few balls and stockings for the pigs to chew on. The side of his face was bruised from his previous encounter with Charles, and he did appear rather mopey with his shoulders drooped and his head low. But as he conversed with his busy friends, he maintained an informal tone that struck Louise with its casual bearing. After all the time they'd spent together, Royce had never used that easygoing manner with her—even when he was sotted. Royce was plainly carefree in his tiny city, as happy as a man could be.

Louise understood now why Charles had planted himself outside the room instead of charging inside. Breaking a man's body was one thing; breaking his spirit was another.

She placed her hand on Charles's shoulder. They shared a speaking look and backed away from the door. In her heart, Louise wished Royce well as she and Charles retreated to the stairs.

They had each mounted their horses when a long and gangly servant came scrambling out of the house after them. The ancient man's knees cracked as he shuffled forth carrying two large sacks in his hands.

"Here are the things you asked for," he huffed, skidding in the dirt. He handed the sacks to Charles, who thanked him. The servant gave the animals their space, scratching at his bald head. "Mr. Bryson said you were asking about these parts," he said, scratching faster. Louise wondered if scratching helped the man think.

"I spent time here when I was a boy," Charles returned, "but I confess it's been a while. I'd be grateful for any tips."

The old man squinted over Charles's shoulder. "Well now, there's a lake not too far, not one of the biggest, but I'd declare it one of the prettiest. It was a favorite of my wife's, on account of the volcanoes."

"Volcanoes?" Louise asked.

He hacked out a chuckle, now scratching at the gray whiskers on his chin. "People say this land swelled with volcanoes, churning and colliding the island to create the peaks and valleys we have today. They say you can see the evidence in the rock, though I've never been able to figure it." He winked at Louise. "My wife and I were always too busy doing other things when we hiked up that way. Much too busy to be worrying about what color a rock was. Anyway"—he yawned, placing his hands on his lower back to stretch his chest wide with astonishing *pops!*—"it's a nice ride. Shame not to see it if you're over this way. The weather isn't always this accommodating, you know?"

Charles laughed, replying that he most definitely did. He tipped his head to the man and turned to Louise. "What do you say? Are you up for it?"

That smile. Louise's heart rammed against her rib cage. She knew what she should say, what the safer option was. But she couldn't bring herself to call forth the words. Maybe everyone was right. Maybe she wouldn't be able to take care of herself on her adventure. She couldn't even guard her heart against one man. Charles was anything but ordinary, though; he was pure temptation.

"Yes," she said finally.

Charles smiled. "I was hoping you'd say that."

Chapter Twenty-Four

The elderly servant hadn't been teasing when he said the lake was pretty. If anything, he'd been downplaying the incredible, breathtaking tableau. With the mountains bordering it, the lake felt hidden and magical, like a place children read about in stories when characters slipped through stones to other places and times. The high sun shimmered across the placid water, making everything shiny and vibrant. Never was a lake so blue, never a hill so green. It was a place where dreams were made and then forgotten, a place where yesterday and tomorrow didn't exist. Only today. Only now.

Charles stopped them near the water's rocky edge and left the horses to drink. He investigated the hefty sack and, with a satisfied chuff, took out a couple thin blankets and a small parcel wrapped in thick paper.

"What's that sound for?" Louise asked. Her back to him, she already had her slippers and stockings off and her feet were in the water. Charles couldn't wait to do the same. He could ignore his blisters, but that didn't mean they weren't there.

"What do you want to do first—eat or bathe?" he asked.

Louise spun around, her brow raised in question.

Charles tossed her the small package. A smile grew on her lips as she brought it to her nose. "Soap," she breathed. "You asked for soap, you lovely man!"

Charles laughed, feeling like his insides were made of honey. Honestly, it didn't take much when she looked at him like that, all sweet and languorous. "I thought we might want to wash our clothes while we're here," he said.

His words floated expectantly between them. Neither needed to point out that if they were washing their clothes then they wouldn't be wearing them.

Charles's stomach clenched. It seemed like the fate of his world rested on how she answered this question. Louise made him wait for it, but when the apples of her cheeks turned pink, he released his breath.

She hooked her hands behind her back. "I think it's time to wash these clothes," she said. "Do you agree?"

"Yes …" Charles returned. "In due time." He let the sacks fall from his hands with a thud. He walked to stand in front of her. Holding the back of Louise's neck, he kissed her, leaving nothing to the imagination.

She pushed away, gasping for breath. "In due time?" she said cheekily. Her baby hairs frizzed around her face, and Charles was back to thinking she looked like a goddess—the true Lady of the Lake. "Just this morning I was told my clothes stink. I think the time is now."

Charles licked her lips, sinking into her warm depths. Lord, he wanted her so badly. He'd planned to wait until later, but seeing her this way, fun and carefree, with her delightful smile and the passion in her eyes—for him … He was grateful he wasn't bursting out of his pants.

It was time for them to come off anyway.

He stepped back and began stripping. "I thought we would start with washing ourselves and then make our way to the clothes." He was naked in seconds. Naked and throbbing, not an inch ashamed of his blatant desire. Why keep it a secret? Let Louise know what she did to him. She'd told him that she felt powerless around him; that couldn't be farther from the truth. She held all the power. It was time for her to embrace it.

Her gaze went directly to his cock. And for a second, Charles worried that he'd moved a little *too* fast. Christ, they'd only been at the lake for a few minutes!

He waited as Louise took her fill. "Take off your clothes," he said quietly. "Let me wash you."

Her eyes turned stormy as she debated with herself in her head. Was she as overwhelmed by her craving for them as he was? Did it frighten her too?

Charles had never been so greedy before; he'd never wanted anything as much as he wanted Louise. Had never wanted anyone to know the real him—his dreams, hopes, insecurities—as much as he wanted her to.

As Louise remained silent, Charles coaxed her forward. He went slow, unlacing and unhooking, unwrapping her gown and petticoats so as not to startle her any further. This wasn't just sex. Of that, Charles was positive. Something was happening between them, a tether being formed and strengthened, forged by a penetrating awareness that whatever was about to happen would be right.

"Don't be afraid," he said when she stood before him in her shift.

"I can't help it," she said plaintively. "Why can't I say no to you?"

"Because you vowed to say yes to everything."

"It's more than that," she replied.

Charles allowed his hands to roam, sliding them up her sides, admiring the downy skin through the barely there undergarment. Louise's curves were bountiful, her hips wickedly full. She was a veritable wonderland. "I know," he said. "And I will be grateful for that every day for the rest of my life."

"Don't say things you don't mean."

"For the rest of my life, Louise. Not just now. Not just forever. For now *and* forever."

Tears fell, lonely diamonds dropping onto the rocks, lost forever in the lake. Good, Charles thought. Let the lake wash her fear away. Let this place baptize their love, forever changing who they were into who they would be together.

Charles stripped Louise's last layer and scooped her into his arms before any more bashfulness could take hold.

He waded into the water. The temperature wasn't ideal—it was damn near freezing—but nothing could stymie the heat in Charles's veins. He was burning so deep he figured he could turn the whole pool into a hot spring.

Louise rested her head against his chest. "It's cold," she remarked, shivering for extra measure.

"I'll warm you up in no time," he promised.

When the water was up to his stomach, he placed Louise on her feet, facing him. Her pink nipples puckered, and the water brushed over them in an intoxicating rhythm that Charles's mouth would emulate soon enough.

"Do you like that feeling?" he asked.

She smiled shyly. "What feeling?"

He nodded to her breasts. "The water against your skin."

Louise attempted to cross her arms, but Charles interceded before she took the lovely vision away. "It's different," she said. "Everything is always different when I'm with you."

"Different good?"

"What do you think?" She handed him the soap. "Now, are you going to wash me or just stare?"

"Can I do both?" he replied with a wolfish smile.

"I certainly hope so."

Charles claimed the soap and worked a furious lather in his hands. When he placed it on her pale skin, they gasped in unison like they'd been shocked. Goosebumps covered her, and Charles's mission was to comfort every last one, sweeping a path over her body, luxuriating in the treasures that lurked in every crevice and around every corner. Finally, he was the swashbuckling explorer he'd warned her about, revisiting a land he'd feared would be closed to him forever.

Charles learned much from Louise while he bathed her, like

that she had an adorable mole under her left armpit. And an adorable birthmark on her right elbow that was in the shape of a moon. And also a smattering of adorable freckles on her back, though none reached her front. How had he missed that enchanting fact before? Charles wanted to kiss the sun for shining a light on all these new details. He would cherish them to the day he died.

Louise trembled under his ministrations but showed no other signs of being cold, and nor did she ask him to stop. Her lips were as rosy as her nipples, and the goosebumps had disappeared. Under his care, her skin was glossy and pink, rubbed and abraded until it glowed.

Charles cupped water in his hand and ladled it over her shoulders and breasts, mesmerized as the droplets trickled over her mounds and valleys. Her breathing came faster now, her chest pumping. Holding her gaze, Charles leaned down and caught one glorious nipple in his mouth as his hand sank into the water, bringing the soap between her legs. He washed her there, stroking her inner thighs and nether hair with growing pressure. Louise's arms circled his neck, and she tangled her fingers in his hair.

"Isn't it time for me to wash you?" she asked huskily, tugging on his ear with her teeth. Charles's balls ached and his entire body convulsed in the energetic hold.

"Later," he said, tossing the soap to the shore. "I need you to help me with something else first."

Louise threw her head back and let out a joyous laugh as Charles palmed her behind. He hoisted her up so her legs could hook around his lower back. She was wide open for him, and his cock was ready, positioned at her entrance. His hands shook as he held her. He was everywhere all at once, massaging her arse, tickling down the slope of her long back, squeezing her so her breasts rubbed against his chest. He couldn't stop. He needed to feel Louise, hold her, savor her, make her understand the love he intended to provide her for the rest of her life.

When she could take it no longer, she held his head still and kissed him, grazing her sex along his cock. Charles groaned in her mouth.

"I like the sounds you make," she confessed in that low, sensual way that made Charles think he was already inside her. "Do you like it when I pet you like that with my body?"

He closed his eyes, devastated by what she was doing to him. Holding her up, he didn't force her movements—rather, he let her work her power all on her own. And it was fucking magnificent.

Louise continued to nibble on his ear. Her breath was warm and hypnotic, and Charles was reminded of the stories he'd heard when he was younger about mermaids luring men to their deaths with their beguiling songs. He understood them now; he would follow this woman anywhere.

She scraped her nipples back and forth against his chest, tempting him, inciting him further. "Make love to me, Charles," she whispered. Her voice finally woke him from the carnal storm. It was no longer cheeky and mischievous; there was a panic there, a desperation that mirrored his own.

Charles sank into her inch by sacrilegious inch, losing his grasp of reality the more her core sucked his swollen shaft, taking everything he had to give. When Louise covered him completely, they stayed that way without moving, letting him pulse inside her, giving this otherworldly action the moment it deserved.

Louise's strength continued to surprise Charles. She locked her arms around his neck, kissing his ear. "Don't leave," she whispered.

"Never," he panted, pulling out just so he could thrust again. Louise keened and bucked from the effort. That was it. That was the spot. Charles wrapped her hair around his hand and took her mouth with crushing force.

"Never," she breathed, wilder this time as their lovemaking took over, untamed and frenzied. The water waved and splashed around them as they found their rhythm.

"Never," Charles promised. His knees trembled, his legs were weak, but he continued to pound into his woman, hitting that spot that made her cry out, that made her arch off his body like a perfect rainbow in the sky. He'd heard about rainbows in the Sandwich Islands, heard they were bloody amazing. He doubted they compared to the arch of Louise's back when her mouth opened in orgasmic wonder. Nothing on this earth could ever compare to that sight.

Louise's nails cut into his back. "Oh, God, yes. Please, Charles, please."

He rammed into her, and when he felt her muscles begin to twitch, when he heard her cry out, he let himself go, releasing into her with an orgasm that he was certain made him blind for close to a minute.

Louise collapsed into his arms, her limbs losing their tension and falling away, but Charles never let her go.

"Never," she sighed drowsily.

Charles kissed the top of her head. "Never."

CHAPTER TWENTY-FIVE

LOUISE LAY ON a patch of grass near the shore as naked as the day she was born. It was glorious to feel this way, so depleted and unencumbered. Not of this world and yet in touch with every delicious sensation swirling around her. Her skin hummed with life, and she had no doubt she could hear the steady ants marching to their task and taste the whipped cream clouds if she tried.

Never had she been so content. As she lazed over Charles's equally naked body, the sun warmed her back while his ever-present heat soothed her front. Louise was scared to put a word to it, but she felt happy … and maybe a little loved.

Charles trailed his fingers over her skin slowly, starting at the nape of her neck and meandering all the way down to her lower back, just stopping where her bottom began to swell. The delicate treatment had come close to putting her to sleep; however, an impulse to worry began to tug at her conscience. Peace would have to wait.

Like her, Charles was still awake. Even though they'd been stretched together in this blissful repose for close to an hour, his heartbeat remained erratic and uneven. His manhood hadn't relaxed, either. It was as thick and hard as ever. Louise wasn't sure what proper etiquette demanded, but she made a special effort not to bother the alert appendage, positioning her legs around the protuberance.

Louise played with the springy blond hairs on Charles's chest, trying to find the right opening to launch into her question. Naturally, when she found the courage to speak, it was about everything other than what was plaguing her.

"Why didn't you hurt Royce?" she blurted. "What stopped you?"

Charles's chest rose high under her hand. Louise tilted her head to study his features. Utterly beautiful even on his worse days, the Knight of the Sun was transcendent under the limpid sky, bronzed and chiseled to within an inch of perfection. But Charles was so much more than his physical self, had so much more to offer than what he provided by way of his body and ancient title. Louise had always known that, though now she felt confident enough to acknowledge it.

His fingers drew an imaginary line up her spine and across the thin upper edge of her scapula. "You know the reason," he answered. "It didn't seem fair. Watching him sit there, happy as he was to be surrounded by those animals … his friends … I don't know. I didn't want to make him suffer in that world."

Louise nodded. "Royce isn't a bad person. He's just stuck. Everyone wants him to be someone else—his brother—and he has no idea how to be that person. I think that's why he drinks so much and becomes so upset. It didn't seem like his father made anything better for him."

Charles's hand trickled to a stop. "What about your father? Did he make anything easy for you?"

She returned a bitter laugh, resting her head back on his chest. "I think you know my family well enough to know the answer to that question."

"But I'm asking you."

"I suppose if he hadn't been such a great disappointment then I would never have looked at those people critically. The balls, the hunts, the interminable, dull conversations where everyone says the same thing because they're afraid of standing out." She shrugged. "I would have just accepted it all as how things were. Maybe I should thank him for that. Forgive him in my heart."

"Those people?" His tone was casual, but she noted a sharpness. "You mean people like me?"

He tensed underneath her, his stomach muscles locking together like perfectly measured joints. "You're not the same as them," she replied. "You see things differently, remember?"

Charles softened slightly. "Even though I like hunting parties?"

"I suppose," she drawled, affecting disappointment.

"And even a dance or two with you?"

"If you must."

He chuckled, kissing the top of her head. "I don't love the dull conversations, though. But I think I could handle them better with you at my side to laugh with."

"You don't have to 'handle' things, you know," Louise began tentatively, clutching at her bravery with every fiber of her being. It was now or never. "You could ... come with me. Work on your drawings. A writer could always use someone to put pictures to her stories." There. It was done.

"Come with you to the islands?"

Louise squeezed her eyes shut. "Mm-hmm."

"You would, um"—Charles cleared his throat—"want me to come with you?"

Louise's nose itched. Tears were coming. Why was she crying? "Only if you wanted to," she said casually.

His nonchalant manner echoed hers. "So ... I would be the new Royce?"

"No," she replied quickly. "You'd be different from Royce."

"How different?"

"Different."

"How different?"

The burgeoning tears forced Louise to open her eyes. She gritted her teeth to keep her voice level. "You wouldn't have to marry me. I wouldn't ask you to do that. We could be together because we want to—like the island couples. So, if or when we ever grow tired of the arrangement … you can leave."

In an instant Charles swept up and over her, forcing Louise on her back. He loomed high and dominant, his expression dogged and fierce. He raked his hair away from his forehead, and his resolute eyes took over his face, commanding her attention. "Lady Louise, I want you to listen now, and I want you to listen good, because I don't think I can explain this to you anymore. Never means never. I want you. I promised you that I wouldn't let you go, and a knight never breaks his word—"

"But you're not a knight!"

"Fuck yes, I am!" he countered. "Did I not save you at the ball? Did I not aid you when you were lost in the park? Did I not rescue you from Royce?"

"You know you did," Louise cried. "But I'm not staying here—"

"I know that! Christ, woman, you've told me countless bloody times! You're going to the damn Sandwich Islands, so that means I'm going to the damn Sandwich Islands too."

Louise's heart swelled so large it could have choked her. "You … you are?"

His lips tightened in annoyance. "Yes! I thought we'd already discussed this in the water."

"We made love in the water."

"No," he countered. "We made promises in the water. To each other."

It was too good to be true, which was why Louise had to keep fighting. "But what about your estate?"

"Thanks to my father, it runs itself."

"What about your family?"

"My mother runs that and hates when I meddle."

"But what about your life?"

Charles's smile was soft and devastatingly kind. "My darling girl, *you* are my life. It's time you started letting me live it."

Louise opened her mouth with another rebuttal, but Charles

settled on top of her and sealed his proclamation with a kiss.

She completely forgot what she meant to ask. In the end, it didn't matter. Charles had made up his mind. Hadn't *she* hated when people tried to talk her out of her decision?

If the man wanted to start living his life, then who was she to stop him?

THE FOLLOWING MORNING, Louise's body forced her to rise just as the sky was bathing itself in shades of purple and pink. Careful not to rouse Charles, she slid out of the makeshift bed he'd fashioned and found her chemise. Eventually, they *had* washed their clothes yesterday and left them to dry on the flat rocks near their little camp.

Louise headed to the lake and splashed the cool water on her face. She had no intention of running away. After their night together, she would no longer try to leave Charles before he left her. Her trust had been won. Heaven help them both.

She stood at the shore, stretching her aching arms over her head. She took her time admiring the sun as it announced the new day, transforming the lake into a sparkling chest of precious jewels.

Louise's stomach growled, and she grimaced, shooting a look at Charles, who still lay undisturbed. The famished couple had eaten half of the cheese and bread in one of the soul-saving sacks that Merton's servant had gifted them, but she had grown accustomed to much more.

It would be wise to leave soon. There were still a handful of days between them and London, and it was best to get them over with. However, the idea of leaving this celestial haven was as distasteful to Louise as only having one pork pie for dinner. The lake and mountains had acted like a bubble. Everything inside was perfectly clear, while the outside seemed foggy at best. A pledge had been made, she told herself. There was nothing to fear on the road ahead. And yet dawdling in this ethereal spot held a certain appeal that was difficult to cast aside.

Exercises! That was what Louise needed to get out of her head.

Her muscles were tired and sore in places they hadn't been before, but working them always put Louise in the correct frame of mind. Exercising wasn't an arbitrary action, it had a purpose, and it was best if she kept that purpose front and center.

Louise got to the task at hand. She'd been disappointed when she'd had to keep her Indian clubs behind in London; they were simply too large to travel with. However, she was positive she'd be able to find something adequate on the *Clementine* to take their place. In the meantime, she gathered two sticks—each about half the length of her arm and around eight pounds—that would act as perfectly adequate weights for this morning. If there was anything to be learned in the time ahead, it was that she must be adaptable.

But as she started her routine, lifting the weights at various heights around her body, pumping blood into her muscles, Louise found that her mind wasn't as focused as she would have liked. Three times she had to stop swinging the sticks to restart the intricate workout, forgetting the drills that she'd memorized months ago. Her trail of thought—and her line of sight—kept creeping back to the gorgeous, slumbering man. Her breath needed to be steady, and yet she kept sighing the schoolgirl sounds that made her want to swat herself over the head with one of the sticks. When she dropped them for the second time, she took a break, irritably punching her fists into her hips.

Focus! It isn't like you to behave this way! You're better than this!

But maybe she wasn't. Louise had to acknowledge that she was infatuated with the dear man. And who wouldn't be? He was like a Greek god, an Adonis with his golden hair, sculpted shape, and devil-may-care smile. Resisting was futile. And he was hers. Finally, he was hers.

Once more, her gaze drifted to him. She was no better than a moth, obsessed with his flame. Only he'd promised not to burn her.

A frisson of electricity jolted Louise's lower belly as she remembered all that he'd done to her the night before. His pretty words were one thing, but she preferred action. And Charles never disappointed.

"What are you doing?"

Louise jumped, dropping her sticks yet again. She scrambled to pick them up. "I'm sorry. I didn't mean to wake you; I was trying to be quiet."

Charles turned to his side, holding his head in his hand. His lids were half-open as he scratched at his burgeoning beard, his hair disheveled and wavy around his face. "You were quiet. I felt you staring at me."

"I wasn't staring at you!" Louise argued … though not too vehemently, since it was a bald-faced lie.

Charles chuckled through a yawn. "I don't mind. I like when you stare. It reminds me that you want me as much as I want you."

Louise opened her mouth and quickly closed it. The man wasn't wrong.

He took mercy on her embarrassment. "You didn't answer my question," he said, nodding to the sticks. "What are you up to?"

"Working my muscles," she replied, pulling her shoulders back. "After I booked my trip, I decided that I needed to add to my strength and endurance. I wasn't sure how to go about doing that until I read Donald Walker's book, *British Manly Exercises*."

"*British Manly Exercises*?"

"Yes, have you heard of it?"

Charles stopped scratching his beard. "I have," he said, his tone difficult to decipher. "And what did you learn?"

"So much!" Louise answered. "It's a wonderful book; the pictures were so helpful. I couldn't do as much as I would have liked because he speaks about boxing and rowing and wrestling quite a bit, and I didn't have a partner, but the Indian clubs have been a godsend. They were tricky at first, but I got better with time. Have you tried them?"

"I have," Charles said. "You're right. They can be tricky." He paused, seemingly mulling something over in his head. His eyes popped back to her. "Is that how you were able to handle the lance? For the life of me, I couldn't figure out how you were able to hold it up. Half the men I trained with could barely do it as well as you."

Louise was certain she was glowing from the praise. "You weren't the only one surprised by that." She laughed. "I couldn't believe that I carried the armor *and* the lance, but it wasn't easy for me. My arms still sting from the labor."

Charles snorted. "Mine too."

She lowered her head, swirling the sticks lackadaisically at her sides. "To be honest, I'm surprised you didn't say anything sooner. Clearly, you can see the pounds I've put on." She looked up to catch Charles's perplexed expression. "You don't have to spare my feelings; I know I'm much bigger than I used to be. I understand it's not fashionable, but I don't care—I needed to add weight. One can't be strong while still being whittled to nothing. The more I trained, the more I ate. I quite like my figure," she added defensively. "I don't feel like I'm going to faint walking uphill anymore. On the contrary, I feel like I can conquer any mountain in my path."

Charles's frown didn't fade. He studied her like she were a science experiment gone awry. "You say you've gained a lot of weight?"

She sighed. "Honestly, Charles. I don't care if you've noticed. Royce definitely did."

"Come here."

"I'm not done working."

"Louise, come here, darling."

It was the *darling* that did it. The sweet endearment floated over to Louise, picking her up and placing her right in front of him.

Charles moved up on his knees. His rakish smile should have alerted Louise as to what he was going to do, but she was caught off guard when he lifted her shift off and tossed it to the side.

"Now let me see here," he said, placing his hands securely on her waist. Louise tried to curb her shame when his fingers could not wrap around to touch the others. Even with a corset, he would not be able to. Old ways of thinking died hard.

His grasp was commanding and proprietary, nothing delicate about it. "I can't speak to before—"

"Because you never paid me any attention."

"I paid you plenty, don't worry about that," Charles said wryly. He relinquished his hold and moved his hands down her hips, sweeping over her new curves, branding her with their heat. "You were a small thing before, that's true," he said, licking his lips, "but you're still tiny."

Louise slapped his hands away. "I am not!"

Charles wouldn't be deterred. He palmed her backside, settling his face in between her juicy breasts as he fondled her bountiful flesh. "You are," he argued. "But now you're round in all the right places. I've never understood why women go to such lengths to be so thin. Real men want real women." He leaned away, capturing her gaze. "And you, my darling girl, are a real woman."

"Even though I read *British Manly Exercises?*"

"*Especially* because you read *British Manly Exercises.*" His hands came around to her front. "Just look at this," he went on, petting the folds of her sex, swiping his fingers just inside. "Only a real woman could have such a sweet quim, one that sucks and holds me like it does."

Lost for words, Louise could only watch as he played with her, slightly—more than slightly—excited by his use of vulgar words. She locked her knees; her legs were like butter and threatened to collapse at any moment.

Charles placed one single kiss on her mons, flicking his tongue at the last moment to sweep inside her seam. Her head fell back as she keened at the ecstasy of the tiny movement.

Her provocative sounds urged him on, and Charles sank his head in between her legs. His hands returned to her arse as he feasted on her, using his tongue to taste and excite her depths. Louise felt like a pagan priestess with a supplicant before her, standing naked and wanton in the fresh rays of the virginal day. He doted on the little nub at the top of her sex, flickering it rapidly with the tip of his tongue. Quick as a hummingbird's wings he stroked her, building her inner fire into an inferno. Louise planted her fingers into his hair, holding him steady as her hips began to undulate, begging for the sweet torment to be over.

But she was stuck. Teetering on a hilltop, just waiting to fall, Louise couldn't let go. She cried out in frustration.

"What is it, darling girl? What do you need from me?" he asked.

"I don't know," she panted.

"Yes, you do. Tell me."

"Your fingers," she said. "I need your fingers."

"Good girl," Charles said. "I can't read your mind, my love. A real woman tells her man how to please her."

"Give me your fingers, Charles, please," she begged.

The release was swift and explosive. The moment Charles entered Louise, her inner walls clamped down on him, finding the pressure and friction they'd desired. She came with a soundless wail, throwing her head back with a satisfied smile.

Needless to say, the Indian clubs weren't swung again that morning. Louise had discovered a new routine she enjoyed more.

CHAPTER TWENTY-SIX

ALL IN ALL, Charles and Louise spent three days at the lake, swimming and frolicking, making love when they had energy, talking when they'd used it all up.

Love fit Charles well. And that's what this was … pure love. True, Louise hadn't said the fateful words, but Charles knew love when he saw it, only because it differed so much from lust. He'd been lusted after by most of the *ton*. Desire was easy to recognize in the eyes, as it was dark and almost violent at times, scorching him. But love … there was no mistaking it. When Louise's gaze settled on him, Charles's whole body felt caressed. He was the boat stuck in the middle of the ocean, and Louise was the breeze that finally encouraged him to sail.

They no longer spoke about the future in hushed tones and open-ended questions. They would go to the Sandwich Islands as one, and they would figure everything out from there. For a man whose life and legacy had been planned the moment he was born, the ambiguous future seemed like a benediction. The freedom was palpable, scary, but in no way daunting. Blank pages were laid out before Charles to draw his own story.

On their last morning, Charles woke up to another one of Louise's training sessions. At first, he'd been amused when he found her at it, but now he felt nothing but pride. More than anyone, he understood the resolve and determination it took to increase one's physicality. How could he fault her for wanting to be stronger when he'd spent the last year doing the same thing in preparation for the Eglinton Tournament?

As he wiped the sleep out of his eyes, his thoughts strayed to the tournament. It seemed like it had taken place months ago, not mere days. It had been so important to him, and now he couldn't even remember why he'd joined the others in the first place.

Charles hadn't shared Eglington and the other men's dissatisfaction with the queen and her coronation. As an earl, he hadn't felt slighted or maligned when some of the dated traditions were scrapped. He'd enlisted in the tournament for one reason and one reason only—he had nothing better to do. Playing dress-up and bounding down the lists in a knight's costume had seemed like the perfect thing to pass the time. It broke up the monotony of attending balls and resisting all the young ladies being thrown at him by ambitious mothers.

It was no surprise, then, that he'd fallen for Louise so quickly. She was everything Charles wanted before he even knew he wanted it. It was true she used to frighten him with her unyielding behavior and frank opinions, her unremitting desire to be who she was. But then she'd taught him that his life was *his* to lead. Charles might have been the knight, but Louise had all the courage. She showed him who he could be, and Charles grasped at that man with hungry hands. He would never let him go.

He turned to his side, watching Louise swing her sticks around her. She was a maelstrom of intention, but oddly, often a bit unfocused and a little clumsy. It only took a few words from him to make her drop the sticks to the ground.

"You know, if you're determined to wake me up in the morning there are better ways to do it," Charles said, lifting an eyebrow when the sticks plunked to the dirt.

Louise sighed, glaring at the disappointing weights. "You know very well I'm not trying to wake you up. I'd love for you to stay asleep so I can actually get through this without being interrupted."

"I thought you liked my little interruptions."

Her frown abated and a splotch of pink worked its way up from her neck. Her shift was prim and covered more than it revealed, but the innocent garb was enough to make his cock salute. "I never said I didn't like your interruptions," she said, one side of her mouth lifting in a reluctant smile. "I just wish they were more conducive to my training."

Charles wasn't sure he agreed with that. They'd been *training* so much his abdominal muscles ached. He had no doubt hers did as well.

"You don't need to train so hard anymore," he said. "You have me now. I'll protect you."

Louise cocked her head. "I appreciate that, my lord, but you can't be with me all the time. It's important that I learn to take care of myself."

"And how will you do that?" he asked. Starting a fight was not his purpose, yet he could see the question rankled Louise. Still, he needed her to understand that it was best she relied on him—she might be strong, but she was still a small woman. If a man wanted to overwhelm her, he would. "Let's say you were in a tavern—"

"I don't think they have many taverns in the islands."

"Fine. A place of eating. What would you do if a man accosted you? How would you defend yourself? Do you know have a knife?"

Louise gestured to her lack of travel bags. "You know I don't."

He nodded. "Do you have a gun?"

"Do you have a point?"

Charles sighed. "My point is that I want you to be safe, that's all. No more insane theatrics like at the tournament. Let me take care of you. Partners, remember? A smart man knows his limits."

"A smart woman knows what she's capable of, and I know I can do anything. What are you laughing at?"

Charles chuckled, rolling to his back. Making love was preferrable to making war, so he would let her win this one. "I'm not laughing at you! I'm laughing at me, because I think I actually believe you. Oh, fine, then. You've got me there. Carry on, my sweet warrior. If I'm ever in distress, I'll know who to call for."

"Speaking of distress … doesn't that bother you?" Louise asked.

Charles twisted his neck to see her staring at his erection. Not shy at all, it was begging for her aid and succor. "What about it?"

She shook her head ruefully, nibbling her lip. "The fact that it's so … you know … ready … already."

He held back a laugh. Even with all their lovemaking, Louise still had a difficult time verbalizing the finer points. It went to show you could take the woman out of Victoria's England, but you couldn't take all of Victoria's England out of the woman.

"I don't mind it," he replied easily. Casually, he palmed himself at the base, running his hand up and down in a carefree manner. "Although sometimes it's a nuisance."

"When?"

"Like when you're not around to help with it."

"Oh." Louise frowned. He'd expected her to laugh at the joke, but she continued to study his cock with her adorable nose wrinkled up.

Abandoning her sticks, she knelt at his side. When Charles tried to come up on his elbows, she pushed him back down. "Show me how to help."

Embarrassment paralyzed him. "Louise, darling, I was only teasing. Go back and finish your training."

The stubborn minx shook her head. "Did you know in the Sandwich Islands, young men and women are taught about intimacies?" she asked. Charles confessed he must have missed that chapter. "It's not in any chapter you would have read. Some sailors explained it to me when I was booking my passage and inquiring about the islands."

He had a violent urge to ask why in the hell she thought it would be a good idea to have a conversation like that with men down by the docks, but held his tongue. He could get to that later. "Go on," he replied instead.

Louise placed her hands at the base of his shaft, and he almost jumped out of his skin. "They are not taught to fear these intimacies; they look at them as a gift you are giving the other person. And it is a gift. You've taught me that. However, I haven't returned it."

"Louise ..." Charles's voice was choppy and coarse. "You have given me more of a gift than you can ever understand. There is nothing else you could possibly do—" ... *to make me love you any more.*

Her pink lips screwed up to the side. "That's all very lovely, but I'm determined. If you don't help me, I'll just figure it out on my own. I've never done it before, but I've watched Cook wring a rooster's neck. I assume it's like that—"

He lashed out, halting her motion before she could test her barbaric theory. "It's not *quite* like that," he said, his hand securely over hers. "Different kind of cock, my love. Mine requires a bit more finesse."

Louise arched a brow. "Well, then?"

Charles exhaled deeply. He couldn't believe he was still hard after the terrifying mental picture she'd given him. Oddly enough, his shaft was fit to bursting. Slowly, he regained his sanity and began to show the intrepid woman how to pleasure him. He guided her movements, up and down his rod, explaining how to manipulate the thin skin without tugging it.

"And this feels good to you?" she asked like a polite apprentice.

He collapsed on the ground, his arms folded over his forehead. "My God, yes," he gasped. Was there nothing this woman couldn't do? Louise caught on fast and, in no time, had him writhing for release.

"But what about these?" Dear Lord, she was pointing to his balls. "Do you want me to touch them too?"

"No ... I ... You don't ..." Charles was flummoxed. He'd

never had someone fondle his balls before, and wasn't sure if he'd like it—

Christ! I like it! I fucking love it!

Louise licked his balls with her raspy tongue. "I hope you don't mind, but I thought I would try this too," she said, lengthening her tongue to stroke the base of his shaft.

"Christ … n-o-o," he choked out. "Keep going. Please, keep going."

Louise wasn't done experimenting. Ever the overachiever, she took his shaft into his mouth, swallowing him whole. By the skin of his teeth, Charles held back from bucking inside her. He tried to keep a modicum of control, but she sucked it out of him. He was clay in her hands, a puppet on her strings. He danced to the tune from her lips.

When Charles was ready to blow, he tore himself from Louise's mouth and grabbed her hand to take over again. She had him coming in two strong pumps.

It was yet another advertisement for women's training, Charles concluded. Strong hands were never a bad thing in the bedroom.

LOUISE AND CHARLES arrived in London a week later. With two days to spare before the *Clementine* left port, the couple used their time wisely, stocking up on basic supplies for their journey—which was more difficult than Charles had anticipated. In his experience, women never had any issues spending money, nor asking that he spend his on them. Louise, true to nature, proved not to be like any other woman of his acquaintance. She held an irrational frugality that bordered on mania when it came to using a single penny. Her savings were all she had to get through the trip, she argued. She would make do with what she had.

Even with Charles offering to pay, the stubborn girl balked mightily, saying she couldn't take advantage. When he argued that it wasn't taking advantage to allow him to buy her an ensemble that didn't smell like a stable of horses and weeks of dried mud, Louise finally relented. The soap at the lake might have helped, but there was no mistaking her clothes had taken quite a beating since Scotland.

Charles had surmised that living with her father's reckless spending habits had made Louise so cautious about her own. However, after they'd purchased just enough and not an item more, he came to realize that it wasn't all about the money. Louise was uncomfortable with his buying things for her. It didn't matter if it was a simple comb or a seductive new shift—she had trouble giving up any sort of autonomy related to her epic journey. At first, Charles had thought that love would solve everything—it was the end point of any fairy tale—but now he understood love was just the beginning. He and Louise could recount every inch of each other's bodies with avid detail, and yet they were still mastering how to maneuver around each other with their clothes on. Learning to adapt would not be easy, nor would it be over soon. He imagined that it would take years of patience and compromise. However, Charles didn't count this as a hardship—in fact, he couldn't wait to get started.

They rented a room at one of the nicer inns near the docks so as to keep their whereabouts a secret. With the Season complete, the *ton* had officially retired to their country homes, but Louise was still terrified someone might recognize them and send word to Lady Delilah. She didn't even want Charles to go to his townhouse to collect his things, though he convinced her that he would be careful. Louise's wits were frayed; she was so close to her goal, and he wanted to be sensitive to that.

He left her in the inn, where she was diligently packing her new pens and paper into the trunk that he'd bought her, and made his way down the docks, where he purchased his ticket for the *Clementine*. It seemed surreal, holding the document in his hand, almost impossible to believe. Charles was doing it—he was actually leaving everything he knew behind and traveling to the

Sandwich Islands with Louise. Wonders would never cease.

Next, he went to his townhome, where he informed his staff of his departure. He couldn't leave without settling his business— it was only right for his family and employees. While his valet helped secure his personal necessities, Charles confined himself to his study, drafting letter after letter. His mother, his accountant, his lawyer, his estate manager ... everyone who would be affected by his lengthy departure. He saved the most important missive for last.

Charles stared at the paper for several minutes, wondering the best way to tell Edward that he was running off with his sister. He had no doubt that Edward would approve of the match—in time. Edward knew all the rakish stories about Charles, and he also knew that most of them weren't true in the slightest. Still ... Charles had to handle this delicate situation with kid gloves. Not only was he whisking Louise away (or, rather, she was whisking him), but he was accompanying her someplace that was deemed rough, wild, and completely inappropriate for a woman of her station. Not to mention, Louise was embarking on a career while she was there. It would be a juggling act of communication, where Charles had to downplay the dangers while simultaneously playing up his protective strengths.

In the end, when he was increasingly frustrated by his lack of eloquence, he began the letter the same way this whole serendipi- tous engagement started and prayed that Edward would be in the mood for understanding and forgiveness.

She kissed me first, Charles wrote at the top of the page. *And though I didn't admit it then, I knew that I would follow her all over God's great earth in the hopes that she would take pity on me and grant me another. Because she is the only person who makes me feel like I am already the person I want to be.*

Charles frowned at the drying ink. A bit maudlin. A bit poetic. But wasn't he a knight? Hadn't he told Louise that every knight had a little poetry in him? As it turned out, when it came to her, Charles had a lot of poetry.

He came out from behind his desk feeling like a new man, lighter, ready to be shaped and molded by the journey—and ready to return to his lady. Charles only had one final errand to run.

A hansom cab dropped him off at Bond Street a short while later. Charles entered Hickman's—his family's jewelry store of choice—and asked for the owner. Mr. Jeremiah Hickman had opened the eponymous boutique ten years before and swiftly became of the most sought-after jewelers in the city. He'd studied for years in Italy before settling in London, and his pieces held a one-of-a-kind grandeur that most of the *ton*'s ladies salivated over.

As Charles waited, he could feel the stares of the other customers, feel their whispers biting into his skin. He was used to low speech; however, it usually accompanied smiles and puffs of adoration. He couldn't be certain, but he thought he heard the occasional snicker while he perused the glass cases.

Hickman's face erupted in a smile as he met Charles at the counter, his thin mustache curving up at its ends. The short and pudgy owner's shoulders sloped forward as if he was constantly admiring his wares or ready to bow. Either way, his clientele loved it.

"Ah, Lord Somerset," Hickman said grandly, opening his short arms wide. "It's been a long time. I didn't expect to see you in the city. To what do I owe the pleasure?"

The entire store stopped to watch the conversation. Charles lowered his voice, ducking his head. "I'm in the market for a ring," he said, getting a jolt of satisfaction out of saying it out loud. If he felt this elated just buying the piece, he couldn't imagine what he would feel like slipping it on Louise's finger. She hadn't mentioned marriage lately. Actually, she'd done her damnedest to shy away from the subject. She still held reservations about declaring something permanent together, almost as if she was superstitious and afraid to jinx their future. But Charles wasn't spending one night on the ship without Louise as his wife. And it had nothing to do with her honor or being proper. He wanted the first night of their adventure together to begin as husband and wife. Despite Louise's appreciation for how the islanders did things, their match would be as never-ending as the gold ring on her finger, end of story.

Hickman clapped his hands. "Ah, wonderful," he replied with his signature giddiness. "Well, I can help you there. A special ring for a special lady, no? Thanks to you, our medieval pieces have become quite popular, and contain lovely options. You can have flowers, grapes, or even leaves circling the stones, which provide a great romantic effect."

Charles tapped his teeth together, inwardly debating. It didn't take a genius to realize that the medieval motif might not fit with Louise's aesthetic. Though, to be honest, he wasn't sure *what* her aesthetic was. Before, when he'd witnessed her in public, she wore plain ensembles, nothing flashy or attention-grabbing. But Charles would never consider her plain. Louise shone despite her clothes, not because of them. She needed a ring that exemplified that extraordinary power—something small and delicate, brilliant but understated.

After he'd explained all that to Hickman, the jeweler nodded, leafing through all the choices in his mind. Soon, Charles had five pieces in front of him, and Louise's spoke to him in an instant. It was a diamond cluster with a pearl-shaped center stone sitting on a gold band. Startling in its simple beauty, just like Louise.

Hickman laughed when Charles announced that he'd take it at once. "You're the easiest customer I've had in months," he said, sliding the other rings away with careless flare, as if they weren't each worth a small fortune. "Yes, your lady will love this, I have no doubt. I'm overjoyed for you, my lord. I'm glad you're focusing on this happiness. It can't have been easy for you, these last few days."

Charles had been lost in his imagination, dreaming about what Louise's surprised joy would look like when he presented the ring, and it took him a moment to land on what the jeweler was saying. He shook his head *and* the silly grin off his face. "I'm sorry?"

Hickman's expression became downcast as he went about packaging the item, his fingers losing their nimbleness. "No, I'm the one that's sorry. I can't believe what she wrote about you. You didn't deserve it. It's not like *you* made it rain. That reporter should be ashamed of herself. None of the newspapers were particularly forgiving ... but she was the worst."

Rain? It hit Charles like a lance to the chest. He'd been so absorbed with Louise that he'd forgotten about the event. As he'd expected, the newspapers must have eviscerated the knights and their shoddy participation. But the articles couldn't have been *that* horrible. Obviously, the knights hadn't been perfect, but they'd done their best with the lamentable situation.

"Oh, do you mean the tournament? Yes, it was ... regrettable how it all turned out," Charles said politely. "It wasn't my best day."

"Nor was it anyone else's, by the tell of it," Hickman went on. "The article didn't hesitate to call out all the men. You all tried, and that's what counted. I doubt that you looked like the buffoons she made you out to be."

Hickman said it again. *She.* Was he really implying the reporter was a female? In all the articles Charles had perused leading up to the event, he hadn't noticed a female writer working for the papers. The only female writer he knew was—

Charles leaned his elbows on the counter, his chest still fluttering but with none of the anticipatory enthusiasm of before. "You don't still have that newspaper lying around, do you?"

CHARLES FOUND LOUISE sitting alone in the inn's tavern, her nose lost in a small book on the table. She didn't tilt her head up until he was towering over her.

"I told you not to leave the room," he barked. Had he meant

to say that? No, not at all, but the damn woman never listened to him. Hadn't she learned anything? The last time she'd sat by herself in a tavern, she came away fleeced.

Louise disregarded his surly tone. She smiled at him as if she knew a secret he didn't. It was then that Charles noticed she wasn't just reading any book—she had *his* sketch journal open for all and sundry to see.

"Please don't be angry," she said, covering the pages with her hands. "You left it behind in the room, and I couldn't help but be nosy. I always knew you were gifted, Charles, but these are exceptional. The way you find the beauty in the ordinary … I can't wait to see what you draw on our trip. The National Gallery will probably award you an entire wing to show off your talent!"

Her words stung him like a swarm of angry bees. Because Charles wanted to believe her. He hungered to bask in her esteem, and that pathetic feeling was like a personal betrayal.

"Charles," she said slowly, her tone growing nervous. "Why are you standing there? Sit down and share some food with me. Please, don't be angry that I left the room. I know you told me to stay, but I was starving and couldn't wait. I ordered plenty hoping you would be back in time. It should be here shortly …"

Her words trailed off as Charles continued to stand like he was chiseled in stone, locked in his disappointment. With her or him? He wasn't sure, and that just made him more furious.

His upper lip curled as he grinned. All teeth. No feeling. "Why would you want to sit with me when I'm"—Charles cocked his head to the ceiling, scratching his chin—"what were the words you used in your article? *As incompetent as Don Quixote, who at least had insanity to excuse his ridiculous behavior.*"

Louise's nervous smile vanished. "What … what are you talking about?"

Charles bent his upper half until they were nose to nose. "You know exactly what I'm talking about. You painted quite the picture of the knights for the *London Town Crier*, didn't you? Described all of us as blundering idiots who couldn't even mount our horses without the use of stairs."

She swallowed glumly. "Well, some of the knights couldn't," she replied sotto voce.

He slammed his palm on the table. "You made me a laughingstock," he railed. "You tore into me like I was nothing more than a foppish, deranged dandy."

"I didn't," she cried, placing her hand over his. Charles swiped his away. He didn't want her to touch him. He didn't want her to soothe him. His anger was the only thing keeping the hurt from destroying him.

Louise took a deep breath, lifting her chin in the air to keep tears from falling. "Fine. I did. You're right. But I never intentionally meant to hurt you. I made a deal with Harvey to write the article. In exchange, he said he would print everything I wrote when I came back from the trip. He was the man I'd been celebrating with the day you found me in the square. We'd just sealed our deal. I had a job to do. I'm sorry you got caught in the middle of it. I barely mentioned you at all; everything was rather general—"

"You call that an apology?" Charles asked. "Why do you even want me to come with you, Louise, when you clearly don't respect me? Was this all just a ruse to get me to take Royce's place after you lost your protector? Is that why you told me I didn't have to marry you? The brilliant, know-it-all Lady Louise wouldn't dare lower herself to marry a man who was"—he huffed, searching his memory again for the worst of her comments—"*so stuck in the past he resembled the flat portraits found in the ancient churches, lacking dimension and scale.*"

"I wasn't talking about you," Louise choked out. Her hands balled to fists in her lap. "I told you, you're nothing like them."

Charles tore off his hat, running his hand through his hair. "But I am! That life is a part of me as much as that journal is. I am an earl and an artist. I can't just run away from my birthright as easily as you. I have responsibilities." He ripped the article from his pocket and tossed it on the table. "I thought you saw the man

I truly was—both sides of me—but it's clear that you're always going to think of me as the silly knight chasing windmills. A man lacking a moral compass, a man … like your father. And I'm"—the words clogged in his throat—"I'm afraid that if I go with you now, I'll always wonder if you can ever love me as much as I love you. Or if I will always feel the need to prove myself."

Louise leapt from her seat, grasping at his coat. "I do love you, Charles. You know I love you more than anything. I was stupid and proud, and arrogant, assuming I knew everything. But I can't do this without you. You promised not to leave me. Do you remember that? And a knight never goes back on his word."

She waited for him to speak, her eyes wide and frantic. Even as angry as he was, Charles was still mesmerized by the way her lovely skin seemed to radiate with promise. Promise of a new day. Promise of what was to come. His hands itched at his sides as he held himself back from holding her. He was a traitor to himself because he wanted to. But he couldn't do it. As he'd said, it was clear what Louise really wanted. And it wasn't him.

With astonishing detachment, Charles unpeeled her fingers from his coat. "You can handle everything yourself, remember? You don't want a knight, my lady. You never did."

CHAPTER TWENTY-SEVEN

H E'D LEFT HER. Just as he had sworn he never would.
So much for a knight's promises.

After Charles exited the tavern, Louise slumped in her chair, paralyzed in the knowledge that she was alone. That she had spoiled everything. That her entire world had turned upside down in a matter of minutes.

Her first inclination was to run after him, but her body had a mind of its own, fusing her to her chair in utter shock and defeat. Besides, she told herself, *he'd* made his decision. Thanks to her story, he didn't want her to chase after him. He wanted her out of his life. His trust—something he'd gifted to Louise freely and readily—was broken. She'd crushed it as easily as a flower petal.

Feeling like she'd been punched in the stomach, Louise struggled to breathe and pick her self-respect off the floor. She couldn't regret writing for Harvey. She'd done her job, but she *had* let her personal bias get the better of her. She'd gone into the event blinded by her own prejudice. What would have happened if Louise had tried harder, as her mother had insisted? What if she had had more conversations with the other ladies-in-waiting or taken a step inside the circles instead of priding herself on remaining on the outside? Looking back, she couldn't blame the other ladies for not having any real interest in her ... she'd never attempted to get to know them, either. Her mind had been made up before the first flag was lowered.

Yes, some of the knights had been ridiculous—comical, even—but some of the men had truly aspired to build a moment for history. Lord Eglinton had attempted to devise something beautiful. As a writer, Louise could understand that now … that urge to create. Charles was no different with his sketches. In the end, weren't we all just looking for people to see us, to form a conversation as we journeyed through life?

And Louise hadn't seen anything. Worse, she hadn't *wanted* to see anything. She was no better than Ephraim Eveleth and his one-dimensional account of the people of the Sandwich Islands.

"What a bastard," she heard a voice say. "That idiot should have never talked to you like that. You're well rid of him. Mind, I wasn't eavesdropping. I just heard the juicy bits here and there."

She deserted her grief long enough to slide her gaze across the table. A swarthy character leered at her from the other end. His face was long and thin and marred by deep pockmarks.

Louise was dead inside, and her words were vacant and ghostly to her ears. "That sounds like eavesdropping to me."

The man snickered, showcasing a gold front tooth. He started to talk, but the barmaid came back to the table, delivering Louise's two steak and kidney pies.

He stole a pie, swiveling it in front of him, and flashed Louise a smile. "Thanks, darling," he said. "I'll just go ahead and take this, since your man left you."

He dug in, not waiting for a response. He was a sloppy eater, completely devoid of manners. Within a few bites, he had gravy spilled on his front shirt and running down his chin. Louise's cheeks grew hot. She wanted to retch … but at least she didn't want to cry anymore.

"Leave my table," she said.

The man chortled, forking in another messy bite. "It's too late for that, girlie. You and I are just getting started; we're going to be friendly tonight. I might even let you buy me more food. It's not like you need it."

Louise wasn't taken aback; she didn't even flinch. If she had a pound for every time a man remarked on her weight, she'd be able to buy steak and kidney pies to her heart's content.

She rested back in her chair, placing her hands on the table. The inn was hushed. Everyone seemed to be interested in the inappropriate conversation, but no one lifted one finger to ascertain if the lady needed help. Louise didn't flinch at that either.

"I'm going to tell you one more time," she said, taking a fork into her hand. She played with the tines, pricking them over her fingers one by one. "Leave my table."

"Or what?" the wastrel replied, spitting pastry out of his mouth.

Louise chucked to herself. She continued to play with her fork, slow and methodical. She could hear a pin drop. "Sir, you don't want to test me right now," she drawled, turning the fork down, sliding the tines across the old, stained wood. "I've had a terrible day. I've managed to lose my best friend and the love of my life. And I'm tired, so bloody tired, of disgusting toads like you who think they can tell me what I should and shouldn't eat. Because I'm hungry, I'm always damned hungry, and this food smells delicious, but my heart is too wrecked to let me enjoy it, and probably will be forever." Tears scalded her face.

The room held its breath. The man stared at her long and hard, his chewing slowing until it eventually stopped.

And then he burst into laughter.

Quick as a flash, Louise shot from her seat, lunging over the table. She grabbed the bastard's collar with one hand while jutting the fork below his pock-spackled chin with the other.

She spoke clearly, enunciating each syllable with bone-melting venom. "I'm alone and I have nothing left to lose, and if you don't leave—right now—I will stab you in the neck with this fork. You may think I'm weak, you may think I'm a coward, and you may think I'm just a woman, but what you really need to do is ask yourself is if I'm capable." She pressed the tines in more, making tiny points on his neck turn white. "Let me assure you, sir, I am more than capable."

"All right now, that's enough," a man called out from behind the bar counter. Louise assumed it was the owner. "I run a respectable place here. We don't want any blood tonight. Leave the woman alone, Mick."

Mick's Adam's apple bobbed under the tines. He licked his lips while his nose flared furiously. He refused to meet Louise's eye. "I didn't want to fuck you anyway," he spat, throwing his head to the side and worming out of his seat.

Louise deflated on the edge of the table as he sauntered away, trying—and failing—to reclaim his dignity. "My loss, then," she replied while Mick kicked open the door and left the inn.

Her hands were shaking. Quietly, she placed the fork on the table and wiped her sweaty palms on her skirt. She sat down, ignoring the crowd. Everyone was staring at her—of that she was certain.

A whistle caught her attention. Why was it so difficult to be left alone? Why did everyone think a woman needed company when she was sitting by herself?

Louise wiped the tears from her cheeks and looked up. An old man, bald as a newborn baby, with skin as tanned and weathered as old leather, leaned off his chair toward her.

"Two bastards in one day, honey. What did you do to deserve that?" He handed her a *relatively* clean handkerchief.

Louise accepted it readily, mopping her face. In her haste, she knocked Charles's journal, ruffling the pages. Handing the handkerchief back, she replied, "The first one wasn't a bastard. He's a knight, and he was right. I humiliated him."

The old man's eyes were as bright as sea glass. "On purpose?"

"No. Yes." She shrugged. "I don't know. All I do know is that he hates me now and will never forgive me."

The old man winced. "It doesn't look like he could ever hate you." He nodded toward the journal. She followed his gaze to a page she'd never seen before, one of his last entries. It was Louise, but different. Charles had captured her in profile, just as he had so many years ago. Her hair was down and windblown over her shoulders, her eyes determined. She looked like the kind of woman that would stop at nothing to fulfill her destiny. She looked like the woman that Louise desperately wanted to be. A woman with no boundaries, a woman with no tether. Fierce and hard.

"He's quite the artist," the old man remarked, craning his wrinkled neck to the journal, and the gold hoop in his ear twinkled against the light. "That's a beautiful woman there."

"Really?" she said, caressing the page with the tips of two fingers. "She looks sad to me."

He frowned, inching closer to the picture. "I don't get that at all."

"I do."

"I see someone ready for adventure," the old man countered. "I heard you tell the barmaid that you're set for the Sandwich Islands on the *Clementine*. I work on that ship," he announced proudly. "This will be my third time going to the islands. You couldn't have picked a better place."

"Oh?" Louise said. "Why is that?" Her lips were moving, but she wasn't sure if sounds were coming out. She was still struck dumb by what had happened. It was like she was wading underwater: everything around her appeared slow, dark, and murky.

The man's face lit up, shaving ten years off. "It is an untouched land, wild and magnificent. The fruit is juicier, the ocean is bluer, the air is sweeter." He slapped his lap. "Ha! The adventures to be had. It's a playground. Even for women. You know they ride astride there? Wouldn't even think of riding like ladies in London do, but they're so much stronger on account of all the swimming. And there's so much to see! The waterfalls are so big and astonishing you'd think they were crafted by giants. And don't get me started on the volcanoes. I could talk your ear off for an entire month about those. You can walk right up to the lava as it bubbles and floats by into the water. Those islands have the kind of beauty that people around here never get to taste."

That wasn't true.

In the last week, Louise had encountered volcanoes and waterfalls, had ridden astride and swum until her lungs and limbs burned. She'd also learned how to trust and love, take pleasure and give it. But she kept those cherished memories to herself.

"I just hope you still go," the old man said, returning to his table, his voice growing wistful. "Don't let what that man said ruin it for you. Either of them. You still are *going*, aren't you? Going to the islands?"

Yes. That was the word that had started it all. That was the word that had guided her decisions like a beacon for the past six months. But as Louise's mouth opened, the word evaporated on her tongue. The thought of encountering any volcanoes or other natural wonders filled her with complete despair because they could never come close to the perfections she'd experienced with Charles.

Now she could see how absurd it all was. Louise hadn't ruined Charles; it was he who had ruined her. This trip was worthless without him. She didn't want to see the world unless she had him by her side. She still had her hopes and ambitions, but they were lackluster without him. Thin and anemic, void of strength.

So when "no" slipped from Louise's lips, she couldn't lament the death of her dream. Because the Sandwich Islands were not going anywhere. There would be more boats, but there would only ever be Charles. Her friend. Her lover. Her soul mate. Her brilliant knight.

She launched from her seat, tucking Charles's journal under his arm. He couldn't have gotten far. She would search all night if she had to. She wouldn't rest until Charles understood how much he meant to her. And the only way she could convince him of that was to give up the trip. Then he would know that he was the most important thing in her life.

She was out the door and ten steps down the docks when she hit her first snag.

"Oh, there she is," Mick taunted her from his sullen perch near the beginning of the pier. He pushed through a gaggle of men to block her path. "I hoped we'd be seeing each other again, and look how soon!"

Louise gritted her teeth. She had a distinct feeling that he'd been waiting for her. The tavern owner had said he didn't want any blood in his establishment; he didn't say anything about outside.

"Please," Louise groaned, "I don't have time for this right now."

Mick reached out, plucked a lock of her hair, and flicked it behind her shoulder. The suggestive look on his dirty face made her insides curdle. "I think you'll find you have all the time in the world for me."

"Get out of my way."

His black-crusted nail trailed down her neck. "What are you going to do to make me?" he asked. "I don't see any forks around."

Louise cocked her head. "I thought you didn't want to fuck me?"

Mick's expression crumpled in displeasure. "The mouth on you," he sneered. "There's only one thing that's good for." His finger continued its way down over her bosom. "And I'm just the man to show you."

Louise reacted quickly and mercilessly. She lashed out, snatching Mick's finger and bending it all the way back until she heard a lovely *snap!*

The bastard howled like an animal, falling to his knees. "Fuck!" he cried, holding his mangled hand in front of him. "Look what you did, you filthy bitch! You're going to pay for this!"

Disregarding his taunts, Louise searched around her and serendipitously located a lovely piece of wood, broken off from one of the shipping boxes being unloaded. It was half the size of her arm and roughly eight pounds. She bounced it up and down in her sure grip.

"When a lady tells you to leave her alone, she means it," she said grimly. She didn't want to use the stick. She just hoped to scare Mick and warn him off—but when she moved past him, he grabbed her skirts with his decent hand. Louise reacted immediately, winding the stick high above her head, ready to make a strike.

But she was too late. A figure zoomed in front of her, knocking Mick straight on his back with one mighty punch.

Charles!

He stood above Mick's prone figure, his chest heaving. Charles's fist was red at his side, but he wouldn't release his tight grip. It stayed there, waiting for another chance, but Mick was out cold.

"My love?" Louise asked, gently taking his fist into her hand. Slowly, she worked his fingers loose, until they tangled with hers. "You shouldn't have done that. You could have hurt your sketching fingers, and then where would you be?"

Charles looked down on their hands, as if only just realizing that Louise was speaking to him. It took a few more breaths for his anger to dissipate, for the fires of rage to calm inside his tense body.

Eventually, Louise felt his fingers twitch and caress hers. "I would be with you," he replied, "and that's all that matters."

He pulled her down one of the piers next to a ship that was bustling with people unloading the cargo. They were hemmed in on either side, but those piercing green eyes were only on her. "Why does something always happen to you the moment I turn my back?" he said irritably.

"Because I need you," Louise replied, hugging her middle. She rested her head on his chest, alarmed by how fast his heart was beating. Was he back to stay, or was he only rescuing her for a final time?

"You don't need me," he whispered, placing his chin over her head. It took way too long, but eventually he wrapped his arms around Louise as well.

"I do," she sobbed.

He shook his head. "You don't. But I don't care, because I need you."

Louise squeezed her eyes shut as tears fell.

Charles went on. "I don't care what you wrote. I don't care what you thought. I'm not like those other men, and I don't need you to tell me that. I have a different perspective, and it's that perspective that helped me see you. I can recognize your strength and independence and fearlessness and love you even more for it. No other man can do it like me. No other man can love you like me. So, I don't care if you think I'm like the others too. It doesn't matter to me, because I've got six months to prove to you otherwise."

Louise looked up at him. His face was resolute. Sure. About her. About them.

"Six months?" she squeaked. "No, Charles. We don't have to go to the islands. They mean nothing to me. I want to stay here with you. I accept everything about you and want to share your world with you. We can go to all the balls and hunts and laugh through all the ridiculous conversations at night together."

Charles sighed. "Well, that's too bad, because I'm going to the islands, and you're going with me. We've got the rest of our lives to attend balls and hunts. Now is all that matters, and we have a ship to catch. You've put the wanderlust in me, and I won't rest until I've sketched every last waterfall there."

His words were a balm to her heart, but it was too much. Louise didn't believe she deserved to be let off the hook so easily, not after everything she'd put him through.

"You were right to leave—" she began.

"I didn't leave," he said, his jaw tense. "I took a moment. I needed a moment."

"Charles, you left. And you had every right to," she said. "I keep pushing you away. I don't deserve you—"

He placed his hand over her mouth. "I needed to catch my breath," he countered. "You aren't the easiest woman, you know."

Louise kissed his fingers. "I know that. But you'll stick with me?"

Charles gave her one of his signature smiles that melted her insides. "Yes, yes, and more yes. You're stuck with me. Now and forever, remember? I'm not him, Louise. I'm not your father. I know what he did to you and your family. I know how your mother suffered, but I will never do that to you. Sooner or later you're going to have to start believing that. You don't have to protect your heart from me. I will always take care of it."

Louise ducked her head, so ashamed of this fear that kept ruining every facet of her life. Charles wasn't anything like her father. He'd never shown her to be like that man in any way. He was everything that was honorable and trustworthy. When he gave his word—his love—he meant it. Louise had wasted too much time and effort battling her insecurity. It was time to lay all her old fears to the side. They had no place in the new world with Charles. She owed him that. She owed herself that.

"I do believe you, my love," she said. "I think I always have. That's why you drove me crazy for so long. I knew I had no chance. Loving you has always been the easiest thing in my life. All I've ever wanted was you."

Charles cupped the sides of her cheeks and brought their noses together. "And now that you have me?" he whispered.

Louise kissed him. She couldn't help herself. His lips were too close and enticing. "All I want is to keep you. Can you ever forgive me for what I wrote?"

"There's nothing to forgive," he said. "You were doing your job. Can you ever forgive me? We knights have thin skin. That's why we wear such heavy armor."

She grinned. "I thought it was to protect your hearts."

"I don't need armor for that, my love. I just need you."

Charles kissed her with such aching sweetness that Louise

forgot where they were until a few whistles woke her up to the sailors skirting around them.

"I love you," she said.

"I love you too."

Charles kissed her one more time before they turned to the docks, their hands twined, their future brilliant before them.

Louise felt like she was floating. She couldn't wait to board the *Clementine* and spend the next six months in a cabin with Charles. They would exercise so much that she would be in the best physical shape of her life when they reached the islands.

Speaking of exercising... "Do you know what I want to do right now?" she asked playfully.

Charles laughed, kissing her hand. "Yes, and I think we can make that happen."

"Good, because I'm starving. Some dastardly villain ate my pie."

He arched a brow. "I do hope that was the man you almost knocked senseless with the stick?"

"The very one."

"Well then, dearest, it will be my greatest wish to purchase you another pie, but first we have to do one last thing before we go back to the inn."

Louise had been too captured in her love to realize that Charles had been directing them toward one person in particular. They stopped in front of a gentleman who was elegantly dressed in a crisp black coat and cap. His bearing was regal and his expression inscrutable under his puffy white beard.

She hugged Charles's side. "Who is this?" she asked shyly.

Draping a protective arm around her shoulder, Charles cradled her closer. "Oh, that's just the captain of the *Clementine*. When I took my moment, I wasn't only catching my breath, I was fetching him. We're getting married, my love. As much as you appreciate the romantic culture of the islands, I believe I'm an old-fashioned British boy at heart. I will need more than a shake and your word before we enter in this ... arrangement.

When I take you to bed tonight, it will be as my wife. Your brother will have my balls if I don't."

Married? Never had anything felt so right.

"Now, Charles?"

"Yes, my darling. Right now."

"And forever, Charles?"

He gazed at Louise and wiped a lock of hair off her face. "Yes, my love," he said tenderly. "For now and forever. Do you think you'll be able to handle that? Handle being loved and cherished for the rest of your time of this earth?"

"Yes."

EPILOGUE

September 8, 1841
London, England

LOUISE CAST A frustrated look behind her. "Why are you shuffling your feet? You're yards behind me now."

"Hardly yards," Charles mumbled. "I'm two steps behind you."

Though he could only see the back of her head, he could practically feel his wife roll her eyes. "You're almost a full block behind," Louise replied with a laugh. "Do you need me to hold her?"

Charles scoffed, hoisting the red-headed one-year-old higher in his arms, eliciting a squeal of delight. "I can walk down the street and manage our pint-sized daughter at the same time. Besides," he railed, "I wouldn't be much of a gentleman if I let you hold her in your condition."

Even from the *considerable* distance, Charles heard a disgruntled noise come from his wife's throat. "Such nonsense. I'm stronger than I've ever been," she returned.

Charles had no ready response to that, partially because she was right. Even three months pregnant, Louise was in the best shape of her life, and their year in the Sandwich Islands could take credit for it. During the life-changing experience, Louise had done everything she'd said she would. She'd ridden horses bareback, hiked to volcanoes, and swum in the ocean nearly every day—mostly naked—while conducting the writing and researching for her book. And she was all the better for it. Charles was as well, considering he'd been at her side for every adventure… when he wasn't looking after the cherub in his arms, of course.

Isabella tugged on the seashell pendant hanging from Charles's neck with her chubby little fingers and promptly stuck it in her mouth. "I think your daughter is hungry," Charles called to his wife, knowing that would be the only thing to slow her feet. Why she was in such a hurry to get to her brother's townhouse was beyond him. They hadn't seen the marquis in two years. A few more minutes would hardly matter. But Louise had acted like a fire was nipping at her heels all morning. As soon as the *Manu Ihu* had docked, Louise had been champing at the bit to get started. She tried to hide it, but a husband knew. She was nervous. Incredibly nervous.

Louise's steps halted at his words, and she swiftly turned around. Not for the first time, Charles wondered if Louise's brother, Lord Edward, would even recognize his sister. She still maintained the same rich red hair and uppity, blue-blooded features, but a seismic shift had taken place. Her time on the islands with the indigenous peoples had unleashed something even more beautiful in his wife. Louise had blossomed into her true self. Her pale skin was now tanned and adorably freckled, and her body—though softened by motherhood—was lean and honed by everyday exertions and purpose. She stood before Charles not a new woman, but a more modern one. One unafraid to speak her mind and unwilling to temper that voice. To put it simply, Louise had grown in confidence.

Though she was having a difficult time exhibiting it now.

"Isabella can't possibly be hungry," Louise said, bending over to study her daughter's content and curious features. "I fed her right before we left the boat."

Charles touched a gentle hand to the side of his wife's face, holding it softly. "I know," he said. "I just wanted you to slow down and catch your breath."

Louise blanched. "I *am* catching my breath. My breath is perfectly caught. What do you mean?"

Charles merely stared at her, admiring her courage. Louise had done her own hair that morning and done it badly. It had already fallen out of her bun and was whipping wildly around his face, just as he liked. She hadn't used a maid in two years. Charles already found himself feeling sorry for the new maid he would have to hire while they were in Town. Louise wasn't easy at the best of times.

"It's perfectly fine to be nervous," he said. "But just remember. Your brother loves you. Your book will soon be published to great acclaim, and you are back home. Just relax."

"I am relaxed!" Louise snapped before closing her eyes and sucking in a sharp inhale. She brushed the long hair off of her face and kissed her daughter on the cheek. "I am relaxed," she said again, quieter this time. "You're the one that's nervous."

"Me? What do I have to be nervous about?"

"Well," Louise began slowly, cocking her head. "You *did* steal his sister away."

Charles leveled his wife with a wry look. "I didn't exactly pull you by your hair in front of the captain and force you to say your vows."

"And," Louise went on as if she hadn't heard a word, "I am me, and you … well, you're *you*."

What the hell was that supposed to mean? Charles transferred Isabella onto his other hip. "If you mean that I am the Earl of Somerset, then you are correct. Your brother couldn't have hoped for a better match for you," he added, rather pompously.

Louise's shrug irritated the hell out of him. "I'm sure he had some duke in mind."

Charles caught her smile a second too late. "What duke could you possibly have married that would have been a better catch than me? And don't you dare shrug at me again."

Louise laughed instead, retying Isabella's bonnet around her perfect round head. "The Duke of Wembley would have surely married me."

"The Duke of Wembley!" Charles blurted with an acerbic cackle. "He's ancient! He spends a reckless amount of money on ridiculous, dangerous animals like they're fine china." Hugging his daughter closer to his chest, he began to walk down the street again, leaving his wife in his tracks. "You know what? On second thought, you would have been perfect for the duke. You're both insane."

The soft, musical lilt of Louise's laughter managed to release the constricted muscles in his chest—but just barely. Charles hadn't realized they were so tight. *Was* he nervous? *No.* Edward was his best friend. If the marquis was still holding a grudge, then Charles would know it.

"Husband," Louise called after him, "I'm only teasing you; you know that. I'm trying to calm you before you see my brother."

Charles let out a huff. "I told you, I'm not nervous. *You* are."

Soon, Louise was back by his side, taking his hand in hers. She didn't force him to stop, just gave him a comforting squeeze. "You're right. Maybe I am a little nervous. Do you really think he'll be all right?"

Out of the corner of his eye, Charles saw Louise's brow furrow, and he returned a squeeze to her.

"You have nothing to worry about," he said. "You've shared plenty of letters and explained everything. If he was angry at us, he isn't anymore, and when he sees you, all he'll want to do is hold you and his gorgeous new niece."

Louise nodded, though her expression was still marred in concern. "You're right," she said, straightening her shoulders. "I'm a woman and not some silly little sister."

Charles smiled at her confidence. "You're also a wife and mother—"

"And soon to be a world-famous author."

"And that too," he said dryly.

"I have nothing to be afraid of."

"Nothing at all," Charles concurred.

"Nothing …" Louise's voice faded as she stopped. They were there. She looked at Charles and raised her chin toward the door, five heady steps away from them. "Why am I acting like this?"

"I have no idea."

She leaned in and kissed him soundly. Not to be left out, Isabella joined in the fun, lodging her head next to theirs in a familial embrace. They were all laughing when they backed away.

Charles nodded at the door. "Are you ready?"

"Of course."

"Then after you."

Louise didn't move. "Why do I have to knock? I think you should be the one to do it."

Charles didn't move either. "He's your brother."

"He's your best friend! Oh, fine!" She pounded heavy footsteps up to the townhouse entrance before giving the door a few demure knocks. Demure wasn't usually a word Charles would use to describe his wife. He wondered if she thought that if she knocked lightly that no one might hear.

As they waited, he had his hands busy calming Isabella, who seemed to have sensed the gravity of the event. She raised her arms high above her head, screaming at the top of her lungs.

Charles bobbed her on his hip, swaying her back and forth while shushing in her ear as he climbed the steps to stand at Louise's side. She sent him a sympathetic smile. "I don't think anyone's home—"

Her eyes widened as the door creaked and suddenly swung open. Expecting a butler to greet them and give them a few more minutes of reprieve, Charles was surprised to witness the austere countenance of the marquis himself staring back at them with the same amount of shock.

Lord Edward's dark gaze stumbled over Charles and the baby

before landing on Louise. Without warning, Edward's long arms reached out and he grabbed her, smushing her into his chest. His mouth was tight, his throat locked, and his eyes closed as he hugged his sister. Charles could only hear Louise's sobs as they embraced in the doorway.

"I'm so sorry, Edward," she cried into her brother's chest. "I missed you so much. But I had to go."

"Shh, shh," he answered in a clipped tone. "None of that. You have nothing to apologize for. I'm just so happy you're home." Holding her shoulders, he pushed her away to meet her face. "For good, maybe?"

She laughed, swiping at her tears. "Maybe." She shrugged. "I don't know. There's so much of the world to see. For *us* to see."

She turned away from her brother and took Isabella's hand. The little girl was confused—stunned, really. In all her months, she'd never seen her mother cry. Clearly, she didn't know what to make of it. "I'd like to introduce you to your niece and goddaughter, Isabella."

Edward's entire body went rigid. With hands locked behind his back, he issued a regal bow to the small child. "Lady Isabella," he said gallantly. "It is a pleasure to make your acquaintance."

Isabella drooled loudly, blowing a giant bubble from her mouth.

Edward lifted an eyebrow at Louise. "Yes, I should have expected that."

It was then Charles noticed the raucous noise coming from inside the house. Shrieks and screams reverberated off the walls, to which Edward merely smiled.

"Brother," Louise said, "in your letters, you've said the mine is beyond successful now. I know you hate spending money, but please tell me you've at least hired a butler. Aren't you too busy to be opening doors all day long?"

Edward crossed his arms with a put-upon smirk. "The butler is busy playing hide-and-seek with Astrid and John. He volunteered after I told them I needed a break."

Louise's mouth dropped open. "A break? *You?* From playing?"

"A lot has changed, little sister," Edward replied. He placed a hand on her back, taking her inside. "Georgiana is out, but she should be home soon. We weren't expecting your ship until next week, so Mother and the girls aren't arriving until then. Come inside and see your niece and nephew. They can't wait to meet their intrepid aunt. They go to bed at night with tales of the wild woman."

Louise beamed and, being Louise, didn't need to be asked twice. She barged inside the house, where the screams and hollers only got more deafening.

Charles started to follow her when he heard Edward make a *tsking* noise, blocking his entry.

"Not so fast for you, I think," Edward said in a low, grave voice that even made Isabella's eyes go wide.

Charles sighed. Were they really going to do this? After all this time, and outside Edward's townhouse? As he braced himself for a swift punch to the jaw, his friend surprised him by reaching out for Isabella.

"Let me see this little one," Edward said. His tone had miraculously changed, and the high, singsong pitch made Isabella giggle. Charles released a breath of relief. *Good.* He would keep all his teeth this day. Perhaps Edward was well and truly over his sister's clandestine escape. What could he really do about it, anyway? Charles and Louise had been married for two years, had one child and one on the way. What was done was done.

Edward held the baby like a man who had plenty of practice. "You look just like your mama. Do you know that?" he cooed.

Charles twisted his neck to see if anyone was around them on the street. He almost felt bad for the marquis. When had Edward become so soft? Not that Charles could say anything. He was as soft as pudding himself, when it came to his daughter.

"She's Louise's twin," he said easily, feeling the muscles of his neck relax as the men casually reverted to their effortless relationship.

Edward's lips fell into a winsome smile. "She is. It's amazing how that happens." After a pause, he said, "She looks happy."

Charles grinned. "She's a very happy baby."

Edward lifted his eyes to Charles. "I didn't mean the baby."

Charles's throat tightened. He sensed the hidden conversation happening between them. "I don't think she could be happier."

Edward *humphed*, jostling the baby for more squeals. "Spoken like a true husband."

"That is what I am."

Edward nodded. "Yes," he said gently. "Yes, I can see that. Thank you …" He sucked in a herculean breath. "Thank you for taking care of her."

Charles knew how much it had cost his friend to say that. He hadn't expected it. "I would do anything for her."

"Edward!" Louise called from inside the house. "Bring Isabella. I want her to meet her cousins!"

The marquis twisted toward the voice before coming back to Charles with a shrug. "I think we're needed," he said.

Charles nodded. Again, he tried to enter the house, but Edward blocked him. And that was when it happened; he should have known. His best friend knew him better than anyone other than his wife—and he was a right bastard. One didn't attack when the enemy was expecting it; one attacked the second the enemy let his guard down.

Edward's knee was swift and on the mark. It was a quick movement, one that barely registered to the child in his arms, and hit the bull's-eye in the center of Charles's legs. Right in the balls. The balls that Charles was certain would never father any more children.

He crumpled to the ground.

Ever the attentive uncle, Edward had already turned to the house, having made sure Isabella didn't see a damn thing.

"Do come in when you're ready," he said over his shoulder before slamming the door on Charles's red face.

Charles writhed for a bit. Muttered a few curses. But a smile eventually began to form. And it stayed there until he could feel his legs again and was ready to stand.

"It's good to be home," he said. And then he opened the door and joined his family.

About the Author

I'm a lifelong reader of romance novels. Some of my earliest memories are of sneaking into my mom's room at night and stealing any books I could find.

After moving around quite a bit, I've finally put down roots in New England with my two sons and husband. I've always been a writer, starting out in newspapers, but it wasn't until my sons began going to school full-time that I began working toward my dream of becoming a romance author.

I enjoy crocheting toys for my kids, hiking with my Saint Bernard, and watching Real Housewives on the couch with my very old and very fat pugs.

9 781961 275423